"Let's get on with it," Shaw said. "I've got food coming."

The Mexican gunman sneered at Shaw's words and said with confidence, "Not tonight, you don't."

Shaw stood staring, realizing that for the time being, the constant pain in his head had ceased to pound; his mind felt clearer, his vision sharper. He looked back and forth from one face to another, his hand hanging loose but poised near the butt of the big Colt on his right hip. Maybe this was his most natural state.

The gunman's hand wrapped around his gun butt. He drew the gun with the blinding speed of a striking rattlesnake. But fast though he was, the tip of his gun barrel never made it past the top of his holster. Shaw's Colt exploded before the two other gunmen watching realized it was even in his hand.

The gunman hit the dirt floor, dead, a streak of blood flying out his back with the bullet, lashing the others' faces.

CITY OF
BAD MEN

Ralph Cotton

A SIGNET BOOK

SIGNET
Published by New American Library, a division of
Penguin Group (USA) Inc., 375 Hudson Street,
New York, New York 10014, USA
Penguin Group (Canada), 90 Eglinton Avenue East, Suite 700, Toronto,
Ontario M4P 2Y3, Canada (a division of Pearson Penguin Canada Inc.)
Penguin Books Ltd., 80 Strand, London WC2R 0RL, England
Penguin Ireland, 25 St. Stephen's Green, Dublin 2,
Ireland (a division of Penguin Books Ltd.)
Penguin Group (Australia), 250 Camberwell Road, Camberwell, Victoria 3124,
Australia (a division of Pearson Australia Group Pty. Ltd.)
Penguin Books India Pvt. Ltd., 11 Community Centre, Panchsheel Park,
New Delhi - 110 017, India
Penguin Group (NZ), 67 Apollo Drive, Rosedale, North Shore 0632,
New Zealand (a division of Pearson New Zealand Ltd.)
Penguin Books (South Africa) (Pty.) Ltd., 24 Sturdee Avenue,
Rosebank, Johannesburg 2196, South Africa

Penguin Books Ltd., Registered Offices:
80 Strand, London WC2R 0RL, England

First published by Signet, an imprint of New American Library,
a division of Penguin Group (USA) Inc.

First Printing, February 2011
10 9 8 7 6 5 4 3 2 1

For Mary Lynn . . . of course

Prologue

Little Ester, the Mexican badlands

Lawrence Shaw rode the dusty switchback trail upward nearly a mile, then stepped his big bay onto a rock ledge and looked down, checking his back trail. Beneath him the speckled bay chuffed and shook out its damp mane in a gust of dry warm wind. A wavering white-hot sky lay overhead. Below, a desolate, broken world of stone, gully, hilltop and cutbank was carpeted over with sand—a harsh, unaccommodating fauna that showed no welcome toward humankind.

Home . . . , he told himself wryly.

The bullet wound in his head had mended slowly but steadily for the past four months. The doctor who'd most recently examined him declared it a miracle of medical science that Shaw was alive. Shaw supposed this was true. Leastwise, he had never known anyone to take such a shot and live. As for its being a miracle, he couldn't say. The way he saw it, miracles didn't come around much.

He wasn't even completely certain who'd shot him, and strange though it was, he didn't much care. *It was the young woman, though,* an inner voice told him. He gazed out from his saddle across endless rolling hills bathed in a harsh glare of sunlight and wavering heat. Deep inside, he knew it was her.

Now put it away. . . .

With his being known as "the fastest gun alive," there were more people who wanted to kill him than he ever cared to think about. Getting shot was something he'd learned to take in stride long ago, a part of the life he'd chosen for himself. So was getting killed if it came to it, he reminded himself, watching a lone hawk swing in a lazy circle high above him. He tried not to make a big thing of it, getting shot. It happened to everybody now and then.

He couldn't quite remember what circumstances had drawn him to this fiery Mexican badlands once again, but it was good to be back all the same, gunshot wound or no. His pal U.S. Marshal Crayton Dawson had called this *his* kind of place. "Gun country," he'd said. And he'd been right, Shaw realized. There was solitude here. This was a good place for a man like him. And here he was . . .

The bay scraped a hoof and tossed its head. Shaw touched back on its reins.

The bullet had hit him from a distance just shy of point-blank range, so close that the blast of powder had burned his hair off. But instead of entering his skull, the big .45-caliber slug had only fractured it. Oddly enough, the bullet had flattened, crushed its way upward and bored a path across the top of his head. It split his scalp like a dull hatchet, leaving in its wake a long furrow of cracked skull bone as it made its way out the other side. He winced, thinking about it.

A miracle? Maybe. . . .

He turned the big speckled bay and rode back onto the dusty switchback, reminding himself once again not to think about it. More than likely it had just been a bad bullet, a weak load. Hell, who knew . . . ?

The bullet wound had not left him unscathed. He still went about his day-to-day life partially mired in a dreamy numbness that refused to turn him loose. Peculiar though he found it to be, there were days, even *weeks* at a time that he could not account for. Then, out of nowhere his memory seemed to catch up with him in some jumbled, unsteady fashion, as if he'd been traveling somewhere far ahead of it.

It was strange, he told himself, nudging the bay forward. But he'd gotten used to *strangeness* in his life a long time ago.

Home . . . , he told himself again, this time without the irony. Finally, he forced his thoughts away from the matter and gazed off across the rocky hilltops, into the endless breadth of earth and sky. He took a deep breath and let it out.

"We've still got a long ways to go," he said down to the bay. In truth he had no real destination in mind, only a deep, persistent need to keep moving.

He wore a long corduroy riding duster with leather-trimmed pockets and collar. Beneath the open front, his big Colt stood in its holster on his right hip. A large black bandana was pulled back and tied at the base of his skull, and atop it sat a tall sand-colored sombrero. The broad-brimmed hat was plain, with a fine line of green embroidery the color of pale wild grass on its soft crown.

His boots were caballero-style, high-welled, battered and scuffed to the desert hue. The right boot was simple seasoned leather, but the left boot bore a wrap-around carving—tooled in fine detail were two wild stallions locked in a death battle.

When he arrived at Little Ester, the first town in a string of ancient Spanish settlement remnants, he stepped down from his saddle beside a short stone wall surrounding the town's watering well, hitching the bay to a thick iron ring attached atop the wall. Reaching down under the bay's belly, he loosed its cinch and let it drink.

As the thirsty horse drew water, Shaw pulled a gourd dipper up from an oaken bucket sitting on the wall and drank from it. Behind him an elderly man appeared from the dark shade between two adobes, a frayed straw sombrero in his knobby hands.

"*Bienvenidos a Pequeña Ester, señor,*" he said.

"*Gracias,*" Shaw replied, thanking the man for his welcome. He wiped a hand across his lips and dropped the gourd dipper back into the bucket.

The old man paused, looked Shaw up and down, taking particular note of his finely tooled boot.

"May I ask what brings you here?" he asked in stiff English.

Shaw turned, facing the smiling old man. "Passing through," he said.

"Aw, *sí,* passing through," said the self-appointed

town greeter. "I understand." His eyes went back to Shaw's boot, then back to his face. "Always when men come to Little Ester from the east, they are passing through." He offered a smile, seeing that Shaw had little conversation for him. Shaw glanced at the shade between the two adobes, where the old man had emerged from.

But as the man turned to walk away, Shaw said out of the blue, "Tell me, senor, is there a witch here who carries a covey of trained sparrows?" As soon as he'd asked, he realized it was a mistake. But it was too late; now he had to let it play itself out.

"A *bruja*?" the old man said, curiously. "With trained sparrows?" He considered the question and he rubbed his goatee for an answer.

"Never mind," Shaw said, wanting to let it go. It had been more than a year since he'd seen the witch and her covey of dancing sparrows. And it hadn't been here in Little Ester. It hadn't even been close. These were the things that had been worrying him lately. He knew it was his head wound talking.

But the old man didn't understand. He continued to study the question for a moment longer, then raised a thin knobby finger and said, "Ah, wait! But, yes, I do know of such a *bruja*."

"You do?" Shaw said. Then he insisted quickly, "It's not important."

"She does not come here," the old man continued all the same. "She travels the hills to the south, across the desert basin."

"Yes, *gracias*," said Shaw. "I remember now." He didn't manage to hide the look of concern on his face.

The old Mexican tilted his head and asked, "May I ask why you seek her, senor?"

"I'm not seeking her," Shaw said. "I was just curious, is all."

"Oh," the old man said in disbelief. "I thought you seek her because she is from your country."

"From *my* country?" That perked Shaw's interest. "She's American?"

"*Sí, Americano.* Did you not know that about her, senor?" the old man asked.

"No, I didn't know," Shaw said, stepping closer to the bay to loosen its reins from the iron ring.

"It is a good day when a man learns something new," the old Mexican said, grinning over bare gums.

He wanted money.

Shaw reached into his trouser pocket.

It had been in the dusty adobe village of Valle Del Maíz where he'd seen the old witch wrapped in a ragged black cloth. She had tossed her covey of paper-thin sparrows upward in a circle of glowing firelight, appearing to orchestrate their movements with the tips of her bony fingers. *An American . . . ?* That was a surprise.

"Tell me, amigo," Shaw said, dismissing the witch and her sparrows, "have two American lawmen passed through here?" He took out a small gold coin and placed it in the old man's weathered palm.

"*Americano* lawmen . . . ?" The old man closed his palm over the coin as he gave the matter some thought.

"Yes," Shaw said, "one is called Dawson, the other one is called Caldwell—some call him *Undertaker.* They track outlaws along the border." He reached down under the bay and fastened its cinch.

"Ah, yes, I have heard of these men," the Mexican said, tapping a finger to his head, "but no, they have not been to Little Ester. This I would know."

"You're certain?" Shaw said. He tested his saddle with a gloved hand.

"*Sí*, I am certain," he said. He took a step back from Shaw, as if in caution. "Are they hunting *you*, maybe, these lawmen?"

"No," Shaw said, not wanting to offer any more information about himself or the two lawmen than he needed to. He swung up onto his saddle. "Maybe *I'm* hunting them."

"Oh . . . ," the old man said. Shaw watched the man's eyes go once again to the tooling on his left boot, then back to Shaw's face as he turned the bay and put it forward along the stone-lined trail.

No sooner had Shaw ridden out of sight than three gunmen walked out of the dark shade between the two adobes.

"Who is he, old man?" a young Mexican named Dario Esconza asked. He stood with a bottle of mescal in one hand. His other hand was loosely shoved down behind his gun belt, close to the big bone-handled Starr revolver holstered low on his hip.

"He didn't tell me," the old man said, having buried the coin out of sight inside his ragged clothes. He rubbed his bristly chin as if trying to recall what Shaw had told him. "I cannot remember why he came here." He grinned sadly. "My mind does not work as well as it used to. Life is hard."

Esconza scowled at him, knowing the old man was

fishing him for money. "If you think life is hard now, imagine how much harder it will be when I stamp my boot on your throat." He took a step closer.

"*Por favor*, Dario! Please, no," the old man begged, raising his hands as if to protect his face. "I will tell you what he said."

Esconza stopped and stared at him. The other two gunmen, both Texans on the run from the law, looked on in approval.

The old man said, "He searches for an old *bruja* who carries a covey of trained sparrows in her bosom."

"A witch with sparrows in her bosom . . . ," Esconza repeated, staring flatly at the old Mexican.

"*Sí.*" The old man shrugged, knowing how unlikely it sounded.

Esconza looked at the two gunmen, then turned back to the old man and took a deep breath, running out of patience.

"That's real good, old man," he said, stepping forward again. "First I'm going to kick you back and forth in the dirt for a while. Then we'll start over."

"It is the truth, Dario. I swear it," the old man said, speaking hurriedly now. "He asked about the *bruja*, and I told him she does not come here. Then he asked about the two lawmen you told me to look out for, the ones hunting down the Cut-Jaws Gang."

"The two lawmen, eh?" said Esconza. "Now we're getting somewhere. What did you tell him?"

"I told him they have not been through here." The old man shrugged his bony shoulders. "Because it is true, they have not."

Esconza turned up a drink from the bottle of mescal and passed it to one of the other two gunmen. He stared along the rise of dust Shaw's horse left stirred in its wake.

"What else?" Esconza asked. "Is he running from them?"

"He did not say," the old man replied. "I asked if they hunt him and he said maybe he is hunting them."

One of the gunmen, a Texan named Ollie Wilcox, lowered the mescal bottle from his lips and passed it to the other gunman. "That's no answer," he said.

The third gunman, a Tex-Mexican named Charlie Ruiz, turned up the bottle, swigged from it, then lowered it and said, "Yep, he's on the run, if you ask me."

"Yes, I think he is," Esconza agreed. He furrowed his brow in concentration and added, "I know this man. . . . I have seen him before somewhere."

"Yeah . . . ?" questioned Wilcox. He just stared at Esconza.

Esconza nodded his head in contemplation. "It will come to me."

Ruiz grinned at Wilcox and asked Esconza, "So, what do you want to do? Chase him down and tell him you know him from somewhere?"

"We are looking for good men, eh?" said Esconza. "If he is hiding from the law and he is good with a gun, we will invite him to ride with us."

Ruiz grinned again. "What if he's hiding from the law but is *not* good with a gun?" he said. "What if he's so bad with a gun he has toes missing?"

Esconza shrugged and reached out for the bottle in

Charlie Ruiz's hand. "Then I will kill him, and we will ride away." He looked at the old Mexican and said, "See how life is *not so hard* for those of us who are bold by nature?"

"*Sí*, I do," the old man said. Then he fell silent and stood staring at the drift of dust above the trail.

PART 1

Chapter 1

Shaw knew there'd been eyes watching as he talked to the old man. *Instincts . . .* , he told himself.

Yet, instead of finding out who was watching, or why, he'd simply let the notion slip away. Out of nowhere he'd caught himself bringing up the matter of the old witch and her sparrows. *Jesus . . . Where had that come from?* he wondered, pushing the bay up a thin path overlooking the trail. It had been a year since he'd seen the old witch and her covey of *dancing birds*.

But this was the sort of thing that had been happening since the head wound. The bullet-fractured skull hadn't *outright* cost him his memory or his faculties, as the first doctor believed it might. At no time during the early healing stages of his wound had he forgotten who he was, where he was from, or what his life had been. Yet, as the slow healing began, so had these unpredictable moments of haziness.

The witch and her sparrows . . . ?

He shook his head in wonder. The speckled bay climbed the steep path and stopped on its own when it came to a flat rock bluff, as if it knew what its rider wanted. Shaw was still consumed by what had happened, and why. *Thank God for good horses. . . .* He patted the bay's damp withers with his gloved hand.

Luckily, Shaw was the only one aware of his problem. The old Mexican hadn't seen it. Neither had any of the others, like the bartender in El Paso. Shaw had called him by the wrong name, drifting back into a similar conversation he'd been engaged in with another bartender more than two years prior.

Shaw considered things. This was what the wound had done to him, and fortunately he'd managed to catch slipups and turn them around before anyone noticed thus far. But how long could he keep doing this before someone saw through him?

And what if my condition gets worse . . . ? he asked himself, turning the bay, watching the trail below from the cover of rocks and brush.

He lived in a hard world, where gunmen lay in wait like wolves for the scent of wounded prey. He knew it, and he wasn't about to give it to them. His hand fell idly to the butt of his big Colt and rested there. He still had his gun. *Always the gun . . .* , he told himself.

He watched the trail below until the first sign of dust rose from the switchback farther down the hillside. As the three riders from Little Ester filed past below him, he recognized Dario Esconza in the lead. His instincts had been right. These were the eyes who'd been watching from the darkened shadows. Now they were trailing him.

Dario Esconza . . . A killer—a man who prided himself in being fast with a gun.

Interesting, Shaw thought. Now that he knew *who* was following him, it wasn't hard to understand *why*. He eased the bay around and nudged it upward, taking a meandering rocky path to the next level of switchback trial. . . .

On the trail below, Dario Esconza stopped so suddenly that Ruiz's and Wilcox's horses piled up before they jerked them roughly to a halt.

"*Condénelo!*" he cursed, as the other men struggled to collect their horses.

"Whoa! *Damn* is right!" said Wilcox, repeating Esconza's curse in English. "This is not a place to make sudden stops!" He pulled his horse sideways away from the trail's edge, glancing down at jagged rock and swaying tree tops stretched far below them.

"*By God*, you'll get somebody killed!" said Ruiz, anger in his frightened eyes.

Paying no attention to the two gunmen, Esconza said with a look of revelation on his face, "It's him! By the saints! It is *him*!"

Wilcox and Ruiz looked at each other in surprise.

"Who?" Wilcox asked, his eyes cutting all around the trail and up the steep hillside. His hand went to his gun butt. "What the hell's got into you, Dario?"

Esconza took in deep breath. "Into *me*?" He gave the two a tight grin. "*Nothing* has gotten into me," he said sharply. He tapped his forehead beneath his battered hat brim. "I told you I knew him from somewhere . . . the sombrero-wearing gringo dressed like a *Mejicano*?"

"Hey, easy with the 'gringos,'" Ruiz warned, his palm pistol-butted on his holstered Colt.

"Pardon me," said Esconza with the same tight grin, "I did not realize what a wilting soul you are, Charlie Ruiz."

"I'll wilt *your* by-God soul," Ruiz said, furious, wild-eyed. "You damn near run my ass off a cliff!"

"Settle down, both of yas," Wilcox cut in. He turned to Esconza and said, "You recognized him, all right. Who is he?"

"He is a *dead man*," Esconza said, fiery-eyed. "That is who he is."

"Oh, a *dead man*," said Wilcox. He and Ruiz gave each other a look. "No name or nothing? Just . . . a *dead man*?" he replied back to Esconza.

"*Sí*, just a *dead man*," Esconza said, staring straight ahead with resolve.

"Hear that?" Wilcox said to Ruiz. "The fellow has no name. He's a dead man." He spat in contempt. "I expect that's what folks call him," he added with sarcasm.

"I heard," Ruiz said. He also shook his head in contempt.

"No offense, Dario," said Wilcox, "but I don't see this taking us no damn where. If you won't even tell us who he is, I'd just as soon not even—"

"You will see who he is," Esconza said, cutting him off, "when I shoot open his head and poke my fingers in his dying brains."

The two looked at each other again.

"Jesus . . . ," said Ruiz, as Esconza nudged his horse roughly and rode past him. When Esconza had ridden a few feet forward of them, Ruiz leaned sidelong in his saddle and said to Wilcox under his breath, "Did you know he was *this way*?"

Wilcox considered the matter for second. Then he spread a short, cruel grin and asked as he heeled his horse forward, "What way?"

Shaw had dismounted his bay and led the animal up the steep rocky path. When he'd arrived on the next level of the switchback trail, he dusted himself off, stepped back into his saddle and rode on toward the town on Ángeles Descansan (Angels' Rest). As soon as he arrived in the small hill town, he turned the tired horse over to a young stable tender and paid him with a gold coin that was almost twice the size he was accustomed to receiving. The young man's eyes widened at the sight of it.

Hefting the coin in his hand, appraising the weight of it, the young Mexican asked with a smile, "Who do you wish me to kill, senor?" He looked Shaw up and down, noting the big Colt standing in its holster behind the open corduroy duster. Shaw's trouser leg had risen and perched atop his left boot well, revealing part of the fighting stallions.

"Not my horse," Shaw warned.

"Oh, no, senor!" The young man retracted quickly, looking frightened by Shaw's dead-somber expression. "I am only joking. I would never kill—"

"So am I," said Shaw, cutting him off, the same somber look on his dust-streaked face.

"Oh, *sí*, I understand, of course you are also joking," the stable boy said with relief. He gave a nervous smile. "I will give this fine strong *caballo* extra-special care— as if he is my own." He patted the horse's muzzle as he spoke.

"See to it you do," Shaw said. Drawing his rifle from the saddle boot, he levered it and checked it, letting the hammer down with his thumb.

The stable boy's eyes widened again at the sight of the Winchester. Shaw stared at him, then turned and walked away in the afternoon sunlight, rifle in hand.

"Holy *Madre*," the young man said under his breath. He started to make the sign of the cross on his chest. But then, as if not wanting the horse to see how shaken he was, he stopped himself and gave a light tug on the horse's reins.

"Come with me, *please*," he said in English, as if the horse understood him. "You and I will be very good amigos, eh?"

The bay chuffed, gave a half nod and followed him to a clean fresh stall.

Shaw walked straight to an adobe cantina, knowing it would be the first place the three riders would come looking for him when they arrived in Angels' Rest. On his way inside he passed two well-attended horses tied to the same iron hitch ring beneath a flapping canvas overhang out of the afternoon sun. From inside the cantina, the sound of a guitar and twanging mouth harp reached out to him through open glassless windows.

Upon walking into the adobe, he locked eyes on two drinkers sitting at a table in a rear corner. When he gazed at the two well-dressed men, he took in the ornate shotgun leaning against a wall nearby. They gave him a half nod, which he returned as he stepped over to a bar constructed of two wide planks resting atop a row of large cooperage barrels.

Friendly enough. . . .

But at the end of the bar, a lone drinker did not give Shaw a nod of welcome. Instead he avoided Shaw's eyes, set his empty wooden cup down and walked away toward the rear door. Shaw stood at the bar and waited until the door closed behind the man.

"Rye and beer, *por favor*," Shaw said to a short, broad-shouldered bartender. As he ordered, he eased along the bar and stopped where the lone drinker had been standing, commanding a better view of the open front door.

"*Sí*, rye *y cervesa* coming," the bartender said, part Spanish part English, noting Shaw's shift to the end of the bar.

The bartender placed a bottle, a shot glass and a mug of beer in front of him, and Shaw paid him, watching him pour the shot glass full. Shaw drank the beer as if it were water. Then he laid his Winchester on the bar beside him, took off his dusty sombrero, slapped it once against his leg and placed it atop the rifle.

"There will be senoritas here shortly," the bartender said privately to Shaw. He gazed at Shaw for a response, as if he understood the needs of a man in their most natural order. But when Shaw didn't reply, the bartender only nodded slightly and stepped away.

Shaw raised the shot glass to his lips and tossed the rye back in one drink.

At the table in the rear, the two men turned their eyes away from the thirsty newcomer and back to the twanging mouth harp and the strumming guitar. Shaw kept an eye on the open front doorway. He drank sparingly.

A quarter of an hour later, he watched through the

open door as the three riders gathered and stepped down from their horses at the hitch rings out front.

"Is there something else I can get for you, senor?" the bartender asked Shaw. "Some food perhaps? There are *frijoles* and roasted *cabra* warming in the *cocina* out back."

"*Gracias*. Beans and roasted goat sounds good right now," Shaw said, without taking his eyes off the three men out front.

"Coming up," said the bartender.

Shaw only stood staring as the three filed inside, Esconza in the lead, and took the positions they thought would best suit their purpose.

Ollie Wilcox stood at the middle of bar. Charlie Ruiz stayed close to the open doorway. Dario Esconza stopped in the middle of the floor and stood scowling at Shaw. Wilcox waved the bartender away as he stepped over to ask what they wanted to drink. "Make tracks," Wilcox growled menacingly.

The bartender seemed to vanish through the rear door almost before Wilcox's words had left his mouth. In their own back corner, the mouth harp and the guitar stopped short. The two musicians stood staring. From the open rear door, the smell of roasted goat meat wafted in on the hot air.

Wasting no time, Dario said, "You're Fast Larry Shaw."

"I'm Lawrence Shaw," Shaw said quietly. "You're Dario Esconza."

"They call you 'the fastest gun alive,'" said Esconza, cutting right to the point.

Fast Larry Shaw? Jesus . . . ! This was the first Wilcox

had heard of it. He stood stunned, barely managing to swallow the hard knot in his throat. He shot Ruiz a frightened look.

But Charlie Ruiz didn't return Wilcox's stare; instead he gazed straight ahead with surprise and terror on his face. His gun hand eased up away from the butt of his holstered revolver. *The fastest gun alive? Whoa . . . !* Though Ruiz was looking directly at Shaw, Wilcox could see he wanted no part of this.

"Do you *believe* that?" Esconza said to Shaw in a tight, clipped tone of voice. "That you *are* the fastest gun alive?"

"The question is, do you?" Shaw said in his quiet tone.

"No," said Esconza, showing no fear. "That is why I have come here. To kill you."

"I saw you trailing me," Shaw said. "I've been waiting here for you."

Esconza was a little surprised, but he kept it from showing.

Shaw asked him calmly, "Who are you riding with these days, Dario? I heard you were working with Santana and his Cut-Jaws."

"We—we are," Wilcox cut in, hoping to head this off before it went any further. "The fact is, we were following you, wondering if maybe—"

"Shut up, Ollie!" Esconza snapped at him over his shoulder. "It's none of this man's business who we ride with. I am going to kill him."

Damn. . . . Wilcox fell silent. He and Ruiz looked at each other.

"Fast Larry," Esconza said to Shaw, "I cannot tell you

how long I have dreamed of catching you alone like this." He worked the fingers of his gun hand open and closed, loosening them.

Shaw took one step away from the bar and stood facing Esconza, while affording himself a partial view of the two men at the rear corner table. "Let's get on with it," he said. "I've got food coming."

The Mexican gunman sneered at Shaw's words and said with confidence, "Not tonight, you don't."

Shaw stood staring, realizing that for the time being, the constant pain in his head had ceased to pound; his mind felt clearer, his vision sharper. He looked back and forth from one face to another, his hand hanging loose but poised near the butt of the big Colt on his right hip. Maybe this was his most natural state.

At the corner table the two men sat watching as if frozen in place, the ornate double-barreled shotgun still leaning against the wall. One of them whispered to the other, "Is that really him?"

"I believe so," the other man whispered in reply. "I'll tell you for certain in a minute—"

Before he could finish his words, Esconza's hand wrapped around his gun butt. He drew the gun with the blinding speed of a striking rattlesnake. But fast though he was, the tip of his gun barrel never made it past the top of his holster. Shaw's Colt exploded before the two men watching realized it was even in his hand.

"Dear God!" one of the well-dressed Americans whispered, as if in a prayer.

"Yep, it's him all right," the other whispered in reply, batting his eyes at the sound of Shaw's big Colt.

Esconza hit the dirt floor, dead, a streak of blood flying

out his back with the bullet, lashing both Wilcox's and Ruiz's faces.

"Don't shoot!" Wilcox shouted as Esconza's body settled in a puff of floor dust. His hand already chest high, Wilcox now reached straight upward toward the dusty ceiling.

"Please!" shouted Ruiz, speaking in a fast frenzy. "*It wasn't our fight this fool Esconza was crazy I don't know why we let him ride with us that's the gospel truth!*" He jerked his head toward Wilcox. "*He'll tell you the same thing!*"

"Easy, the both of you," Shaw said calmly. "It's over." He'd already seen that these two had wanted no part in Esconza's plan once they'd realized who they were up against. Besides, he reminded himself, they might have information on Santana and the Cut-Jaws that could be useful.

Wilcox looked relieved. He let his hand come down a little and started to step toward Esconza's body. "Want me to check? See if he's dead?"

"No need," Shaw said. He spun his Colt backward into his holster. He glanced first at the two men at the table, and then at the mouth harp player, all standing and staring at him. Behind the rear door, the bartender stood peeping inside warily.

"How's my food coming along?" Shaw asked him.

Chapter 2

———

At the bar, Shaw ate beans and chunks of roasted goat with a wooden spoon. In the rear corner, the guitar player had reappeared and began accompanying the twanging mouth harp once again. From the back table the two men still watched Shaw as he talked with Ollie Wilcox and Charlie Ruiz. The bartender and a cook from the *cocina* out back dragged Esconza's body onto the street and left it lying in the dirt. A skinny hound appeared, as if out of nowhere, and licked hungrily at the dead outlaw's bloody shirt.

"Someone else will have to move him," the bartender said to Shaw when he and the cook walked back inside dusting their hands.

"*Gracias,*" Shaw said. He nodded and turned back to Wilcox and Ruiz. "Go on," he said to Wilcox.

Wilcox continued what he'd been saying. "See, Charlie here and I both told him, as bad as we need good gunmen, we ought to be talking about hiring you, not killing you." He shrugged. "But we couldn't make the dumb jackass listen to anything." He looked at Ruiz. "Ain't that right, Charlie?" he said.

"Right as rain," Ruiz said quickly. He paused, looking at Wilcox, and then said, "But I'd be lying if I didn't say we never heard of Fast Larry Shaw ever riding with a gang like us Cut-Jaws."

"It's *Lawrence* Shaw, and I always keep who I ride with to myself," Shaw corrected him. He raised a spoonful of beans and goat meat to his mouth, moving his eyes from one man to the other as he spoke. He knew that the Cut-Jaws had long been on the list of border gangs that his friends U.S. Marshal Crayton Dawson and Deputy Jedson Caldwell were trying to wipe out.

"Oh, we understand that," Wilcox cut in. "I say a man who doesn't watch his tongue might damn well end up losing it."

"Watch his tongue . . . ?" Shaw said, staring coldly at him over the spoonful of food.

"That's just a way of putting it," said Ruiz, cutting in. "The point is, we wanted you to join up before we even knew who you are. Now that we know . . . well, hell, we *doubly* want you with us."

Shaw took his time, chewed his food, swallowed and gazed off in contemplation for a moment.

Wilcox said, "We mean, that is, if you think we'd all get along, not crowd one another or otherwise I—I—I—I!" His words turned into a shriek as Shaw's big Colt staked up toward him and fired.

"Lord God!" Ruiz shouted, falling back against the bar, Wilcox right beside him. The lone barman who'd left the cantina earlier had rushed back in through the open door, his rifle raised to his shoulder.

Shaw's shot picked the rifleman up and slammed him backward beside the door. He sank down the rough adobe wall, leaving a wide bloody trail behind him.

Again Shaw's Colt leveled toward Ruiz, smoke curling up from the barrel. "Friend of yours?" he asked in a soft but menacing tone.

"No! No, he's not," said Ruiz, his eyes growing wide again. "I swear he's not with us. We don't know him! We had nothing to do with this."

Shaw said, "I'd hate to think that you two were setting me up, ensuring that he'd catch me off guard."

"No, sir!" Wilcox cut in. "Like Ruiz said, we had nothing to do with—"

"They're telling you the truth," said one of the well-dressed men, who'd stood up from the rear corner table and begun walking forward. "I believe this man intended to kill *me*. It was his misfortune to run into you first."

"Oh?" Shaw looked at him, letting the barrel of his Colt tip upward. "And who might you be?" he asked, seeing the other man had also stood up and walked toward him. Both men stopped and stood facing him, and Shaw looked them up and down.

"I'm Howard D. Readling, sir," the first man said, "of Readling Mining and Excavation Enterprises, among other things."

Readling grinned with perfect white teeth, taking off a new-looking black bowler hat and holding it at his chest. In spite of his finely polished demeanor, Shaw detected a hardness to the man, a trait not uncommon among the wealthy elite. He noted a bone-handled nickel-plated Remington sitting in a shoulder rig at Readling's left arm under his opened black suit coat.

"I couldn't help hearing this fellow call you Fast Larry Shaw?" he said, turning his statement into a question.

Shaw only nodded. He looked at the second man, who now stood off to one side, as was the custom of most hired bodyguards he'd known.

Noticing the questioning look on Shaw's face, Readling introduced his companion. "This *well-armed* gentleman is Willis Dorphin, my personal assistant." To Dorphin he said, "Say hello to Mr. Shaw, Big T."

Big T . . ., Shaw said to himself, recognizing the man's name right away.

"*Mr. Dorphin* to *you*," the broad-shouldered man said to Shaw, as if he'd heard his thoughts. "Only my best friends call me *Big T.* He tried to appear unimpressed by the shooting he'd witnessed only moments earlier.

Shaw let it go. He knew that part of Dorphin's job was to keep his boss thinking he was the best protection money could buy. "Mr. Dorphin," he said with another nod.

To keep himself and Charlie Ruiz from being left out of the conversation, Ollie Wilcox cut in, saying innocently, "Is that *Dorphin*, like the big fish?"

"What?" Dorphin stared coldly at him.

Ruiz rolled his eyes slightly and looked away, embarrassed. In opening his mouth, Wilcox had made a fool of himself.

"You know, *Dorphin*?" Wilcox plodded on, making his blunder even worse, "like the big fish with the pointed nose?"

"My name is Dorphin, you foot-licking idiot," the big gunman lashed at him, "not *Dolphin*." He glared at Wilcox with fire and venom in his fierce eyes.

"Pardon my mistake, Mr. Dorphin," said Wilcox. The inept gunman slinked backward along the edge of the bar like a scared hound.

"Damn ignorant rube," Dorphin grumbled under his breath, tearing his hard stare away from Wilcox. He wore a black leather glove on his left hand. His right hand was bare, Shaw noted, seeing the glove shoved down behind his gun belt. He also saw the tied-down holster on the big gunman's hip, housing a black-handled Colt, similar to his own.

To defuse what Ollie Wilcox had clumsily managed to turn into a dangerous situation, Shaw moved his eyes and attention to Howard Readling, who stood watching intently. "Tell me, then, Mr. Readling, why would this man want to kill a wealthy fellow like yourself?" Shaw questioned.

Dorphin said quickly, "That's none of your damned business—"

But Readling cut him off, saying, "Come now, Big T. Mr. Shaw was gracious enough to spare us both from having to kill this man." He smiled affably and gestured toward the smear of blood running down the wall beside the door. "I believe he deserves an answer."

Shaw spooned beans into his mouth and gave a slight shrug. He felt his patience begin to wear thin. "Not if it's inconvenient," he said.

"Nonsense. It's no inconvenience at all," said Readling. He looked at Dorphin and said, "Why don't you be a good personal assistant and see to it I have a full glass in my hand while I'm speaking to Mr. Shaw? Hail us a bottle and glasses."

Dorphin caught the threat in Readling's stern, brittle look. "Yes, sir," he said obediently, and backed away, his gun hand resting atop the bar. "Bartender," he called out, "three glasses and a fresh bottle, pronto."

Wilcox and Ruiz looked at each other, unsure of where they stood now that Readling and his body-guard had entered the scene. They both searched Shaw for an answer. He gave them a nod that directed them to the other end of the bar, and they made their way across the room. Once there, Wilcox cursed under his breath.

"Damn Esconza's hide, he got us into this mess, then went and got himself killed," he said.

"How long are we going to stay here kowtowing to Fast Larry?" Ruiz asked in a whisper. "If the rest of the Cut-Jaws ever hear about this, we'll be in a tight spot for sure."

Wilcox stared at him coldly. "We're in a tight spot right now, in case you haven't noticed," he whispered. "I was hoping to get Shaw to ride off with us—catch him unawares and bash his head in. Now we'll just have to hope another chance doesn't pass us by."

The two stopped whispering when they looked down the bar and saw Shaw's piercing eyes sweep across them, as if he'd heard every word.

"*Unawares?* Jesus," Ruiz whispered, tightening his grip around the shot glass in his hand. "Did I miss some-thing here, or did you?" He glanced at the blood on the wall, the floor and out on the street, where heel marks were left behind from the bodies being dragged away.

"All right," Wilcox conceded, "he's fast. He's deadly. But did you get a look deep in his eyes the way I did?"

"Evidently I did not," said Ruiz.

"Well, if you had," said Wilcox, "you'd seen that he's not all here."

Not all here . . . ? Ruiz jerked his head around and gave Wilcox an incredulous look. Above them Shaw's gun smoke still loomed on the ceiling. "If he ain't *all here*, I hope to hell I'm gone before the rest of him shows up."

As Shaw finished his food and washed it down with a drink of whiskey, Readling stood close by his side and spoke in a guarded but straightforward manner. "A wealthy man who doesn't have people wanting to kill him must not have his whole heart in making his fortune, Shaw."

"I understand," Shaw said. He looked down the bar at Ruiz and Wilcox. They were trying hard to listen, but Shaw could tell they weren't hearing much of the conversation.

With a smug grin Readling continued quietly. "The man you killed is a paid assassin by the name of Karl Herstadt, known as 'the Hun.' Perhaps you've heard of him?"

"I might have. . . ." Shaw gave a short shrug, wanting to hear more. Of course he'd heard of Herstadt—he was no saddle tramp or local thug. He'd made his living killing for top dollar among the business elite.

"You *might* have heard of him?" Dorphin cut in, sounding irritated. "Herstadt 'the Hun' just happens to be one of the most dangerous gunman on either side of this planet."

"Not anymore," Shaw said flatly. He nodded at the smear of blood Herstadt had left down the wall beside the door.

Readling chuckled and said, "Quite true, Mr. Shaw." Then he turned a sharp look to Dorphin. The bodyguard took the warning in his employer's eyes and settled down to his glass of whiskey.

"You must understand," Readling said to Shaw, "Mr. Dorphin was looking forward to killing the Hun for me." He flashed a white, smug grin. "We even spoke of a bonus for his efforts. But you beat him to it."

"Another second and I would have killed him myself, make no mistake on that," Dorphin said grudgingly, brooding over his whiskey glass.

Shaw wondered why a man like Readling tolerated so much directness from his hired help. But he made no comment on the matter.

"Be that as it may," said Readling, dismissing Dorphin's remarks, "former business acquaintances of mine paid the Hun to kill me, Mr. Shaw. Now that he's dead, I can expect there will be others hired to do the same."

"Sounds like a tough business you're in," Shaw said quietly.

"Amassing a great fortune on a wild frontier isn't a gentle game," said Readling.

"I never supposed it to be," Shaw said.

Readling studied his face for a moment, then said with resolve, "Allow me to speak freely. I need a man like you, Shaw."

Shaw cut a glance to Dorphin as the gunman grumbled and looked away. "You already *have* a man like me, Readling," Shaw said. "You've got Big T here."

"That's true. I have Big T, and I have access to many others just like him," said Readling. "But I need *more* men like you and him for a project I'm venturing forward." He paused and then said in the same guarded tone, "I recently purchased a gold mining facility from the French. As soon as I arrive at the mine, the French will pull out their soldiers and I'll be responsible for my own security. Of course, the Mexican government have committed to providing *federales* until I have adequate security in place."

"Watch your words," Shaw said cautiously, a warning that reminded Readling of Ruiz and Wilcox, who were still struggling to hear whatever they could.

Readling lowered his voice and went on to say, "The mining operation is up above San Simon, near the city of Hombres Malos."

"City of Bad Men," Shaw translated.

"Yes, are you familiar with the area?" Readling asked.

"Well enough," Shaw said. He gave a dismissing shrug, seeing Dorphin turn and stare at him coldly.

"How well?" Readling asked.

"Well enough not to buy anything the French offered to sell me there," Shaw replied, "even with the Mexican government providing security."

Readling only smiled slightly, then said, "I didn't ask you what investments I should or should not purchase. If you worked for me your job would be to look after my personal safety. Put yourself and your Colt between me and men like the Hun when the time comes."

Shaw considered it. He looked down the bar at Ruiz and Wilcox. Santana would find out that the mine was changing hands, if he hadn't heard it already. It was the sort of situation men like Santana and his Cut-Jaws lived for—catching a mining operation short on guards.

"I appreciate your offer, Readling," Shaw said. "But I'm not looking for work."

"What *are* you looking for, then, if I may be so bold as to ask?" Readling questioned.

Shaw wasn't about to tell him that he already had a job, that he carried a deputy marshal's badge inside his clothes. Instead he said, "All I'm looking for right now is a good night's sleep and a fresh start in the morning."

"A man with your talent . . . ?" Readling looked shocked. "I can't accept that you're turning me down. I need your gun skill and I'm willing to pay you top dollar for it."

"Would I make the same as Big T?" Shaw asked. "Would I have to take orders from him?"

Dorphin snapped an even colder stare at Shaw.

"You'd both be on the same level," said Readling. "You'd take orders directly from me—no one else."

"Same level, same pay?" Shaw asked.

"Yes, for a man with your reputation," said Readling. He eyed Dorphin. "I'll pay you what I pay Big T." He looked Shaw up and down, waiting for an answer. "What say you, sir?"

"I'll think about it," Shaw replied.

"You'll think about it?" Readling seemed a little put off by Shaw's attitude.

"We're headed in the same direction—toward the

City of Bad Men," Shaw said. "Our trails will be crossing plenty along the way."

"So if you decide to take my offer you'll let me know at your convenience?" Readling asked, frustration in his voice.

"That's right," said Shaw. "I'll let you know."

"I don't do business that way, Shaw," Readling said, his countenance stiffening, a hard edge coming to the corner of his eyes.

"I do," Shaw said calmly.

"Putting people off is bad business. It won't make you many friends, Shaw," Readling said.

"Oh . . . ?" Shaw caught the slightest warning in the man's tone. He glanced down the bar at Ruiz and Wilcox, then back to Readling and said, "I've been in town less than an hour, and I've had two job offers."

Chapter 3

"After you, men," Shaw said, ushering Charlie Ruiz and Ollie Wilcox out the cantina door ahead of him. Readling and Dorphin watched the two outlaws gather their horses from the hitch rail and lead them away, down the dusty street toward the town well.

Dorphin said to Readling, "It's just as well if he doesn't join us, sir. The Johnson brothers will be here most any time—Doc Penton too. There's plenty of damn good gunmen looking for work these days."

"Yes," Readling agreed in a stiff tone, turning back to his drink sitting on the bar, "but they're not Lawrence Shaw, are they, Big T?"

"They may not be the *fastest gun alive*," Dorphin said in a critical voice. "But truth be known, neither is Shaw."

Readling gave him a hard icy stare. "Do I look like a fool, Big T? Do you take me for some sort of imbecile?"

"Well, no—no, sir," Dorphin stammered. "I only meant—" He tried to explain himself, but Readling cut him off.

"Do you suppose I actually *believe* there is such a man—the *fastest gun alive*?" he asked, his voice growing heated.

"No, indeed, sir," Dorphin said stoically. "We both know there is no such man. It's just something to call a man like Shaw, who is—"

"Somewhere, every gunman has a bullet with his name on it," said Readling, cutting him off again, "the same way every businessman has a charge he must answer for someday."

"Of course," Dorphin said, agreeing in order to placate his employer.

Readling fell silent. After a moment of dark contemplation, he said, "As soon as Penton and the Johnson brothers arrive, you come tell me." He clasped a hand around a bottle of rye. "Until then, I'll be in my room with the woman." He gave Dorphin a level stare. "I don't want to be disturbed."

"Yes, sir," Dorphin said. He watched as his employer swung away from the bar with a knowing wink and walked out the front door.

Walking along the dirt street, Shaw had made it a point to stay behind the two gunmen. Noting a tense silence, Wilcox said over his shoulder, "Where are you taking us, Shaw? Are you still thinking about riding with us? If you are, you're going to have to learn to trust us behind your back."

When Shaw didn't answer, the two slowed and looked behind them. They saw him standing ten yards back in the street, staring aimlessly toward the hotel.

"What the hell . . . ?" said Ruiz, his hand going almost to his gun butt.

"Don't try it, Charlie," Wilcox whispered, "not yet. He's got eyes in the back of his head and the speed of a rattlesnake."

"I know it," said Ruiz, letting out a breath.

Shaw stood swaying slightly. But as the two gunmen watched him, he caught himself and shook his head as if to set his mind back in motion again.

"Shaw?" Wilcox called out. "Are you all right back there?"

Shaw turned as if nothing out of the ordinary had happened and walked on to where they stood waiting, their horses' reins in hand. "Yeah, I'm all right," Shaw said.

"We need to know, Shaw," said Wilcox, "are you going to ride with us Cut-Jaws?"

"I'm still thinking about it," Shaw said, walking right between the two and on to the well.

"Still thinking about it . . . ?" Ruiz said to Wilcox. The two looked at each other and followed along behind Shaw. Only moments before, it had seemed Shaw wasn't about to turn his back to the two; now it appeared as if he couldn't care less.

"You heard him," said Wilcox. He looked at the hotel, then back at Ruiz with a bewildered shrug.

At the well, Shaw saw the livery boy filling a large wooden bucket to carry back to the barn. As the boy lifted the bucket, Shaw stepped forward and handed him a gold coin. "Bring my horse to me, *por favor*," he said.

"*Sí*, I bring him right away, senor," the boy replied, hurrying his pace as he shoved the coin inside his loose ragged shirt.

While Ruiz and Wilcox began watering their horses, Shaw watched a sheet of dust billow up and drift side-long, revealing four riders making their way into town at an easy gallop. When they slowed their horses to a walk, they looked Shaw and the other two over and made their way on to the iron hitch rail out in front of the cantina.

Having seen the four riders step down from their horses, Dorphin turned and said to the bartender, "Set up four whiskey glasses for my associates, and bring in a tall drink of milk from your *cocina*."

"*Leche*?" said the bartender, sounding surprised that a man might want milk when there was plenty of whis-key at hand. He quickly pulled four glasses from under the bar and stood them next to Dorphin's bottle.

"Yes, *milk*, and make it quick," said Dorphin.

Hesitating on his way to the rear door, the bartender said, "But I have only *cabra* milk, senor."

"Goat milk?" Dorphin made a sour expression, but then said, "I don't give a damn if it's dog milk. Get it in here."

The bartender rushed out the back door as the four riders walked in, looked around and spotted Dorphin at the bar. "Where's Readling?" asked a tall man with a drooping thin mustache and a wide, low-crowned hat.

"Good day, gentlemen," said Dorphin, gesturing a hand toward the four glasses on the bar top. "Mr. Readling is in his room. Have some whiskey. You look like you could use something to cut the dust."

The four men spread out along the bar, each catching a shot glass as Dorphin slid it to them. He handed the bottle to the man with the thin mustache. The man poured his glass full and stood for a moment looking back and forth expectantly.

"Don't worry, Doc. Your *leche* is on its way," Dorphin said. He managed to keep any personal disdain out of his voice.

No sooner had Dorphin spoke than the rear door opened and shut and the bartender hurried behind the bar and set a tall wooden cup in front of Dorphin, who pushed it sidelong to Doc Penton.

The other three men stood staring as the tall gunman raised the wooden vessel to his lips, sipped deeply and then lowered the glass in satisfaction. "Ah, *leche la cabra*," he said, licking a drop of it from his mustache. He pushed the whiskey bottle on to the man beside him as he savored the taste of the cool thick milk. Only then did he raise the whiskey glass to his lips.

A powerfully built man named Aldo Barry stood at the end of the line of gunmen. He curled his lip at the thought of goat milk, but he kept quiet about it and filled his whiskey glass when the bottle finally made its way to him.

Brothers Elvis and Witt Johnson drank greedily and ran their hands across their lips, letting Doc Penton do the talking.

"We'd have been here sooner," Doc Penton said, "but Aldo here shot a man in the territory. A sheriff kept him overnight, made him write down all that happened." He shook his head in disgust. "It's getting to where you can't have a square fight without some lawman pulling out a fistful of paperwork on you."

"He didn't make me do a damn thing," the young gunman cut in, sounding offended. "I wrote it down so's everybody would know. I shot Fred Colvin fair and square—one shot in the liver. *Bang!*" he added, making a gun of his right hand.

"You killed 'Hot' Freddie Colvin?" Dorphin asked, half surprised, half impressed.

"Dead as hell," Aldo said with a crooked grin. "But he wasn't the first. And he won't be the last."

Realizing the two men had not been introduced, Doc Penton said, "Dorphin, this is Aldo Barry." Nodding toward Aldo, he said, "Aldo, this is Willis Dorphin."

The two acknowledged each other. "My friends call me Kid," said Aldo.

The Johnson brothers barely kept themselves from smiling sarcastically. They both stared at Dorphin with their whiskey glasses in hand.

"Likes to be called Aldo the Kid—get it?" said Witt Johnson.

"Get what?" Aldo said testily, stiffening at Witt's comment.

"Nothing," Witt shot back, the same testy tone in his voice, "just that you like being called 'the Kid.'"

"Yeah, I got it," Dorphin cut in, noticing the tension between the two. "Glad you could join us on such short notice, *Kid*."

"Yeah, well, I had plenty of other offers," Aldo said, disregarding Dorphin and looking out through the open front door at the men they'd passed while riding in. "The men at the well, are they with us?"

"No," said Dorphin. He nodded at the dried blood on the floor and said, "Two of them came in with another fellow. The other fellow threw down on the man wearing the sombrero and got himself killed."

"Yeah . . . ? The man in the sombrero?" Aldo stared toward Shaw in contemplation. "Mexican . . . I figured when we rode in."

"He's dressed like a Mexican, but he's not one," said Dorphin. "That's a Texan named Lawrence Shaw. They call him the fas—"

"Damn, son!" said Aldo, cutting him off. "That's Fast Larry Shaw? The fastest gun alive? You're not joking with me, are ya, fellow?"

Dorphin didn't answer. Instead he gave Doc Penton a look.

Doc Penton cautioned, "Aldo, Mr. Dorphin here doesn't *joke*."

Aldo just looked at the two as if he hadn't heard the warning in Doc's statement. "I've wanted to kill Fast Larry Shaw since I first heard his name." He grinned and gave Doc and Dorphin a questioning look.

Witt and Elvis Johnson looked at each other and sipped their whiskey.

"Some other time, Aldo," said Doc. "We met Dorphin here to take on a job. That's all we're here for."

"Yeah? Well, I'm betting Mr. Readling would like to see what he's spending his money on," said Aldo, staring at Dorphin and ignoring Doc.

Dorphin gave a slight shrug. He was already starting to dislike Aldo Barry. "I'm in no hurry, *Kid Aldo*," he said. "If you think you need to prove something, have at it."

Aldo grinned. "Which room is Mr. Readling in? I think he ought to see this for himself."

"Hold on," Witt Johnson chimed in as Aldo turned and started toward the front door. "You'll make us all look bad if this doesn't go your way." He looked at Dorphin for support.

But Dorphin only shook his head. "Let him go. If it doesn't go his way, he'll be dead in the street. I saw a lot out of Shaw earlier. If this *Kid* kills him, he deserves to be the top dog."

Aldo grinned with confidence and adjusted the Colt in his holster. "Fill my glass, bartender," he said. "I'll be right back for it."

From his hotel room, Howard D. Readling heard his named called out through the partly open door leading onto a front balcony.

"What the blazes is this?" he said, sitting up naked in his bed. The woman lying beside him sat up as well.

"It is one of your men calling you," the woman said with a half sigh. She swung over onto her side of the bed, sat on the edge and wrapped a sheet around herself.

"I'll have his eyes for this," Readling growled, as he heard the voice call out his name again on the dirt street. He sprang up from the bed and snatched a robe from a chair on his way to the balcony.

"Who are you? And what do you want?" Readling shouted down, taking a sweeping glance along the street and seeing Dorphin and three other men step out of the cantina, watching. In the other direction, he saw Shaw standing at his horse beside the town well, the livery boy handing over his horse's reins.

"There you are, Mr. Readling," Aldo called out, seeing his new employer step onto the balcony.

"Beg your pardon, Mr. Readling," said Aldo, seeing the woman watching from the half-open doorway, wearing nothing but a sheet. "I'm your new security man. I want you to see that you got your money's worth hiring me."

"This idiot!" Readling growled under his breath. "Why doesn't Big T kill him?" He started to turn and walk back inside, but when he saw that the man was walking directly toward Shaw, he mumbled to himself, "Oh . . . I understand."

"What is it, Howard?" the woman asked, walking across the short balcony and standing beside Readling. She clutched the sheet at the center of her bosom.

On the street, Shaw saw the gunman walking toward him with deliberation, his gun hand poised near the butt of his holstered Colt. He'd seen all of this before. He knew what it meant without the man saying a word. Yet, even as the stranger drew closer, Shaw turned his eyes away from him, and up to the balcony.

My God, Rosa, it is you. . . .

He saw the dark-haired woman return his gaze, looking down on him as if from some higher sunlit plain. The sight of her held him transfixed.

"Well, well, if it ain't Fast Larry Shaw!" Aldo called out in a taunting voice as he advanced along the dirt street. Even a skinny hound who sat scratching himself in the street by the boardwalk seemed to hear the threat in Aldo Barry's tone of voice. He stopped scratching, cocked his head in curiosity and slinked away, looking back wearily over a bony shoulder.

"Rosa . . . ?" Shaw whispered to himself, handing the reins back to the livery boy, his eyes still turned upward to the balcony, seeing only the woman.

Chapter 4

Out in front of the cantina, Doc Penton stood beside Dorphin, holding the tall wooden cup of goat milk he'd carried with him from atop the bar. Looking down the street toward the town well, he said, "So, that's Fast Larry Shaw in the flesh."

"Yep," said Dorphin, staring right along with him. The Johnson brothers stood nearby, following suit.

"For a man singled out for a gunfight, he doesn't seem to be much beside himself," Doc mused.

"There ain't anything that seems to faze him, Doc," said Dorphin. "I'll give him that."

"Fast, huh?" said Doc.

"Yep, as the name suggests . . . ," Dorphin said with quiet speculation, seeing Shaw finally turn his eyes away from the balcony and on to an approaching Aldo Barry.

"I'm here to kill you, Fast Larry," Aldo Barry called out, stopping thirty feet away and spreading his feet shoulder width apart.

Ruiz and Wilcox hurriedly led their horses off to the side and stood watching with rapt interest.

Shaw didn't answer Barry's threat—didn't pay him any notice. He gave his horse a firm push on its rump as the livery boy quickly pulled the animal out of the line of fire. Then he started walking toward the gunman, a look of dark resolve on his face.

"Did you hear me, Fast Larry? Stop right there!" Aldo Barry called out, watching Shaw advance with no sign of slowing down, let alone stopping.

Barry had positioned himself at just the right distance from Shaw. No sound gunman ventured any closer than this. But Shaw reduced the distance between them with each step.

"Damn . . . ! What's wrong with this fool?" Aldo remarked to no one in particular. He couldn't let Shaw force him back in front of Readling and the others. "I said stop right there, Shaw!" he bellowed.

Shaw didn't even slow down. He stalked closer, fifteen feet . . . twelve . . . nine . . . six.

Aldo could wait no longer. *If this fool won't stop and fight . . . !* He drew his gun from his holster with blinding speed. But it was too late; Shaw was upon him. As Aldo's gun came up, Shaw snatched it from his hand, made one vicious swing and crushed Aldo's nose flat to his face with the edge of his own gun butt.

Out in front of the cantina, both Doc Penton and Dorphin winced at the sight of the blow.

"Holy Mother Hannah," said Elvis Johnson under his breath, seeing Aldo fly to the ground in a spray of blood.

"Aldo is down," said Witt Johnson, shaking his head.

"And out," said Elvis, also shaking his head. "Felled by his own shooting iron."

At the well behind Shaw, Ruiz and Wilcox stared at

each other, dumfounded. "We're in a bad spot here," Wilcox whispered, "and it keeps getting worse."

On the hotel balcony, Howard Readling smirked at the downed gunman and watched for a second longer, a bemused look on his face. It was clear that the man wasn't going to get up for a while. He nodded down toward Dorphin, and turned to the woman beside him.

"Well, that's that," he said. He wrapped an arm around her waist and guided her back inside the room. As she turned, the woman looked down at Shaw standing in the street over the unconscious gunman. The man's Colt hung in Shaw's hand.

"Did you see what he did?" the woman asked, unable to take her eyes off Shaw as she stepped inside the door.

"Oh, yes, I saw," said Readling. "Shaw coldcocked that fool with his own pistol."

"No, I mean the way he grabbed the man's gun instead of drawing his own," she said, noticing Shaw's eyes following her own until the balcony door closed between them.

"Yes, I saw that too," said Readling. "Shaw is a remarkable man."

"He—he grabbed the gun because he did not want to risk a stray bullet hitting someone," she remarked to Readling, as if in disbelief. "I have a strange feeling that he did it for me. . . ." Her words ended in a wistful tone.

"Don't kid yourself," said Realing. "A man like Shaw looks out for no one but himself. It's what keeps him alive. That, and always being faster than the person standing in front of him." He jerked the sheet from her and tossed it onto the bed. "There, you see? I'm pretty fast myself."

She stood naked, her arms open to him. "And he works for you, this man Shaw?" she asked.

"No," said Readling. He stepped forward and took her in his arms. "I offered him a job, and he turned me down."

"Oh, so there *is* someone you can't hire?" she teased, a hand on her bare hip. "There *is* someone even you cannot persuade to do your bidding?"

"Nobody can persuade a gunman like Shaw to do anything unless he sees something in it for himself," said Readling.

"Oh? Perhaps you gave up too easily," she said, drawing circles on his chest with her fingertip. "I bet if you asked him again he would accept your offer."

"What makes you think so?" Readling cocked his head and gave her a curious look.

She shrugged a naked shoulder. "It is just something I feel."

Readling edged her toward the bed as she loosened his robe and spread it open. "We'll see," he said. "Now, where were we?"

Aldo Barry awakened, sprawled out on the dirt street where he'd fallen nearly an hour earlier. He opened his bleary eyes as water from a wooden bucket splashed onto his throbbing face. "*Go-d . . .*," he managed to groan brokenly, batting his eyes, trying to get them to focus on something, anything. Slowly, he shifted his head toward a voice that addressed him.

"You must wake up, senor," said the boy from the livery stable, an empty bucket in hand. "It will be dark soon and a wagon could run over you."

Aldo struggled back and forth, trying unsuccessfully to lift himself up. Finally the boy set the bucket on the ground, took the dazed gunman's right hand in both of his and pulled him into a sitting position. Aldo shook his pounding head a little to clear it.

"How—how long . . . ?" His voice had taken on a thick nasal twang.

"I do not know, senor," said the boy. "It has been some time now. Everyone thought that you were dead. But when they went to drag you from the street, they saw that your heart was still beating."

Aldo looked confused. Gently, he touched a palm to his smashed and swollen nose. "So, they . . . they just left me lying here . . . because I'm alive?"

The boy only shrugged. "I do not know. I only know that your *compañeros* paid me to bring a bucket of water from the well and throw it on you." He gestured a hand toward the cantina. Now only a lone woman stood out front smoking a short black cigar.

"*Compañeros?*" said Aldo, turning slightly and looking toward the cantina. He spat in disgust. "They're not my companions, the sonsabitches."

The boy only stared at him.

"I'll show them whose *compañeros*—" Aldo instinctively ran his hand down to his holster and gazed ahead at the cantina, but to his surprise, his Colt was missing. "What the . . . ?" He looked down at the empty holster, his head throbbing with pain from his crushed and swollen nose.

"He took your gun, your *compañero*—" The boy caught himself and said, "I mean the man they call Big T."

Aldo gritted his teeth and shoved himself to his feet in spite of his pain. He staggered in place for a moment, wiping water from his face. His eyes glowered wild and red with pain and fury.

"Well, then, I'll just have to go get it back, won't I?" he said.

"Senor, your hat?" the boy called out as Aldo began to stomp off toward the cantina.

Aldo forced himself to turn around and walk back to the boy, who was holding out his dusty hat. The boy stared expectantly at Aldo, anticipating a tip. But the staggering gunman only snatched the hat from him and slapped it against his thigh. Dust billowed from both hat and trousers. He looked all around until he eyed his horse standing at the iron hitch rail. His rifle butt stood up from its saddle boot.

"*Gracias,*" Aldo said in a gruff voice.

At the sight of Aldo Barry rising from the dirt, the lone woman at the cantina blew out a long puff of smoke, turned and walked back inside.

Dolphin, the Johnson brothers and Doc Penton sat at a round table off to one side of the bar, where they could see the comings and goings of both the front and rear doors. Dorphin had walked over to the hotel only a few minutes earlier to check on Readling. He had returned and seated himself as Doc Penton raised another cup of goat milk to his lips.

"Readling says we're leaving in an hour," Dorphin told the others, making a swift grab for his shot glass.

Doc and the Johnson brothers looked at one another.

"It'll be dark when we leave here," Doc said. "Why not stay the night . . . ? He's already wasted the day between the sheets with some *puta*. Why not head out in the morning?"

Dorphin stared at him. "I wouldn't be calling her *some puta*, Doc," he cautioned the dapper gunfighter. "Traveling with her is costing Readling more than an entourage of French chorus girls."

"A whore is still a whore," said Doc. "The cost is incidental." He sipped his tepid milk and licked it from the lower edge of his mustache. Then he toasted a shot glass toward the Johnson brothers and tossed back its fiery contents.

Before Dorphin could reply, the woman who'd just made her way back inside approached him and whispered, "The dead man in the street is coming here."

Dorphin picked up a gold coin from the tabletop and handed it to her. "*Gracias*, Juanita," he said.

"*De nada*," Juanita replied, thanking him, her cigar clenched between her teeth. She dropped the coin into the bosom of her low blouse.

Dorphin rose from his chair as the woman gave a short curtsey and hurried away. "Hear that, gentlemen?" he said with a smile to the other three gunmen. "The dead man in the street is coming."

Doc Penton shook his head a little. "I'm thinking the boy's not all there."

"I bet he wants his gun back," said Dorphin.

"You're not giving to give it back to him, are you?" Elvis asked.

Dorphin grinned and started to respond, but he was

interrupted by Aldo's enraged shouts. "Who's got my damn gun in there?" Aldo yelled, his voice ringing from out front.

Dorphin looked along the bar at the few customers watching, then replied, "It sounds like he won't take *no* for an answer."

Out front, Aldo jacked a round into his rifle chamber and held its butt propped against his thigh. "Bring it out, or I'm coming in shooting!" he bellowed.

After a pause, Doc Penton called out, "Aldo, is that you?"

"Hell, yes, it's me," shouted the pain-racked gunman. "Who else would it be? Who else got left for dead by his *pards* . . . lying in the dirt like some damn worthless animal!"

"You sound upset, Aldo," said Doc, "but I don't know why." He stifled a chuckle, then added, "Come on in. We've all been wondering when you'd wake up."

Huh . . . ? Aldo shook his head again, as if to clear it.

"Who's got my gun?" he shouted, not about to be pacified so easily. He stomped forward toward the open door of the cantina, his rifle out and ready. "I'm taking it back! You're every one of yas lucky I don't kill ya!" He paused for a moment, waiting for a response. When he heard none, he called out, "Dorphin, *you're mine!*"

He entered the cantina and started toward the table where he saw three men sitting, but it dawned on him that Dophin was missing. The realization came too late. As he hurried forward through the door, his boot toe tripped over Dorphin's outstretched foot; he flew forward and down to the dirty floor while Dorphin quickly snatched his rifle from his hand.

Dorphin clamped a heavy boot down onto Aldo's chest and pointed the gunman's own rifle an inch from his bloody purple nose.

"Let me make sure I understand this, Aldo," he said. "You come in here to kill *me*, because I took your gun, to keep somebody from stealing it while you're lying out there in the street unconscious?"

"Damn it, mister," said Aldo, angry, humiliated, his nose and head pounding in blinding pain, "I ought to kill every one of yas! You men are my pards, my sidekicks! But you just stood here and did nothing while Shaw knocked me cold! Then you left me for dead!"

"Sidekicks?" Dorphin said with a cruel grin. "A man who gets clubbed with his own gun is no sidekick of mine." He tightened his grip around the rifle, ready to shoot the injured young gunman. "We weren't *pards*, Aldo. You made an ass of yourself, and you made the rest of us look like fools. It's all I can to do to keep from spilling your head over the floor."

"Don't shoot, Mr. Dorphin!" pleaded Aldo. "I'll make it up! I'm going to kill the man who did this to me. You can bank on it."

Along the bar a few drinkers stood watching, wide-eyed and tensed. The other gunmen sat staring coolly from the table.

"The man who did this to you rode out of town while you lay in the street with your nose bleeding," Dorphin said, letting out a tense breath. "You're too pitiful to kill."

Dorphin took his finger off the trigger, his anger subsiding a little. He levered round after round from the rifle chamber. Bullets rained down and thumped onto the floor around Aldo. When the rifle was empty, Dorphin tossed it onto the young gunman's chest.

"There's your rifle," he said. He reached behind his back, raised Aldo's pistol from the waist of his trousers and emptied its bullets onto the floor. "And there's your six-shooter. Now drag yourself on up out of here. Mr. Readling said you're fired."

"Fired . . ." Aldo stared at him. "I ain't been on the job long enough to even get—"

"You're leaving," Dorphin said, cutting him off. "We've seen all we need to see from you."

"But—but I've got no money, no supplies," said Aldo. "How am I supposed to get by?"

"A smart fellow like yourself? You'll figure something out," said Dorphin. "Now get moving before I change my mind and decide to kill you anyway."

Aldo half crawled across the floor until he struggled to his feet, empty rifle in one hand, empty revolver in the other. "All right, I'm leaving," he said, cutting a sharp glance toward the other three gunmen. "But you haven't seen the last of me. I'll be back, and when I do, it'll be with Fast Larry Shaw's head on a stick!"

"On a stick!" said Elvis Johnson with a mock look of excitement on his face.

"Hear, hear!" Witt Johnson said, raising a shot glass toward Aldo in a toast.

Doc Penton just stared hard, licking a fine line of milk from the bottom edge of his thin mustache.

Chapter 5

As darkness sank upon the baked and broken land, Shaw sat atop a flat sand-stuck rock overlooking a stretch of flatlands and gazed back along their trail. His horse stood beside the rock, its reins hanging to the ground. Behind Shaw, Charlie Ruiz and Ollie Wilcox were busy setting up camp, spreading their saddles and blankets on the ground, while a pot of coffee boiled over a fire.

"I tell you, this man ain't natural," Wilcox whispered to Ruiz.

The two stared over at Shaw, who sat as still as a statue. Ruiz shook his head.

"I've seen so much lately, I can no longer say what's natural and what ain't," he whispered in reply.

"Well, this one *ain't*," said Wilcox. "If you can't see it, you can take my word for it." He scooted closer to Ruiz and said, "We've got to kill him and get on away. Else we need to get him to the Cut-Jaws and let Santana deal with him."

"*Umph,*" said Ruiz, grunting at the thought of trying

to kill Shaw, having seen how unsuccessful everybody else had been.

Wilcox stared at him coldly. "What do you mean, '*mph*?" he said.

"Nothing," said Ruiz.

"Are you afraid of him?" asked Wilcox.

"I don't know," said Ruiz. "Maybe I should be. Maybe it would be wise if we both were a little afraid of him."

"*Wise?* What do you mean?" questioned Wilcox.

"Every man who *wasn't* afraid of him today ended up dead by nightfall," said Ruiz. "That ought to tell us something."

"All it tells me is my pard is starting to turn yellow on me," Wilcox replied.

Ruiz ignored the remark and gazed over at where Shaw sat, seemingly immersed in thought. "Look at him," he said. "He ain't even concerned enough to keep his eyes on us anymore."

"There's been other talented gunmen who've died making that same mistake," said Wilcox. As he spoke, he eased his gun up from his holster.

"Yeah, except I'm thinking that Fast Larry Shaw does it on purpose," said Ruiz, "just his way of catching us trying to get the drop on him—so's he can kill us with justification."

Wilcox eased his gun back down into its holster. "You really think so?" he said. "All this crazy staring and wandering around is just for show—just so he can kill us? Why does he have to *justify* killing a man?"

"Some people just have to," Ruiz whispered, "I don't know why."

"Jesus . . . ," said Wilcox, bewildered. He crossed his arms and sat staring into the fire.

Finally, Shaw turned in surprise when the horse nudged its muzzle against his left shoulder, as if warning him to pay attention. He looked at the two gunmen sitting in the circling light of the fire. It wasn't that he'd forgotten they were there—only that for a long moment his mind was clear of everything but the woman, who had reminded him so much of his deceased wife, Rosa.

He noted how much darker it had grown since he'd sat down on the rock. The night had set in and surrounded him.

"*Gracias*," he whispered to the horse, rubbing its curious probing muzzle.

The big horse grumbled, scraped a restless hoof and shook its mane.

"All right, I best get you attended," Shaw said, standing and lifting the reins from the ground.

Hearing Shaw's movement, the two men turned and watched him lead the bay toward the fire.

"Coffee's boiled," Ruiz said cordially.

"Obliged," Shaw said, walking his bay toward a stand of wild grass between two towering boulders where the other horses stood.

"*Coffee's boiled* . . . ," Wilcox whispered, mocking Ruiz in a sarcastic tone. The two watched as Shaw dropped his saddle and bridle from the bay.

"What'd you want me to say?" said Ruiz. "Stay on your toes, Shaw. We're fixing to kill you."

Shaw smiled to himself, knowing they were talking about him. He took out a handful of grain from his saddlebags and palmed it to the bay's wet mouth. "Sorry, boy," he murmured under his breath. "I was off my game there for a minute."

The bay crunched on the grain and ate hungrily.

When he'd finished attending to the bay, Shaw set the animal loose to graze alongside the other two horses. He carried his saddle and blanket over to the fire and dropped them on the ground across from the two gunmen. Spreading his blanket out beside the saddle, he filled a tin cup he'd taken from his saddlebags and took a seat on the ground.

The two gunmen watched Shaw sip his coffee, not knowing what to say. After seeing how unpredictably he'd walked right up to Aldo Barry, snatched his gun and knocked him senseless, they were aware that anything they said could set him off.

"So," Shaw said, lowering his tin cup of coffee from his lips, "who wants to tell me all about Mingus Santana and the Cut-Jaws?"

"Does—does this mean you want to join up with us?" Wilcox asked hesitantly.

"It means I'm still thinking about it," Shaw said. "The more you tell me about the Cut-Jaws, the easier it will be for me to decide." He sipped his coffee and waited.

"That makes sense to me," said Wilcox. The two gunmen looked at each other with an air of relief. "What is it you want to know?"

Shaw gave a shrug. "The usual stuff. Who's Santana's right-hand men? What big jobs have they pulled? What jobs are they planning on pulling?"

"Whoa," said Ruiz, "some of that's awfully powerful information. Santana would cut our throats and stick our legs down them if he ever found out we—"

"I understand," said Shaw, cutting him off. "You've got my word, nobody in the gang will ever know you told me."

"You're swearing on that?" Wilcox questioned, still with a hesitant tone.

Shaw just stared at him; his gun hand fell easily to the butt of his big holstered Colt.

"Damn it, Ollie!" said Ruiz, looking worried. "He gave his word. What more do you want?"

"Pay me no mind," Wilcox said to Shaw. "I know you're a man to be trusted." He continued quickly. "We hardly ever even see Santana. He lies low and stays away. He gives his orders to the two lead men under him. One is James Long. The other is Morgan Thorpe." He paused, then said, "I'm betting you've heard of them both."

"Yep, I've heard of Long," said Shaw, sipping his coffee. He repeated the names to himself, needing to remember them so that he could pass them along to Dawson and Caldwell when next they met. "Long was a prison guard at Yuma. They called him 'the Fist.'

"That's right," Shaw continued. "His right fist is twice the size of his left. They say it comes from beating so many prisoners with it."

The two looked impressed that Shaw would know this. They had no idea he'd learned about the men from the other lawmen at the American consulate in Matamoros while riding as deputy with Marshal Crayton Dawson.

"What about Thorpe?" Wilcox asked.

"Never heard of him," said Shaw. He had heard of Thorpe, but he'd decided to hold back and see what information the two had to offer about the man. Morgan Thorpe was a gunman who'd ridden with the Younger brothers after the war. Soon after Cole Younger's arrest following the holdout at Northfield, he'd disappeared. A year later he'd turned in Mexico, running guns, kidnapping the rich and robbing payrolls.

"Thorpe is Santana's right-hand man," Ruiz said. Then he lowered his voice as if Thorpe might be standing nearby listening. "He's the one you don't mess with. He's a straight-up killer."

"He's a straight-up *lunatic*," Wilcox cut in, also in a whisper. As he spoke of Thorpe, his eyes instinctively moved around, as if he were on the lookout. "But don't ever let him know I told you so."

Shaw just stared at the two.

"Listen to us go on," said Ruiz, looking a little embarrassed. "We're talking to Fast Larry Shaw. I don't expect we need to warn him about Morgan Thorpe."

Wilcox said, "Forewarned is forearmed, though, no matter who you are or how you see it." He looked at Shaw, wanting him to agree.

Shaw remained silent for a moment. When he did speak, he asked, "What kind of big jobs is Santana planning?"

The two fell silent; they gave each other a guarded look. "I want to know I'm not wasting my time riding with him," Shaw explained. "I don't want to get stuck here stealing *federale* mules for a living."

"Nor do we," said Wilcox.

Ruiz leaned in a little and said, "You remember hearing about the big gold robbery at the Banco Nacionale last year in Mexico City?"

"I heard about it," Shaw said.

"That was Santana's setup. We pulled it off, under Thorpe's lead," said Wilcox.

Shaw studied their faces in the glow of firelight, then said, "Setup is right. Word has it, there was more German gold coin lying in the bank that day than there's ever been before or since."

"*Amen*, it's true." Wilcox grinned with pride.

But his grin waned when Shaw asked, "If you two were in on that, how come you're not rich?"

Ruiz looked disturbed. "We were in on it, but not for a big share. We were paid a cut for being ten miles outside of town with fresh horses."

Shaw sipped his coffee. "So you two were *horsemen* for the rest of the gang," he said flatly.

Ruiz and Wilcox looked at each other again. "Well, yes, sort of," said Ruiz. "But that was then. We've garnered ourselves more important positions since—"

"I don't want to hear about what happened in the past," Shaw said, cutting him off. "What's in the works right now?"

The two thought about the question for a moment. Finally Wilcox said, "We don't know. But whatever it is, it will be big."

"You don't know," Shaw said with finality. He gazed out across the dark quarter-moon night.

The two gunmen sat in silence, watching intently until Shaw took his last drink of coffee and slung the grounds from his cup. Neither spoke as he set his cup down and lay back against his saddle. He stared across the fire at them as he drew his Colt from its holster and set it on his chest. Then he pulled his blanket over himself and tipped his sombrero down over his eyes.

After ten minutes of silence, Ruiz finally whispered, "What do we do now?"

Wilcox tossed the grounds from his battered tin cup, lay back against his saddle and whispered in reply, "Damned if I know."

The two gunmen spent a tense and wary night, each wrapped in his blanket with his gun drawn and clasped to his chest. As the first thin slice of sunlight mantled the eastern horizon, Wilcox awakened and lay stone-still for a moment, listening for any sound of snoring or rustling from Shaw's side of the fire. After a while he sat up slowly and squinted through a curl of smoke atop the glowing embers.

"I'll be damned," he murmured.

Ruiz's eyes snapped open, startled. Then he too eased up on his blanket, six-gun in hand, and whispered under his breath, "What is it?"

"He's gone," Wilcox said in his normal voice. He sat staring at the spot on the ground where Shaw had been lying on his blanket.

"Gone . . . ?" Ruiz rose to his feet and hurried over to their two horses.

Wilcox stood up and stepped around the glowing remnants of the campfire. "Blanket, horse and all," he said, staring down at the ground where Shaw had been lying.

Ruiz returned and stood beside him, still wiping sleep

from his eyes. "Damn, he just lit out in the middle of the night," he said, baffled by Shaw's actions.

"Yeah," said Wilcox, equally stumped. "Did—did we do something wrong?" he asked.

"No," said Ruiz. His voice turned bitter. "But maybe we shouldn't have told him we're just horsemen for the Cut-Jaws. Maybe he figured we're not high enough up to suit him."

"We're not just horsemen," Wilcox corrected him. "We're also hiring agents, remember. We're supposed to bring in some new blood."

The two considered things for a moment. "Well, I say good riddance," Wilcox declared. He blew out a deep breath of relief. "The fact is we were looking to get ourselves shed of him, new blood or not."

"Yeah," said Ruiz, "probably lucky for him he drug up and left when he did. Otherwise, we might've had to kill him."

The two chuckled as they looked all around in the grainy darkness. "I don't like the idea of telling Thorpe about what happened to Esconza," said Ruiz, picking up the coffeepot to prepare a fresh brew.

"We've got to tell him about it, though," Wilcox said, stoking the embers back to life with a stick. "Otherwise he'll hear it from somebody else and be madder than a hornet—"

His words stopped short at the sound of a twig snapping behind them. As they both turned, their gun hands reaching frantically for their holstered revolvers, a familiar nasal voice rang out from the darkness.

"Get your hands away from your shooting irons," Aldo said.

The two raised their arms in the air, Ruiz still holding the blackened coffeepot. They remained stooped at the fire as the battered gunman made his way over slowly, looking all around in the darkness.

"No secret why I'm here, boys. Where is he?" Aldo demanded.

"That's what we'd like to know," said Wilcox. "He disappeared in the night, like he owed us money."

Aldo didn't believe them right away. He walked back and forth, taking note of the fresh tracks Shaw and his horse had left on their way out.

Ruiz looked around at Aldo and said beneath his raised hands, "Just so you know, we had nothing to do with him gun-butting you, mister."

Aldo stepped closer and said in his nasal twang, "If I thought you did, I'd be reloading right now." His gun lowered a little in his hand. He looked down at the coffeepot still in Ruiz's hand.

Aldo's swollen face was illuminated by the glow of the revived campfire, and Ruiz winced at the ghastly sight.

"Damn, he sure put it on you, didn't he?" Ruiz said.

"Not near as bad as I'm going to put it on him," remarked Aldo.

"I'm fixing to boil us up some coffee," Ruiz ventured, gesturing to the coffeepot in his raised hand. "Something hot might make you feel better."

"Yeah, it might," said Aldo, touching his free hand to his shattered purple nose. He let his gun down a little more and stood slumped, taking one more look around. "Left without a word, eh?"

"Yep, that's the size of it," Wilcox said, shaking his head as he lowered his hands and continued stoking the fire. "You're welcome to sit down and have coffee. It looks like Shaw has left us all lying in the dirt."

Aldo stiffened at Wilcox's words. "Are you poking fun at me?" he asked.

"No," said Wilcox, aware that he had rubbed the young gunman the wrong way. "It's just that me and Ruiz were there—we saw what he did to you. We've all three got a bone to pick with Fast Larry Shaw, far as I'm concerned."

"Yeah . . . ? Well, I'm gonna kill him," Aldo said.

"Right you are," said Wilcox. He gestured for Aldo to seat himself at the fireside. "But as you can see, he's not here."

"Fact is," Ruiz put in, "we might just want to kill him ourselves when the time is right."

"The time is already right for me," said Aldo. He released a tense breath and let his cocked pistol slump in his hand. "I could use some coffee, though. That's for sure."

Chapter 6

As Aldo Barry drank his cup of steaming coffee, he told the two outlaws his story, as if neither man had been there to see Shaw knock him out senseless. When he'd finished recounting his version, Ruiz and Wilcox looked at each other knowingly, but said nothing as Aldo continued.

"Had Shaw acted like any gunman is supposed to, I would have left him dead in the dirt," Aldo said in conclusion, tipping his tin cup for emphasis.

"So, you're saying he cheated?" asked Wilcox with a curious look.

"Damn right he cheated," said Aldo. "Way I see it, there's ways to do things and ways not to do them. Shaw should have stood there and drawn with me. And if he had, he'd be dead. You can count on that."

"It's over and done with," Ruiz commented, tired of hearing the story. "The thing is, where are you headed now?"

"I'm headed after him," said Aldo. "And I won't stop until I—"

"Yeah, yeah, we heard all of that," Ruiz said, growing impatient and cutting him off. "Meanwhile, we're riding to la Ciudad de Hombres Malos to meet up with some pals. You want to ride along with us?"

Aldo wasn't pleased that he'd been cut off, and gave Ruiz a scorching stare.

Wilcox cut in to keep down any harsh exchange between the two. "The thing is, when Shaw killed our man Esconza back there, it left us one short. We ride for Mingus Santana. Are you interested?"

"You're Cut-Jaws?" Aldo said.

"Yes, we are," said Wilcox. "You got something against Cut-Jaws?"

"No," Aldo said flatly. "How a man makes his way is his own business."

Ruiz cut in, asking, "You got anything against making money—*big* money?"

"No, I can't say that I've got a thing against making big money." He considered it under their watching eyes, then said, "La Ciudad de Hombres Malos, eh? The City of Bad Men . . ."

"That's the place," said Wilcox.

"It might just be the same place Shaw is headed," Ruiz threw in.

"I've heard of the place," said Aldo, running the prospect through his mind. "I wouldn't mind taking a ride there, 'specially if Shaw might be headed that way."

"It's a good bet he is," said Wilcox.

Aldo looked back and forth between the two. "None of the Cut-Jaws would object to me killing him, would they?"

"I can't see why they would," said Ruiz. "We're a

high-spirited bunch." He grinned. "We welcome a good killing as much as the next fellow."

A smile formed beneath Aldo's swollen, purple nose. "I always wondered, are there really a lot of *bad men* in that town?" he asked.

"There will be when we get there," Ruiz said in earnest.

At the morning's first light, Shaw sat atop his bay, looking out at the main trail that stretched below him. From his position, partially hidden by overhanging juniper branches, he watched four riders step down from their horses and quietly lead the animals forward. They were headed toward a curl of campfire smoke rising from a small clearing among trees and rock.

Readling's camp . . . ? Yes, he told himself, he was certain of it.

He watched the four men spread out as they approached, circling wide around the campsite before moving in. "Interesting . . . ," he murmured to the bay. With a touch of his boot heels to the horse's sides, he turned the animal to a thin tree- and brush-covered path leading down to the campsite.

Among the rocks, the leader of the four men, a gunman known as Silver Bones, raised his hand and brought the others to a halt. They listened intently to the exchange of voices coming from the campsite. Silver Bones' leathery face looked toward the sound of a woman's laughter.

"Did you hear that, Bones?" a young, round-faced gunman called out in a hushed tone less than twenty yards away.

Bones only nodded, and gave him a warning gesture to shut up. "Hell, yes, I heard it," Bones then whispered to himself. He eased forward, a sawed-off shotgun in his gloved hand. "I'm going to have me some of it too. . . ."

At the campsite, out in front of a canvas tent set up beside a wagon, the woman walked off with a robe wrapped around her, a bathing brush and bar of soap in hand. "It's never too cold to bathe," she said laughingly over her shoulder to Readling as she walked away. "Don't be such a tenderfoot."

Readling looked over at the campfire where the Johnson brothers, Doc Penton and Willis Dorphin sat eating breakfast from tin plates. "Dorphin, keep an eye on her," he said.

Dorphin set his plate aside and stood up.

"Don't you dare follow me, Willis Dorphin," the woman said in a threatening tone. She scowled at Readling with a hand cocked on her hip. "Are you out of your mind? You want him to watch me bathe?"

Dorphin looked to Readling for clarification.

"Sit down, Willis," Readling said in defeat.

Dorphin sat down. "Damn . . . ," he whispered, disappointed.

"Eat your breakfast, Dorphin," Doc Penton whispered under his breath. "You can't even afford to look at a woman like her."

"How do you know what I can or can't afford?" said Dorphin.

"None of us can afford that kind of woman," Elvis Johnson said.

"Amen, brother," said Witt Johnson.

Dorphin watched the woman walk out of sight toward a pool of runoff water backed in the rock basin. As soon as he picked up his tin plate and started to spoon his warm beans, he heard Readling call out to him in a guarded tone.

"Give her a few minutes, then go check on her. But make sure she's in the water first," he said.

How the hell . . . ? Dorphin thought. But he caught himself and said, "Sure thing, Mr. Readling." He set his plate aside again as Doc Penton and the Johnson brothers grinned secretly into their coffee cups.

"And mind you, keep your eyes to yourself," Readling demanded before he turned, walked back inside the tent and closed the fly.

"Yes, sir," said Dorphin, his coffee cup in hand.

Doc said teasingly, "Whatever you do, keep your eyes to yourself." He winked.

Dorphin gave a guarded half smile. "Of course I will," he said. He looked off toward the water basin and asked, "How many minutes is a *few* minutes?"

"I expect you'll have to figure that one out to suit yourself," Doc replied. "For me it'd be long enough already."

"I'll wait some. . . ." Dorphin pulled a watch from his vest pocket, studied it, then looked off in the direction of the water, not wanting to get on the bad side of either Readling or the woman if he could help it.

At the edge of the rock basin, fifty yards from the campsite, the woman stepped out of her slippers and touched a toe to the shallow water. It was colder than she'd

expected, but not unbearable. In any case, she wasn't
about to go back now and admit she'd been wrong. Smiling at her stubbornness, she loosened her robe and let
it fall the ground at her feet.

Here goes. . . .

She waded out only a few feet into the water. Goose
bumps covered her naked flesh as the cool crispness of
morning wrapped around her. *Oh, yes, this had been a mistake,* she told herself, swishing the bathing brush around
in the water. Still, she raised the brush and rubbed it up
and down her forearm with determination.

"Good God Almighty," said Silver Bones, who had
slipped from the brush and rocks to the water's edge.
Startled, the woman turned her head toward the voice
and set her eyes on Bones. Without hesitating, he waded
straight into the water, boots and all, loosely holding a
shotgun aimed out at the naked woman.

"We got her covered, Bones," said Bobby Flukes. He
and the other two men, Rady Kale and Dub Banks, were
spread out along the water's edge, guns in hand.

The woman didn't scream as Bones approached her.
Instead she snarled, "Get away from me, you filthy
pig!"

"I got you, *honey!*" said Bones, hurrying, grabbing
the woman's wrist as she swung the brush at his face.
She jerked her arm free for another swing.

But with a powerful grip Bones shook the brush from
her hand and pulled her to him, roughly. She backed
down and shut up, feeling a sawed-off shotgun barrel
jab into her flat, naked belly.

"There, now, honey," said Bones, "you just stay real

quiet for ol' Silver." He looked around at the other three gunmen and said to the woman, "We'll ease on out of here before your friends even know what's happened."

"Ple-please," the woman managed to say, still struggling to catch her breath.

"Bobby, grab her clothes," Bones said over his shoulder as he dragged the woman into the brush and rock where the horses stood waiting. Rady Kale and Dub Banks stood staring, their mouths agape. Flukes managed to take his eyes away from the naked woman long enough to snatch up her robe and slippers from the ground and hurry along behind the others.

"I got her next right after you, Bones!" Flukes said, excited, scurrying past Kale and Banks, right on Bones' heels.

"Well, I expect that'll be up to her," said Bones. "See, I never force my friends on a woman. I like to give a gal some say in it." He grinned. "It's only fair."

"Like hell," said Flukes, not sure if Bones was only teasing him. "I'm carrying her clothes!"

"Bobby! Settle down," Bones said over his shoulder as he rounded a boulder toward their horses. "There's an art to romancing a woman as beautiful as this one. You can't just bend her over a fence rail."

The woman groaned in the crook of his arm, her breath coming back, but not strong enough to offer a struggle.

"You see," Bones continued, "with a good-looking woman like this you need to—"

His words stopped short at the end of Shaw's rifle butt as he stepped around the boulder and caught the brunt of the blow straight into his grinning, unsuspecting mouth.

Blood and teeth flew.

"Drop them," Shaw said to the other three almost before Bones' limp body hit the ground like an empty feed sack. Holding his rifle one-handed as he caught the woman in his left arm, he cocked and aimed it at Bobby Flukes' nose from less than a foot away.

Flukes' gun fell from his hand, so did the woman's robe and slippers. Behind Flukes, Kale and Banks dropped their rifles and raised their hands high. Banks recognized Shaw instantly.

"Don't shoot, Fast Larry!" he said. "It wasn't my idea!"

"Mine neither!" said Kale.

"Fa-Fast Larry?" said Flukes, looking fear-stricken by the news. "You're *him*?" His empty hands reached high above his head in surrender.

"Damn right, it's him!" said Banks. "Shaw, we—we had no idea this was your woman!" he pleaded.

Suddenly a sharp pain stabbed at Shaw's head, just below the mended bullet wound, forcing him to wince. He tried to ignore it, but for a second he felt as if he might black out and drop to the ground. For the woman's sake he couldn't chance it.

"Get out of my sight," he growled at the three frightened gunmen. He waved his rifle barrel toward their horses.

"Yes, sir!" said Flukes.

The three men wasted no time peeling Silver Bones' limp body up off the ground and throwing it over his saddle. Bones cursed under his breath, then fell silent. A string of red saliva swung from his lips. The others leaped atop their horses and raced away through brush and rock, leading Bones' horse by its reins.

"Who—who are you?" the woman asked, clinging to Shaw as the men rode away.

"Take it easy, ma'am," Shaw said quietly. "I'm on your side."

She looked into his eyes; recognition came to her face. "You're . . . the gunman from yesterday. In Ángeles Descansan?"

"That's right. I am," Shaw replied. He picked up her robe and helped her slip into it. As she pulled the sash around her waist and hitched it, the men came from the campsite, having heard the horses' hooves pounding away along the rocky trail.

"Step away from her, Shaw!" Dorphin shouted, in the lead, his gun in hand. Doc and the Johnson brothers gathered around him.

"Put that away, man!" Readling shouted at Dorphin, passing the three gunmen. He shoved Dorphin's gun down and to the side. "Can't you see what's happened here?"

"She's all right," Shaw said as Readling ran up and took the woman from his arm. At first the woman clung to Shaw, resisting Readling. But Shaw turned her loose, his eyes still on hers, assuring her that he wouldn't be far away.

"*Are* you all right?" Readling asked her anyway.

"Yes, I'm all right," she said. She didn't cling to Readling the way she'd clung to Shaw. Instead, she collected herself and stood with her arms crossed, the collar of the robe gathered together in one hand at her throat.

"Four men tried to take me with them. But they failed," she said to Readling, still looking into Shaw's eyes, "thanks to this man."

Noticing the questioning look on Readling's face, Shaw explained. "I saw them coming from up there," he said, pointing toward the ridge above the trail. "I came down and waited for them at their horses."

"I see," said Readling. "You were just happening by, and saw this unfold below you?"

Dorphin and the others looked at Shaw with skepticism in their eyes.

"No," Shaw said, "I was following you. I've been following you most of the night."

"Following us?" Readling half turned toward Dorphin. "And yet no one seems to have noticed you."

"What does it matter if he was following us?" said the woman. "The important thing is, he was *there*. He saved me from a pack of lowlifes." She huddled tighter in her robe as she considered what could have happened.

"Yes, of course that's the important thing," Readling said quietly, consoling her. He looked back at Shaw and said, "I'm most grateful to you, Mr. Shaw. But I have to ask, why were you following us? Did you reconsider my offer? Have you decided to ride for me?"

"I'm still considering the prospect of riding *for* you," Shaw said. "But right now, I'd like to ride *with* you. If I'm welcome, that is." Even as Shaw spoke to Readling, he couldn't keep his eyes away from the woman's. He barely tried.

"Yes, you certainly are welcome to ride *with* us," said Readling. "Perhaps it will help you make up your mind." He showed a stiff smile in spite of the fact that he noticed the way Shaw and the woman were looking at each other, and didn't like it one bit. He knew that the men saw it too, and he wasn't happy with the way it must make him look in their eyes. But he stayed cool and tried to smooth the situation over.

"I don't believe you've been formally introduced to Mr. Shaw," he said to the woman, with the same stiff smile. "Rosa, this is Mr. Lawrence Shaw. . . ."

Rosa . . . ?

My God, Shaw thought, *even her name is the same. Is this some sort of dream, or is this really happening?*

Readling's voice sounded distant and unearthly as he continued the introduction, saying, "Mr. Shaw, this is Senora Rosa Reyes. She is accompanying me . . ."

Shaw continued to hear Readling's words, but he didn't bother trying to make sense of them. He had heard the name Rosa. Now everything around him seemed to slow to a halt as he stared into her dark eyes.

"Ma'am . . . ," he heard himself say as he lifted his sombrero toward her.

Doc Penton, the Johnson brothers and Willis Dorphin stood watching guardedly. Readling stood clenching and unclenching his hands at his sides.

"Well, then," he said, "now that everyone is properly introduced, let's get back to camp, get our horses saddled and see if we can catch these scoundrels."

"Why'd you let them get away, Shaw?" Dorphin asked.

Shaw answered without taking his eyes from Rosa's.

"I was more concerned with Senora Reyes' well-being," he said, "than I was in chasing down a pack of curs."

When Shaw listened to his own words, they seemed to be spoken by some third person on his behalf. For a second, he was no longer standing there in the Mexican hill country. Instead, he found himself in the old Spanish cemetery outside Somos Santos, Texas.

Rosa . . . , he whispered.

And although he'd spoken the name to himself every waking day since he'd seen the letters etched in stone above a bouquet of wildflowers, suddenly there was a newfound hope in the sound of it.

"Curs, eh?" said Readling. He considered it for a moment, and then said, "That's a good comparison . . ."

Readling continued to speak, but Shaw only heard his voice fade further away as he lost himself even further in the warm depth of Senora Reyes' eyes.

"Readling," Dorphin said, "the three of us will get our horses ready—we'll bring yours to you."

"No," Readling said, "I've changed my mind." He stared at Shaw as he spoke. "Let the *pack of curs* go, so long as Rosa is unharmed. We've got much better things to do than chase around in the night after four saddle tramps."

PART 2

Chapter 7

———

U.S. Marshal Crayton Dawson shoved two fresh loads into the ten-gauge shotgun and snapped it shut, smoke still curling from its barrels. At his feet lay the bodies of Logan Decker and Herbert Hartlett, two of five men he and his deputy had been tracking throughout the night. At daylight the fight had begun. Now, at mid-morning, two of the men were dead, one was badly wounded and the other two had managed to get to their horses and ride away, straight north.

Dawson gazed off at the rise of dust from their horses' racing hooves. *See you soon*, he thought to himself.

Deputy Jedson Caldwell walked out from behind a large, half-sunken boulder, shoving the wounded gunman along in front of him. The outlaw gripped his bloody stomach with both hands.

"This one is Dave Furley. He tells me Lawrence Shaw was in Vista Clara a week ago," Caldwell said.

Dawson looked at the sweaty, blood-smeared face of the wounded man. "Vista Clara, eh?" said Dawson, considering it. "Was he alone?"

"He was as . . . far as I could tell," the man said in a labored voice. "Are you going to . . . take me in?" He sat down on a rock, his hands still gripping his midsection. Caldwell stood nearby, his rifle trained on the wounded outlaw.

"Would you make it if we did?" Dawson asked.

"Hell, I doubt it," said Furley.

Dawson nodded and looked again in the direction of the fleeing horsemen. "Give him some water, Deputy," he said quietly.

Caldwell walked over to their horses standing in the shade and cover of a large boulder; he came back with a canteen in hand.

"*Gracias*, both of yas," Furley said. He took a drink of tepid water as Caldwell held the canteen up to his lips.

"Drink slow," Caldwell advised.

When Caldwell lowered the canteen, the gunman let out a breath and squinted at him. "Are you the one they call the Undertaker?"

"Some do," Caldwell said, recapping the canteen.

"Why do they call you that . . . because you're some kind of hard-ass, killing sumbitch?" Furley asked.

"Because I used to be an *undertaker*," Caldwell replied.

"Oh . . . ," said Furley. But he continued staring at Caldwell, as if the answer wasn't good enough.

Dawson half smiled to himself. Caldwell might be a trained undertaker, but Dawson knew that was only part of the story. Caldwell had gained the moniker by facing and taking down some of the most vicious killers the borderlands had to offer.

"So, what's it going to be?" Dawson asked. "You want

to try to ride . . . or do you want us to sit here with you a while?"

"Sit here . . . just for a spell," said Furley. He slid himself to the ground and leaned back against the rock. "I'll tell you . . . who those two are." He turned his eyes north, toward the rise of trail dust.

"We know who they are," said Dawson. "Ned Breck and Carlos Loonie."

"Well, hell," said Furley, sounding disappointed.

"More water?" Caldwell asked him.

Furley's limp, bloody hand waved the canteen away, so Caldwell placed it by Furley's side for later. He turned and began dragging the first body deeper into the shelter of rocks.

"Hartlett and me . . . argued over the horses," Furley said to Dawson. "Sumbitch . . . shot me." He looked at the body of Herbert Hartlett lying dead in the dirt. "For all . . . the good it done him," he added.

"You always rode with Dag Elliot's Wild Boys," said Dawson. "What's got you over here with Hartlett and these Cut-Jaws?"

"Hard times . . . ," the dying outlaw mused. "The Wild Boys are . . . thinning down to nothing. A man needs work. Santana's Cut-Jaws are the ones . . . hiring."

Dawson and Caldwell looked at each other. "We've heard that ourselves," Dawson said. Caldwell took the second body by its boots and began dragging it away to the rocks.

"Anyway, I'm all finished," Furley said with solemn acknowledgment. His voice sounded stronger, his having resolved himself to his fate, and he lay silent until Caldwell returned from among the rocks.

"I tied two of their horses back there," Caldwell said. "Looks like they were a horse short."

"That's what got me killed," Furley reflected. He looked up at Dawson and said, "Marshal, can you . . . oblige me my gun back before you leave?"

Dawson looked at Caldwell.

Caldwell pulled Furley's Remington from behind his gun belt. He opened the chamber and let five bullets fall out into his palm. Then he shut it and said, "I'll leave it at the rocks with the bodies. Can you make it that far?"

Furley only nodded. "Obliged," he said. Then he looked up at Dawson and said, "Shaw acted . . . about half simpleminded when I saw him in Vista Clara— asking in the cantina about birds . . . witches and such."

"He took a bullet in the head," said Dawson.

"Damn . . . that'll do it," said Furley. "Looks like I'm not . . . the only unlucky one." He let his head bob on his chest.

Caldwell stood with the Remington in hand, staring down at Furley. He knew he wouldn't have to carry the gun into the rocks after all. Holding the five bullets in the palm of his gloved hand, he stooped down and raised Furely's bowed head. The outlaw's dead eyes gazed off aimlessly into the harsh sunlight.

Dawson's shotgun slumped to his side and the deputy shoved Furley's Remington back behind his gun belt. He took ahold of the dead man's damp shirt collar and dragged him away into the rocks. When he returned, Dawson had gathered their horses, as well as the two horses belonging to the dead outlaws.

"So Shaw is back," Dawson said.

"Yep, just like you said he'd be," Caldwell replied. He took the reins to his silver gray, and then grabbed for the reins to the outlaws' horses.

"What's it been, six months?" Dawson asked.

"Less than that," said Caldwell, stepping up into his saddle. He adjusted his dust-streaked bowler hat atop his head. The two sat atop their horses for a moment, staring out across the badlands.

"Birds and witches . . . ," Dawson finally said with a sigh.

"His head's still not well," Caldwell said, as if in Shaw's defense. "The doctors all said it would take a long time to heal—a head wound like that. Maybe never."

"Yep," said Dawson. "I figured getting away from here might help. But I knew he'd be back."

"I wonder what became of the woman?" said Caldwell.

"Tuesday Bonhart?" said Dawson.

"Yeah, Tuesday," said Caldwell.

"I expect we'll have to ask him, first chance," said Dawson, nudging up his horse's pace.

Caldwell turned his horse alongside him. "It's darn near impossible to speculate about what Shaw's going to do next."

"So long as he's still carrying a badge, he's still on the job, as far as I'm concerned," said Dawson. "We need to find him, see what he's doing." He turned his horse to the thin trail.

"That's what I was thinking," said Caldwell, riding

beside him. "A man could get himself in an awful fix, the shape he's in."

Having made their getaway, Carlos Loonie and Ned Breck wasted no time in putting a stretch of hill country between themselves and the two lawmen. They pushed their horses steadily until they'd ridden onto a narrow flatlands and reached a watering hole on the trail to Little Ester.

Breck, a tall, rangy Arkansan, looked up from watering his horse, shook his head and said, "How the hell we gonna find Santana? I don't want to spend my life running from these law dogs."

"We might not find Santana before we have to get rid of them ourselves," Carlos offered. "Mingus Santana ain't likely to come forward and show his face just to protect us. He'll wait to hear that we're able to protect ourselves." He shrugged. "If we cannot take care of these lawmen, Santana will decide we're not worthy of riding with him."

"Yeah? And how will Santana ever hear about it, if he ain't around?" said Breck, with a sarcastic turn to his voice.

"Like any smart leader, Santana has eyes and ears all over these badlands," said Loonie. He was a Mexican-Irish gunman, born and raised in the rugged Mexican hill country.

"Sounds like a hell of deal to me," said Breck, a little irritated. "We search every barn lot and pigsty in this hellhole until we find him—he won't even come forward and help us out when we need him to?"

"It is the way we do things," Carlos said. "When you've ridden with the Cut-Jaws for a while, you'll better understand how things are done."

"That's real comforting to know," said Breck, still obviously irked. "I've ridden with some of the best, the Youngers, the Mollyhorns, the Border Dogs. I expect I've been around long enough to know how things are done. I don't need you telling me."

Loonie stared at him.

Seeing he might have pushed too hard, Breck pulled his attitude back a little and said in a friendlier tone, "This heat makes me easily riled." He stood in silence for a moment, working to settle himself down.

Then he asked, "And these two law dogs? Are they the ones I've heard so much about—always sticking their beak into everybody's business?"

"Yeah, they're the ones you heard about," Loonie said in a flat tone. "They're the ones who put the Mollyhorns out of business. They almost did the same to the Border Dogs last year."

"Damn their eyes! I should have figured they were the same two sonsabitches," Breck said, irritated once again. "Why don't somebody do everyone a favor and kill them—be done with them for good?"

"Why don't you?" Loonie asked.

"If I can get half a chance, I damn sure will," Breck declared.

Loonie gave a dark grin. "I'll give you more than half a chance. I'll kill them with you."

When the two had finished watering their horses, they mounted and rode away on an upward trail toward

Little Ester. By late afternoon they had traveled into town, and turned their horses to an iron hitch rail out in front of a cantina.

"*Bienvenidos a Pequeña Ester, señores,*" said an old man, the town greeter.

Loonie and Breck looked the old man up and down, then stepped from their horses, hitched them and stared at the old greeter again.

"I have been here before, old man," Loonie said. As he spoke he untied his saddlebags, slung them over his shoulder and drew his rifle from its boot. Watching him, Breck followed suit.

"Ah, *sí,*" the old man replied to Loonie, allowing a look of cautious recognition to appear on his weathered face.

Aware that the old man knew him all along, Loonie shook a finger and said with a half grin, "You're a wise old man. You remember no one until you see they don't mind being remembered, eh?"

The old man admitted nothing. Instead he fell back on his well-rehearsed lines and said, "May I ask what brings you to Little Ester?"

"No, you *may* not," Ned Breck cut in.

"Easy, Ned," Loonie said. "You are a *friend* of a *friend* of mine," he said to the old man. "I want you to tell my friend that I'm here in the hill country, and I'm looking for him."

"*Amigo de un amigo . . . ?*" the old man said, looking confused.

Loonie grinned again. "Suddenly he doesn't understand me," he said to Breck. Taking a gold coin from his vest pocket, he held it up for the old man to see.

"Fool with me and I will kill you, Miguel," he said,

calling the old man by name. "Do as I ask and you will be rewarded."

The old man only nodded. His blank eyes and expression still admitted nothing, but Loonie knew this was all the response he would get, and flipped the coin to him.

"Go to the stable and have the boy bring us two fresh horses—the best horses in the barn. And tell him to stick some food in a sack for us while we ride."

"*Sí, sí,*" the old man said, nodding. "Food and good horses."

"And move quickly," Loonie said. "We have men trailing us." He looked at three horses standing along the iron hitch rail. Two of the animals were strong-looking desert bays, but the third was a scrawny, mousy-looking range stray.

An accordion stopped playing as the two dusty gunmen stepped inside the cantina and stood staring at four drinkers sidling along the bar. Noticing the look on the barkeeper's face as he stared toward the new arrivals, the four men turned and looked them up and down.

"Carlos Loonie," said one of the men, a Mexican who bore a long, vicious scar down his right cheek. "You are the hombre I have been looking for."

Loonie's hand went instinctively to the butt on his holstered Colt. "Cervo, my cousin," said Loonie. "You better have a good reason for letting my name fall from your lips so freely."

"*Mi primo . . .*" Cervo spread his hands in the gesture of an apology. "I heard that Santana needs good men. We come to join you. I did not mean to—"

Carlos raised a hand, silencing him. He looked the other three men over good, recognizing one of them, a young Texan named Buck Collins. "How good are these men?" he asked Cervo.

The three stared at him coldly. "Good enough not to be questioned about it," said Buck Collins.

"You I have seen before," said Loonie as he and Breck ventured to the bar. "You rode with Junior Lake's gang before that Arizona Ranger killed Junior and his old man."

"You've got it right," said Collins, a sneer on his craggy face. "Had I been with Junior, it would have been the ranger who wound up dead that day."

"Well-spoken," said Loonie. "Who's riding that flea-bitten stray out front? No one who rides with us Cut-Jaws would be seen riding such a sad animal."

"That's my horse," said Buck Collins, looking ashamed. "But don't worry. I plan to trade up the first chance I get."

"See to it you do," Loonie said haughtily. He jerked his head toward the other two men. "Who are these hombres?"

"This is Matt Stewart and Russell Hogue," said Buck. "Two of the meanest sonsabitches I ever took up with."

"What do you say, cousin?" Cervo cut in. "Did I bring you some good hombres?"

Loonie let a slow grin come to his face. "No," he said. "You brought me some *bad* men . . . and that is *good.*" He looked at Breck, who nodded with approval.

"Yeah," Breck affirmed, "come to think of it, some bad hombres are just what we need right now."

"There are two lawmen dogging us," Loonie said to his cousin. "Your first job is to kill them when they arrive."

Chapter 8

It was dark when the two lawmen rode along the hillside trail toward Little Ester. Knowing they were close behind the outlaws, and well aware they were in perfect terrain for an ambush, they remained cautious. Their senses tended to every sound, every rustle of night breeze, every click of hoof or padded paw on the rocky hillside.

When they caught the sound of riders moving quietly on a trail running parallel to theirs, they stopped in their tracks and searched the darkness, listening intently. After a moment they saw the silhouettes of riders highlighted on a trail above them.

"Think it's them?" Caldwell asked in a hushed voice.

"If it is, they know we're down here," Dawson whispered, easing his rifle from its boot and propping it on his thigh. "Let's ride up and meet them on level footing."

"Good idea," agreed Caldwell, his rifle already out of its boot and lying ready across his lap.

The two nudged their horses forward at a walk,

staying on the inside of the trail, close to the steep rock-strewn hillside that reached two hundred feet upward to the next switchback. Less than twenty yards forward, they turned their horses onto a narrow path leading up through a maze of brush and loose-lying rock.

Hidden along the upper trail, Carlos Loonie, Ned Breck and the other four men hurried down from their saddles and stretched out along the cliff's overhang. There they lay in wait for the two riders; they'd already heard the riders' horses moving toward them in the darkness.

"Everybody hold fire until I give the say-so," Loonie whispered sidelong. He grinned at Breck, who was lying beside him, and said, "Now that we've got these law dogs in our gun sights, let's make sure they don't ride out of this alive."

"I'm with you on that," said Breck, checking his rifle. "Be sure you tell Santana that I had a hand in this. That's all I ask."

"I will," said Loonie. "You can count on it. We both killed them. Far as I'm concerned, we'll both take the credit for it."

The ambushers fell silent as the unsuspecting riders moved their horses at a slow walk along the dark trail. As soon as Loonie saw their silhouettes directly beneath him, he raised his cocked rifle to his shoulder and slid his finger over the trigger.

"Fire!" he bellowed, and with a long war cry he sent round after round of deadly rifle fire down onto the trail below.

Beside him, the flash of heavy gunfire lit the cliff line, which was soon shrouded in a swirling veil of silver-gray smoke. From the trail below, the sound of return fire lasted only a second. Realizing the strength of their five rifles against only two unsuspecting adversaries, Loonie stopped firing and ordered the others to do the same.

"So long, *law dogs*," he said, unable to hear himself because of the relentless ringing in his ears.

The rest of the men lay beside him in silence, listening for any sound from below, their ears also ringing as they took the time to reload their weapons.

Finally, Breck said with a short laugh, "I only saw a couple of muzzle flashes down there, Carlos. We've pounded the hell out of them."

"Yeah, we sure did," Loonie said. Fanning smoke with his hat, he stood up and continued staring down into the darkness. "But let's not go getting too full of ourselves just yet, Ned."

"What do you mean?" Breck asked, standing up beside him. "They're both dead. We caught them with their guard down—that's *that*."

Loonie looked at him flatly and said, "Before I call it a kill, I need to see some hair and bone with blood on it."

"If that's all it takes, come on," said Breck, getting more and more confident. He turned and started toward the horses standing hitched a few yards away. "We'll get you some hair and bone right now."

Cervo and the other three men stood as well, dusting themselves and looking to Loonie for orders. "How did me and my amigos do, Carlos?" Cervo asked with a proud smile.

"You and your amigos did just fine, cousin," Loonie

said. "I never doubted any of you for a minute." He looked at the other three and said, "Come with me. Let's make sure this ain't a trap."

They walked over to the horses. Breck had already separated his from the others and stepped up into his saddle. Looking up at Breck, Loonie said, "You better settle down, Ned, and watch your step. These two law dogs are known for being full of tricks."

Breck held his horse back and gave a grin. "That may have been true," he said, "but all they're full of now is bullets."

"You're right," Loonie said, not wanting to appear overly wary in front of his cousin and the three new men. "But it's always best to see some blood first." He stepped into his saddle and turned his horse alongside the restless gunman.

"And so we will," said Breck, barely able to hold himself back.

Once the rest of the men were mounted, Loonie and Breck led them off the cliff overhang and down a path to the trail below. Even in the pale light of the quarter moon, they didn't have to travel far before they could make out four objects lying motionless on the rocky switchback.

Stopping, Loonie and Breck stepped down from their saddles and led their horses forward on foot, their guns drawn from their holsters, cocked and ready. The other four gunmen dismounted and spread out on either side of the trail. They proceeded forward warily, coming to a hault when Loonie and Breck stopped.

Loonie heard the sound of labored breathing coming from one of the dark forms lying spread out beside a dead horse, and aimed his Colt. "Ned! Have you got matches?" he asked in a harsh whisper.

"Yeah," Breck said. He hurriedly took out a long wooden match, struck it and held it out in front of him. The short circle of light illuminated two boots struggling to crawl away through a wide puddle of blood.

"Stop right there, law dog! Your string has just run out," said Loonie, his gun out at arm's length, ready to fire at a distance of five feet.

The crawling man stopped, turned up onto his side and looked back at them in the flicker of the match light. Blood was streaming from either corner of his mouth, but in a broken voice managed to say "Law . . . dog?"

"Oh, no! Damn it to hell!" said Loonie in horror, recognizing the bloody face of James Long. "We've shot the Fist!"

"What?" Breck said in disbelief, stepping closer, the long flickering match still in hand. The other men gathered close around the wounded gunman with stunned expressions, except for Buck Collins, who only spat and shook his head.

"Who's the Fist?" Buck Collins asked Cervo under his breath.

Cervo said, "My cousin told me he is James Long, one of Santana's second in command."

"Just my *gawl-danged* luck," Buck growled. "First day on the job, I've shot the boss."

"Damn, Long," said Loonie, "you've got to believe me. This was a terrible accident!"

"Accident . . . your ass," Long said. He coughed and wiped blood from his mouth. "One of you sonsabitches . . . get me some water," he said brokenly.

Cervo looked at Russell Hogue and said, "Get him a canteen, pronto!"

Russell gave him a look, but then did as he was told.

"Jesus, Fist, what are you doing out here?" said Loonie, stooping down to cradle the wounded outlaw. "Who's the other man?" he questioned, looking over at a lump lying in the darkness.

"That's Tucker Cady," Long said, shoving Loonie away from him. "We were . . . looking for you, you idiot." He coughed again.

"Tucker Cady? Reilly Cady's brother? My God! Hurry up with that water," Loonie shouted at Hogue.

"Are you going to live, or what?" Buck asked out of the blue, stepping in closer, standing over Long and Carlos Loonie, who was still stooped beside him.

"You're damn . . . right I'm going to live," said Long, giving each of the men a cold, threatening stare. "When I tell Santana . . . you sonsabitches . . . are going to wish—"

His words stopped short when Buck raised the tip of his pistol barrel and sent a bullet ripping through his forehead.

"Good God Almighty!" Loonie shouted, Long's blood splattering over his face and chest. "You've killed him! He might have been all right with a little doctoring!"

"Damn right I killed him," said Buck. "You heard what he said. Did you want Santana climbing up our shirts over this?"

"He's got a point, Loonie," said Ned Breck. "Santana would have had us killed for sure. Reilly Cady would kill us, if nothing else."

Russell walked back with the open canteen he'd brought for Long. Breck grabbed it from his hand.

"Obliged," he said. He took a deep swig of tepid water as the others looked on with puzzled expressions. When he lowered the canteen, he said with a threatening tone in his voice, "Loonie, you're the one led us into this. You best keep your mouth shut about it."

Loonie stared. "But you're the one who killed him, not me," he said.

Buck turned his smoking gun barrel toward Loonie and said, "You really want to talk *that* way?"

"No!" Loonie said, raising his hands chest high in submission. "I'm just shook-up by all this."

"Get *unshook*," Buck ordered, lowering his Colt to his side. "You led us into this mess. Now I'm leading us out of it. Any objections?" He looked all around at the gunmen, searching their faces for any sign of dissent, then stared back down at Loonie.

"No," said Loonie, "no objections."

Buck looked at Ned Breck.

"No objections," Breck assured him.

"Good," said Buck. He started to holster his Colt, but then stopped himself, looked down at Carlos Loonie once again and said firmly, "While it's on my mind, you and I are trading horses."

Loonie sat in hangdog silence. Buck nodded and said to the others, "All right, then, hombres. Drag these two dead sonsabitches off the trail and let's get away from here."

When Dawson and Caldwell had heard the shooting, they'd hurried upward to the next level of the switch-back trail. Using caution on the steep, rocky hillside, they arrived less than half an hour after the shooting had ended, the last of it being the single gunshot from Buck Collins' big Colt. The lawmen rode the last hundred yards of winding trail, and came upon the two dead horses lying in wide pools of blood.

"Fire us a torch, Deputy," Dawson said. "These men have hightailed it out of here." They'd both already seen the long streaks of blood leading off the trail in the light of the quarter moon.

While Caldwell took a short torch handle from his saddlebags and wrapped it with a strip of cloth, Dawson followed the smears of blood over to a broken clump of brush. Caldwell soon arrived, a flickering glow of torchlight encircling him, and both men looked down at two bodies lying sprawled a few feet off the trail. Noting the enlarged hand on one of the corpses, Dawson took hold of the torch, walked down closer to the body and rolled it over with the toe of his boot.

Caldwell, stepping down beside him, stopped and said quietly, "James Long, also known as the Fist, Santana's number two."

"Killed by his own men," Dawson added. "No wonder they cleared out of here so fast." He stepped over to the other body and rolled it faceup to him.

"One of the Cady boys?" Caldwell asked, studying the blank, dead eyes on the bullet-chewed face and body.

"Tucker Cady, the younger one," said Dawson.

"Something sure got them stirred up against each other," Caldwell mused.

"Nope," said Dawson, "I believe this trap was meant for us. The Fist and Tucker Cady just happened to stumble into it."

"Talk about *rotten* luck," Caldwell reflected.

"Indeed," said Dawson, well aware that it could have been the two of them lying there in the brush.

"What about the bullet hole in Long's forehead?" said Caldwell, remembering the single shot they'd heard a few minutes after the rest of the heavy firing had stopped. "If it was a mistake . . ."

"He was still alive," said Dawson.

The two stood in silent contemplation for a moment.

"Would you want to leave James Long alive after ambushing him, even if it was an accident?" Dawson asked.

Caldwell only chuffed at the thought. "When Carlos Loonie gets his story straightened out, it'll be *us* who killed these two."

"That'd be my guess," said Dawson. "One thing we can tell from this for sure—Mingus Santana is gettin' ready to make a strike somewhere."

"Why do you say so?" Caldwell asked.

"Because he sent one of his top men out to gather the gang together," said Dawson.

"Yeah," Caldwell said, staring at the bodies lying in the brush and loose rock of the hillside. "Maybe we'll get lucky, catch them when they're all together."

Dawson said, "I'd feel better about that opportunity if we could find Shaw first."

"Since when do we need Shaw to do our jobs?" Caldwell asked.

"We don't," said Dawson. "I'm just thinking . . . if everything starts to come to a head with Santana's Cut-Jaws Gang, and Shaw finds himself right in the midst of it, his head still not working just right . . ."

"Yeah, I see what you mean," Caldwell said. "Sorry. I meant no harm."

"I know you didn't," Dawson assured him. He turned and walked back to the horses. Caldwell followed, the torchlight flickering in his hand.

Chapter 9

———

Riding alongside the wagon on the trail to la Ciudad de Hombres Malos, Shaw watched from his saddle as Senora Rosa Reyes turned to Readling and whispered something in his ear. Readling was in the wagon seat next to the senora. Willis Dorphin sat on the other side of the senora, driving the wagon. When she had finished whispering in Readling's ear, he turned and stared out at Shaw for a moment. Then he motioned for Shaw to come closer.

As Shaw sidled over to the wagon, the eyes of Doc Penton and the Johnson brothers on him, he watched Readling turn and speak to Dorphin. Before he reached the passenger side, the wagon came to a halt.

Readling said in a clipped tone, "I know how you are with a gun, Shaw. How are you with a team of horses?"

Shaw gave the senora a glance, knowing this was her request, not Readling's.

"I'm all right," Shaw said, recognizing the pointless-ness of the question. Readling only wanted to appear to be in charge.

"Good, then," Readling said. "I know you're only riding *with* me, not *for* me, but would you mind taking over the reins for a while? I'm sure Big T could use a break."

"I'm not tired, sir," Dorphin offered, just between himself and Readling. But Readling only gave him a cold stare.

The senora took the opportunity to flash Shaw a guarded smile. Despite the dull pain inside his head, Shaw managed to return the smile. The pain had found him during the night and stayed with him through midmorning. Usually with the throbbing came a detached numbness to the world around him. But not today.

Was it the woman that kept his senses from straying . . . ? Her nearness? Her familiarity? The sense of comfort he felt with her?

Readling turned from Dorphin and watched Shaw step down from his saddle and loop his reins loosely around the saddle horn. As he walked to the wagon, Readling called out, "You can hitch your horse to the tailgate."

"No need," Shaw replied. "He knows where I want him."

The horse stayed at Shaw's heels as he crossed in front of the wagon and stopped on the driver's side. Dorphin stepped down from the wooden seat and started back to where his horse stood hitched to the rear of the wagon.

As Dorphin stepped into his saddle, Doc Penton moved his horse up closer and said quietly, "How long you figure it'll take Shaw before he has Readling tagging along at his heels?"

Dorphin didn't answer. Instead, he jerked his horse around by its reins and moved it away from Penton to the other side of the wagon. The Johnson brothers sat watching, their wrists crossed on their saddle horns as Shaw slapped the traces to the horses' backs and the wagon rolled forward again.

In the narrow wooden seat, Shaw could feel the warm aura of the woman beside him. As surely as he felt Rosa's relaxed warmth, he felt the cool brittleness of Readling sitting on her other side. But Shaw didn't care about Readling. Being near this woman was all he cared about—this woman, who shared a name with his own precious Rosa. . . .

He was not a religious or otherwise superstitious man. Yet, being near this woman summoned up something unexplainable inside him. It was as if his Rosa had come back to him somehow. He wasn't sure how that sort of thing would work, even if that sort of thing was real. He pictured the hands of the old *bruja* as she reached up and set her sparrows loose to dance on the breeze above the racing sparks and licking flames. There was something here, he told himself. *Something . . .*

In the day's heat, Shaw lifted his sombrero enough to let it fall back behind his shoulders on its leather drawstring. With it went the damp bandana that covered his head beneath the sombrero. They rolled on a hundred yards before the senora looked sidelong at the terrible scar just above his hat line. His hair had grown back, covering it for the most part, but it was still visible, and the sight of it caused the woman to wince.

Without turning toward her, Shaw sensed her questioning eyes on him. Ascertaining that the bandana had fallen inside his sombrero, he reached back and pulled it from within the crown and held it in his hand.

"A gunshot," he said sidelong to her. "I try to keep it hidden. It still has some healing to do."

"It is not so noticeable," said the senora. She reached up and carefully fluffed his damp hair with her fingertips to better hide the scar. "There, now it is covered."

Rather than sit there brooding while his woman brushed her fingers along the side of Shaw's head, Readling cut in and asked, "Who did that, Shaw? Some gun-slick out to build himself a reputation, no doubt?"

"To be honest, I don't know who did it," Shaw said, staring straight ahead.

"Uh-oh," said Readling with a smug grin. "It's my experience that a man who leads with the statement 'to be honest' usually isn't telling the truth—not all of it anyway."

Shaw gave a short, sidelong glance past Rosa Reyes to Readling. "I don't lie," he said flatly, keeping his tone as even and cordial as he could, realizing that it still had a bit of a sharp edge to it.

"No, of course not," said Readling, his tone turning more serious, the smugness gone. "I simply meant there must be more to the story than you're willing to share with us."

Shaw stared straight ahead, the silence clearly making Readling uncomfortable. Rosa sat gazing ahead with a demure half smile on her face, as if enjoying the tension Readling had brought upon himself.

Finally, Readling broke the quiet, saying, "Well, if you two will excuse me, I think I'll ride my horse far aways." He looked at Rosa and said, "It appears Mr. Shaw has the wagon well in hand."

The senora only looked away.

Without a word, Shaw drew back the traces and slowed the horses to a near standstill. The riders gazed on curiously as Readling jumped down from the seat and turned to speak.

"Carry on, then," he said, assuming an authority that he knew he didn't really have, not over Shaw, that is. "We'll stop and rest the horses before the last stretch into—"

The sound of the wagon lurching forward cut him off. He hurriedly made his way back to the tailgate and unhitched his horse before Shaw left him standing alone in the trail.

"Boy, oh, boy," Elvis Johnson whispered to his brother, Witt. "Talk about letting a fox into a henhouse."

"Quiet, brother," said Witt. "If I was Readling, I wouldn't be in the mood for hearing any remarks."

Elvis grinned, but fell silent, watching Readling scramble atop his horse and nudge it forward, trying to hide his concern over what Shaw had done.

As the wagon rolled along, Rosa Reyes laughed playfully under her breath and said, "You certainly proved to Howard Readling that *your* wagon waits for no one."

Shaw didn't reply; he continued staring straight ahead. When the woman placed a hand on his forearm, he finally turned and faced her, and she noted the surprised, almost startled look on his face.

Realizing he had not been aware of what was going

on around him for a moment, she asked him quietly, "Are you all right?"

Shaw looked down curiously at her hand on his arm. Then he looked back to the trail ahead.

"Yes, I am," he said. Then he went back to the subject of his head wound, as if nothing else had been done or spoken in between. "Some believe it was a woman who shot me," he said.

Rosa Reyes studied his face intently, and let her hand drift off his forearm. "Do you believe it was a woman?" she asked. As she spoke she appraised him more closely, her eyes going down to his tooled leather boots. *A gunman with stallions fighting at his feet . . .* , she remarked to herself.

"I believe if it was, I probably deserved it," Shaw said, the trace of a wry smile on his face.

Rosa gave a short nod, trying to listen closely and gain whatever understanding his words were willing to reveal. As if to try and plumb the darkness she felt in him, she asked, "What kind of women are in the life of a gunman like yourself?"

In response, Shaw only turned his face to her and asked, "What kind of woman are you?"

"Forgive me," she said. "I had no right to judge you."

"Forgiven," Shaw said. "Now, back to my question. What kind of woman are you?"

She smiled. "I am not *in* your life, Mr. Shaw, and I don't intend to be."

"Careful," Shaw said with his wry smile. "Intentions make a cold breakfast."

She returned his smile and said confidently, "I will not live to eat my words, you can believe that." Then, after pausing for a moment, she asked, "Besides, who are you to speak this way to your employer's woman?"

"You're no more his woman than I'm his gunman," Shaw said.

She tried to move away from the matter. "Oh? When the time comes, you would not take his money to protect him?"

"When the time comes?" Shaw quoted her. "Shouldn't you say *if* the time comes?" He'd seen her try to skirt the subject of her being Readling's woman, but he wasn't going to let her.

"When, if." She shrugged slightly. "What does it matter?" she said. "If you take his money, will you not protect him?"

"I'm not on his payroll yet," Shaw said. "When I am, if I ever am, yes, I will protect him. But that still wouldn't make me his gunman. I don't belong to anyone—not for money anyway." He turned and looked deep into her eyes. "What about you?"

"Money does not buy me either," she said briskly.

"Then what are you doing here?" Shaw asked bluntly.

"It is complicated," she said with dismissal in her voice. "But I am not a *puta*. I am not some woman of the shadows who sells herself to any man who—"

"I know you're not that kind of woman," Shaw said, cutting her off.

"Oh?" She looked surprised. "That is what the others think I am."

"The others aren't driving this wagon," Shaw said.

She let that sink in. But something kept her from opening up any further to him. "As I said, it is complicated."

"Then allow me to try and explain for you?" Shaw said, asking her permission.

"Please do, by all means, indulge yourself," she said in a tone he could not quite discern.

But he proceeded anyway. He looked her up and down and said, "First of all, you're not the daughter of some poor Mexican who sold you into service."

"Oh?" Her interest piqued a bit. "Have I in any way presented myself to be?"

"No," said Shaw. "That's how I can tell. In fact, I'm going to venture that you've never seen Mexico, except from inside a coach, and even then only the larger cities."

She sat quietly, listening.

"This is your first trip into the badlands. Your first time aboard a freight wagon too. No woman from this country would bathe in cold runoff water, not in the early morning."

"You have learned all this from my bathing habits?" she asked with a trace of thinly veiled sarcasm.

"No, senora," Shaw said. "I don't know everything about you. But I know something about men like Readling. Between what I've learned about you and what I know about him, would you like me to take a stab at what this trip is all about?"

She didn't answer; she didn't have to. Her eyes said everything for her.

"Here goes," Shaw said. "You're not Mexican, not by birth anyway. You're from Spain—north-central Spain would be my guess."

She stared at him, trying to mask her stunned surprise.

Shaw said, "Both your English and your Spanish are

too good for you to be from here. You didn't learn either language from some mission school."

"You have not heard me speak Spanish," she countered.

Shaw shrugged. "It doesn't matter, I hear your Spanish through your English. You've been educated properly—it's in your voice."

"Go on," she said.

"You're not Readling's woman, you're a form of collateral to him," Shaw said. "Are you part of this mine deal he made with the French government?"

"Yes, the *mine deal....*" She let out a tense breath and said, "I may have started out as his collateral, but I have become his prisoner."

"Tell me all of it," Shaw coaxed.

"No," she said in a defiant tone. "I have told you too much already. How do I know you aren't going to him with what I tell you?"

"You don't know," Shaw said. He waited. A silence set in.

"All right," Rosa Reyes said at length. "My family owned the mining venture jointly with the French. With the help of the Mexican government, the French forced my father and my brother to sell it to Howard Readling."

"Since Readling bought the mining operation sight unseen," Shaw said, continuing for her, "he demanded that you accompany him here to make sure he got what he paid for."

"You are almost correct," Rosa Reyes said. "My father would never have stood for such an arrangement. Readling's associates are holding my father and my brother hostage in Mexico City. Both the French and the Mexican government are aware of it. They turned their heads."

"With no one on your side, you have to do exactly as he says, even when it comes to sleeping with him," Shaw said.

Her face tightened with anger and shame. "To *service* him," she said. "Not only must I service him, I must act as if it *pleases* me to do so—as if I am his woman." She took in a breath as if to keep from exploding. "If I do not play this role to his satisfaction, his men will kill my father and my brother."

"It's an old game among business tycoons, Senora Reyes," Shaw said. He didn't want to tell her that in all likelihood her brother and father were already dead. He'd wait on that until he knew it with all certainty.

She paused, then said with resolve, "But it is a game I *must* play, as convincingly as possible, for the sake of my loved ones."

"I understand," Shaw said. He stared at the trail ahead, but he heard the sound of horses' hooves moving closer up the side of the wagon. "We'll talk more at another time."

The woman nodded, also hearing the hooves. She lowered her voice. "You mentioned that you have heard my voice before . . . ?"

"Yes. It was a woman like you. She even had the same name as you . . . *Rosa*," he said, his voice turning softer just by saying the name out loud. "Her family lived in Mexico, but they were from Spain." He took a breath and said, "We met under similar circumstances, you could say."

She studied his face from the side, reading the tragedy from both the cut of his jaw and the furrowed slant of his brow. "This woman, Rosa, she was your wife . . . ," she said. It was not a question.

Shaw only nodded, staring ahead. He didn't wonder how she knew this, for it came as no great surprise to him. They both seemed to know a lot about each other. More than two people should, he thought, given that they had never met.

"And she is dead, this woman you speak of . . . ," the senora said softly.

"She is dead," Shaw replied in a low, mournful voice.

Chapter 10

On a dark hillside beneath a silver quarter moon, Bobby Flukes looked away from the racing sparks and licking flames swirling above their campfire. Overhead, a deep purple sky lay wrapped around countless stars stretching higher into an endless universe.

"Nobody ever found anybody by tracking their campfire," Flukes said. "That's pure hearsay, an old wives' tale."

Rady Kale looked first at Dub Banks, then back at Flukes. "Bobby, I can't even *begin* to tell you how stupid that is. I ain't even going to try."

"Yep, old wives' tales," Flukes repeated in affirmation. "Only fools and poltroons believe such nonsense. I don't believe a word of it." He spat and ran his hand across his lips.

As Flukes spoke, Kale began rolling up his shirtsleeves. "I used to believe a man could not kick the living shit out of another," he said. "But then one night I saw it happen with my own eyes, in an alley off of Canal Street, in New Orleans."

Flukes saw what Kale was about to do. His right hand slipped into his boot well and wrapped around the handle of his skinning knife.

Across the racing fire, Silver lowered the wet bandana from his black swollen lips and said with much effort, "Damn it! Shut up, all of yas." His voice sounded wet and airy through the empty spaces where he'd lost front teeth to Shaw's rifle butt.

Kale heard Bones' words, but he paid them no attention until he heard them followed by the metal click of a gun hammer.

"You think I'm playing?" Bones said, pain filling his mouth with every word. "I swear to God . . ."

"Easy, Silver," said Kale, sidling away from the fire, and Flukes' and Bones' cocked revolvers pointed at him, glittering in the firelight. "I'm just trying to look out for all of us."

Flukes' hand eased up from his knife handle. He said to Kale, "Besides, don't you think it helps Bones' face, getting some heat on it? Hell, look at what an awful shape the poor sumbitch is in."

Kale and Banks looked at Bones' battered mouth from across the fire. Banks shook his head in pity and looked down into the crackling fire bed.

"Can I say something?" he asked. Then without waiting for anyone's permission, he said, "Anybody with enough sense to pull on a boot knows that a firelight burning in the dark of night has led wild Indians to kill many a white settler."

"Ha! There are no *wild* Indians around here," Flukes threw in quickly. "If there were, so what? Are we afraid of wild Indians? Hell, no! Not me anyways."

Kale and Dub Banks looked at each other.

Before Kale could speak, Silver Bones lowered the wet bandana from his mouth again and in his pained, distorted voice, said, "Let it rest, Kale. The man has strong opinions."

From the outer darkness beyond the wide circle of firelight, a voice called out, "Everybody freeze up! We've got guns on you!"

Startled, still standing, Kale almost made a grab for his holstered Colt. But he caught himself before going too far.

"Watch it!" the voice called out again. "We'll kill you where you stand."

Silver Bones half rose, his gun still cocked, in hand, from pointing it at Kale. Squinting, barely making out the black silhouettes moving forward from the purple darkness, he said, "Who the hell are you, sneaking up like this, on *honest* pilgrims?"

"Drop it, you sumbitch, or fall with it," the voice called out. "We want Fast Larry Shaw! We're going to kill him! Send him out to us and the rest of you can keep on living."

"Shaw . . . ?" Rady Kale gave the others a bewildered look. "They want us to give Shaw over to them," he said in a bemused tone. "Says they want to *kill him*."

"These stupid sumbitches!" Bones growled through his pain. Lowering his gun to his side, he struggled to his feet and said, "Who the hell is out there?"

Recognizing Bones in the firelight with his bandana lowered from his mouth, another man called out, "Silver Bones? Is that you?"

"Hell, yes, it's me," Bones said, his pain keeping him

irate. He squinted at the darkness. "Is that you, Charlie Ruiz?"

"Yes, it's me," Ruiz said with a sense of relief. To the dark figures near him, he said, "Aldo, don't shoot. This is Silver Bones. He's one of us."

"Holy cake and candles," said Kale, also sounding relieved. "Charlie, what are you doing roaming around in the dark, stirring up trouble?"

"Looking for Fast Larry Shaw, just like the man here said," Ruiz called out as he, Ollie Wilcox and Aldo Barry walked forward, leading their horses. Barry still held his gun cocked and leveled toward Silver Bones.

As the three drew closer, Wilcox looked at Bones and exclaimed, "Good Lord, man, what happened to your mouth?"

"This is what Shaw did to me," Silver Bones said in his strained, distorted voice. "No matter how bad you fellows want to kill him, I want to kill him worse."

"Huh. Look at my damn nose," Aldo chuffed, as if Bones' battered face meant nothing.

"Who is your pard, Charlie?" Bones asked testily, staring at Barry and his broken purple nose. "And why is his gun still pointed at me?"

"This is Aldo Barry," said Ruiz. "And that's what Shaw did to him." He gestured a hand toward Aldo and added, "Knocked him cockeyed with his own gun."

"He snuck up on me, caught me unawares," Aldo offered in his own defense.

"Damn," said Bones, "he smacked me in the mouth with a rifle butt." He settled a little as Aldo lowered and uncocked his gun.

"He's dead the minute I lay eyes on him," Aldo said in a menacing tone. He spun his revolver backward on his finger, bringing it to a halt inside its holster.

"What's got into Shaw?" Bones asked. "He's supposed to be the fastest gun alive. Don't he shoot anybody anymore?"

"Well, fastest gun or not, he's dead the minute I find him," said Aldo.

"They heard you, Aldo," Wilcox said. "Howdy, fellows," he called out to Banks and Kale. "Looks like you're all headed where we are."

"Oh? Where's that?" Kale asked, fishing for information before giving any up.

"La Ciudad de Hombres Malos," Ruiz cut in with a crafty grin. "I'm not bashful about my destination—or about my intentions once I arrive there."

"City of Bad Men," Kale translated.

"That's where we're headed too," said Banks, gesturing the three men to join them around the campfire. "Coffee's hot, and strong enough to float a pistol. Help yourselves."

"Just out of curiosity," said Kale, as the three men gathered around the fire, "how'd you find us here, *in the dark*?" He glared at Flukes as he asked.

"Are you kidding?" Wilcox grinned, warming his hands out above the flames. "You could see this fire plumb to the desert floor."

To change the subject, Flukes asked, "Any of you heard from Santana yet?"

"No, but he's sending the rest of the bunch to the City of Bad Men," said Wilcox. He grinned and added slyly, "Or so I've heard."

"He's most likely sent the Fist on ahead by now. We ought to be seeing him anytime," Ruiz said.

"Your mouth is a mess, Silver. Why'd Shaw rifle-butt you anyway?" Wilcox asked.

"It was over a woman we was running off with," Bones said, not really feeling like talking. "He caught me by surprise."

"Caught us all by surprise, to tell the truth on the matter," said Kale. "Before we could rally behind Silver, Shaw had knocked him cold, and had us covered."

"The same way the sumbitch done me," Aldo said, still brooding over the incident.

"Not exactly the same, Aldo," said Ruiz, getting a little bolder with the young gunman now that more Cut-Jaws were around him. "He just walked up, grabbed your gun and coldcocked you, as I recall."

Aldo had enough savvy to realize he was greatly outnumbered now, and Ruiz and Wilcox were growing fed up with him. "I'll kill him," he offered in a more tame response than he'd given. "That's all I've got to say on it."

Ruiz turned to Silver Bones. "Fact is, last we talked to Shaw he mighta been considering riding with us." He shrugged. "Santana sent us to find good men."

Bones spat and grumbled a bit under his breath. "I'm not making any idle threats. When I get him, I'll do something instead of just talking about it."

Aldo looked away as Bones' eyes and the eyes of the others sought him out.

"Umm-umm . . ." Banks shook his big head slowly and said under his breath, "Took the man's own gun and dog-smacked him with it."

Silver Bones chuckled a little in spite of his pain and said with much effort, "I suppose you fellows will stay the night with us—ride on into Bad Men City come morning."

"Yeah, we'll ride in with yas," said Ruiz, a dark grin spreading across his face, "and if it ain't the City of Bad Men when we get there, it will be by the time we leave."

Lawrence Shaw sat beyond a wall of rock at the edge of a wide cliff overhang, staring down in the night at a distant glow of firelight. He'd taken a faded, striped poncho-style *serape* from his saddlebags and pulled it down over his shoulders. His head was bare, his sombrero resting at his feet. His rifle lay across his lap. Behind him, on the other side of the rocks, the camp slept—Readling and Rosa together inside their own tent.

Doc Penton and Witt Johnson both lay snoring in their blankets near the low, flickering campfire. Elvis Johnson, who'd just stood watch, was now lying down, a blanket wrapped around his body. Willis Dorphin came walking up behind Shaw carrying a cup of coffee.

Shaw didn't bother looking up as Dorphin sat down on a rock a few feet away and gazed out at the firelight with him.

"You figure those are the ones who tried taking the woman?" Dorphin asked, gesturing a nod out across the darkness.

"Like as not," Shaw said, judging the fire to be a good three miles away, across a stretch of rocky valley between the two steep hillsides.

Dorphin sipped his hot coffee. "I'll be on guard until

morning. No need in you being up. Elvis said you sat watch all through his guard. Can't sleep, eh?"

Shaw didn't answer. Instead he continued staring out at the distant firelight. When he spoke it was still in reply to Dorphin's first question.

"If it is them, they'll be late sleepers come morning," he said.

Dorphin considered the amount of time it had taken Shaw to answer. *Peculiar. . . .*

He gave Shaw a curious stare and said, "Oh? How do you come to that?"

"Nobody keeps a fire stoked that high at night unless they're all still awake."

"Only a damn fool would build a fire that big out in the open at night." Dorphin looked back over his shoulder, judging their own fire. "Ours is higher up and sheltered behind these rocks. Whoever they are, we can see them but they can't see us."

Shaw continued to stare out in silence like a man in a trance.

Dorphin sipped his coffee, but Shaw's quiet was beginning to unnerve him. Then, as if he'd hit upon Shaw's reason for being awake at such an hour, he said, "So . . . if you want to get some sleep, I've got everything covered here."

"What's the story on the woman?" Shaw asked out of nowhere.

It caught Dorphin by surprise. "Oh, the *woman*," he said. He offered a slight chuckle. "Yeah, I see you looking her way an awful lot." He grinned in the darkness above a curl of steam from his tin cup. "Don't think Mr. Readling doesn't see it too."

"What's the story on her?" Shaw asked again, this time more demanding.

"She's not what you think she is," said Dorphin. "So don't trouble yourself thinking about her. . . ."

Shaw stared at him.

"All right," Dorphin said with a shrug. "Men as rich as Mr. Readling don't like sleeping alone, that's all. He gets the best his money can buy, whether it comes to gunmen or whores." He shrugged again. "I don't blame him. I'd do the same."

"Why do you say she's a whore?" Shaw asked.

"Why . . . ?" Dorphin was taken aback by the question. "Because he paid cash *in advance* for her, bought her from Madam Javelina's Sporting House in Matamoros."

"You were *there*? You saw him pay Madam Javelina for her?" Shaw asked.

Dorphin only stalled for a second, but his slight hesitation was enough to convince Shaw that he wasn't telling the truth. "Yes, I was there. I saw him buy her. I loaded her travel bag onto a buggy. I helped her onto her seat. I even—"

"You're lying," Shaw said flatly, cutting him off. They were both aware of what Shaw's accusation meant. Calling a man a liar was no less disrespectful than spitting in his face. Shaw stared at him, coolly, the rifle across his lap, his hands hidden beneath the faded striped poncho.

Dorphin stiffened at the words. He dropped his cup from his hand. He started to grab for the big revolver on his hip. Though he'd barely moved, Shaw saw Dorphin's reach in his eyes. But Shaw also saw the gunman rethink his actions. He clenched his hands tight on both knees to keep from making what he must've decided would be a deadly mistake.

Shaw continued to stare at Dorphin. His gaze was both a dare and a warning. The thing Dorphin did not see in Shaw's eyes was any trace or fear, hesitation, anger or even excitement. These were the eyes of some stone-cold killer, ready to do what he no doubt *could* do. Dorphin knew the look. He'd felt that same expression on his own face, always when someone was about to die. In the past, Dorphin always knew that someone wasn't going to be *him*.

But this time was different, Dorphin told himself. Shaw hadn't called him a liar or bad-mouthed him in front of the others in order to show his toughness. Shaw was ready to kill him, here and now; he was sure of it.

Dorphin eased his clenched hands and let them lay at rest on his knees. The imprint of his fingers still lingered on his trousers. Shaw's eyes stayed locked on his.

"All right, just hold on here, Shaw," he said, keeping his voice low and level. "You're right. I didn't see it . . . I wasn't there. But Mr. Readling told me where she came from, and he had no need to lie about it."

"Neither did you," Shaw said quietly behind his iron-like stare, "but you did."

"I did," Dorphin said. "I shouldn't have, but I did. This is the best job I ever had, Shaw. I'm not doing anything to mess it up."

"There're other jobs," Shaw said.

"For you, sure there are," said Dorphin, a trail of envy and disdain in his voice. "You're the *fastest gun alive*. But this is all I get. Leave it alone. I'm asking you—" He paused, then said humbly, "Please."

"I heard about Mexico City," Shaw said, recounting his own version of the story. "About Readling holding Rosa's father and brother there, about him having them killed after he left with her." He watched Dorphin's worried eyes, sounding them for the truth.

"I heard that too," Dorphin said, sounding as though he was coming clean. "But I don't think it's true. What's true to a rich man isn't always the same as what's true to the rest of us."

Shaw stared at him intently.

"I mean, *yes*, he was holding them there, but I don't think he had him killed."

Shaw's stare wouldn't let up.

Even in the chill of the night, Dorphin sweated.

"All right, it might be true . . . I—I think maybe it is." He swallowed, looked off in the direction of the tent and tried to judge if Readling was listening. "Hell, it's true . . . he had them killed—it wasn't me who killed them, though. I swear it wasn't."

Shaw finally relented. He let out a breath and nodded slightly, letting Dorphin know he had accepted his answers at last.

Dorphin also breathed easier. "If he finds out I told you this . . ." He shook his head and let his words trail.

"He won't hear it from me," Shaw said. He turned and looked back out across the purple night toward the distant fire glow. "I'm taking the woman," he said over his shoulder.

"He'll turn the three of us loose on you," Dorphin said, noting that Shaw hadn't said *how* or *when*.

"I know," said Shaw, "that's why I'm telling you now. It's time for you to decide how much this job is really worth to you."

Dorphin stood up, knowing that he'd just received as much warning as Shaw intended to give him. After a moment of silence, he said, "Shaw, I have to tell you . . . the way you handled those two fellows in Angels' Rest. I never seen anything so—"

"Get out of my sight," Shaw said, cutting him off. There was neither threat nor anger in Shaw's voice. Dorphin stood behind his left shoulder looking down at him. Shaw seemed undisturbed. His eyes didn't so much as flicker when he heard the gunman turn to walk away.

"One thing, Dorphin," he said without turning. "If Readling *does* hear about this, guess who I'm going to kill?"

Chapter 11

———◆———

As the first silver glow of dawn wreathed the eastern horizon, Shaw still sat on the edge of the cliff overhang, his rifle still across his lap, his hands still hidden beneath his poncho. But his eyes had been closed for the past hour—sleep had finally crept up and found its way inside his stalled, trancelike condition.

A rock landed on the ledge near his left boot, then rolled forward off the edge.

"Hell, is he dead?" Elvis Johnson asked his brother, Witt. The two stood atop the short rock wall behind Shaw and observed how still and unguarded he looked sitting there.

"I don't know," Witt said. He called out, "Shaw, wake up. It's morning."

Shaw still didn't stir.

"If he's not dead, a man who wanted to kill him would never get a better chance," said Elvis.

Shaw's eyes had snapped open at the sound of the rock thumping near his boot, but he remained as still as stone. Wherever his dreaming mind had wandered to, it had come back to him and the sound of Witt calling his name. Yet he remained motionless, unsure whether or not he could move even if he wanted to.

Elvis gave a short grin, staring at Shaw, his hand resting on his holstered revolver. "If I killed 'the fastest gun alive,' think what that would make me."

Witt cut a sidelong glance at his younger brother. His arms were hanging at his sides, his right hand holding his rifle.

"The *new* fastest gun alive?" he replied.

"No," Elvis said, his hand sliding down from his holstered revolver. "It'd make me a back-shooting son of a bitch."

Witt gave a trace of a proud smile. "That's what I was thinking, but I didn't want to say as much."

"Hey, you shoulda known better," Elvis said, giving his brother a mock shove on his shoulder.

"I did *know better*, damn it," said Witt shoving back at him. "Had I thought you meant it, I would have bent this rifle barrel over your head."

"Shaw! Wake up," Elvis shouted loudly, clapping his gloved hands together. "We're getting ready to pull out of here and head to the mines."

They both watched as Shaw began to rise shakily to his feet, swiping his sombrero up off the ground. "I'm— I'm up," he said, in a strained, cloudy voice.

"Are you, now?" said Witt. He and Elvis looked at each other and chuckled.

"You sure as hell don't look like it," Elvis said, laughing. He gave his brother a nod back toward the camp and the two turned and walked away.

Shaw stood for a moment to collect himself. Then he

turned and walked back through a break in the rock wall to the campfire, where the others had gathered.

Stopping a few feet before the group, Shaw stared back and forth as if sobering up from a night of heavy drinking. A dull pain pounded deep inside his head. He didn't notice Doc Penton approaching him, leading both Shaw's horse and his own, until Doc held the reins out to him.

"Hard night, eh?" Doc said.

"Yeah, hard enough," Shaw managed to reply thickly, his eyes still not completely focused.

"I thought so," Doc said between the two of them. "I got your horse ready for you."

"Obliged, Doc," Shaw said, taking his horse's reins from him.

Readling stood near the fire, eating from a plate in his hand. Beside him, Rosa was sipping coffee from a tin cup.

"Glad you can join us for breakfast, Shaw," Readling said. Shaw noted that Readling had dropped the *Mister* and begun calling him *Shaw*. But he didn't care.

He led his horse closer to the fire and lifted his rifle from the saddle boot. As he lifted the rifle, he saw Dorphin walk away from the fire as if he'd just thought of something he needed to do. The others didn't seem to notice.

Shaw said to Readling, "It looks like I'll be leaving you this morning."

"Oh," said Readling. "That means you won't be riding for me." He shook his head in disappointment. "That's too bad. I don't like hearing it."

Shaw thought he caught a slight threat in the man's

voice. He watched Readling bend over and set his plate on a rock.

"Here's something else you're not going to like," Shaw said. "The senora is coming with me."

"What?" said Readling, taken aback. He took a side-step closer to the woman.

"What?" the woman echoed with a stunned look on her face. She actually moved closer to Readling.

"You can stop playing this man's game, senora," Shaw said. "I hate telling you like this, but your father and brother are dead. Readling had them killed soon after you left Mexico City with him."

"What are you saying?" the woman said in a shaky voice. "What are you trying to do?"

"I'm setting you free," Shaw said. Seeing Witt Johnson's hand move close to his holstered revolver, Shaw quickly levered his rifle with one hand, swinging the tip of the barrel toward Witt and his brother. "Don't do something stupid," Shaw warned them.

The Johnson brothers looked at Doc Penton, who stood with his gun hand chest high. "You heard the man," Penton said. "Don't get stupid."

The brothers seemed to settle.

"My God, Mr. Shaw," the woman said tearfully. "You don't know what you are doing!" She cut her frightened eyes to Readling. "Please! This is not my idea. I knew nothing of this!"

"Take it easy, Rosa," Readling said, now standing close beside her. He looked at Shaw and said, "You need to take it easy too." With his hands chest high, he gave a slight snap of a finger. Shaw turned at a sudden sound coming from the brush and rock surrounding the campsite. He saw a circle of mounted Mexican *federales* encircling them, rifles up and ready to fire.

"Surprise, Shaw," Readling said with a crafty, chuckling grin. "Look who happened to join us just before dawn, while you were stargazing." He gave a nod toward the young captain sitting atop his horse, holding out a big Remington revolver.

"Howard, don't, please," the woman said. "Don't kill him. Can't you see he does not know what he is doing?! He is out of his mind!"

But Readling ignored her and said to Shaw, "This is Captain Fuente and his men. They're here to see to it I have no difficulty taking over the mines."

The captain stepped his horse forward, boldly. He kept the big Remington revolver pointed toward Shaw.

"Lower your weapon, senor!" he demanded, staring at Shaw from less than ten yards away. "Or my men will cut you down where you stand."

Shaw felt the dull pain begin to throb harder inside his head. "The woman's coming with me, Readling," he insisted, "even if I have to kill you first."

"Shaw," Readling said in a confident, bemused tone, "stop being a fool. Look around you. If I say the word, you're done for. Give it up. Don't make me do it."

"If I die, you die first, Readling," Shaw said, his gaze moving all around, as if he'd found himself stuck in some sort of mental haze. He pointed the rifle toward Readling, the hammer cocked, his finger on the trigger.

Doc Penton said calmly to the others, "A dollar says he pulls the trigger." The Johnson brothers stood up, staring at Shaw.

"You'll get no takers here, Doc," Witt said. "He'll pull it."

Shaw watched them start to edge forward. There was no fear in their eyes, only a knowing look.

"It's over, Shaw," Readling called out.

"Please, stop this!" the woman begged both Readling and Shaw.

"Stop it? No, I don't think so," Readling said with a thin smile. "It's just getting interesting. Well, *Fast Larry*, what's it going to be? Are you going to die alone, or take me with you?"

Shaw pulled the trigger, ready to take what the soldiers threw at him, so long as he could kill Readling and set the woman free. But when the hammer fell and no shot exploded from the barrel, he stood in surprise for just a second, seeing the widening smile on Readling's face.

"You've got sand, Shaw," Readling said. "I'll say that for you."

Shaw dropped the rifle to the dirt and drew his Colt so quickly that nobody could make a move to stop him. The Colt shot up toward Readling. But as Shaw pulled the trigger, he heard the same hollow metal-on-metal sound. His gun was empty.

"Need these, Shaw?" Dorphin called out as he came walking back toward the campfire. He held out his hand, and let Shaw's six bullets fall to the rocky ground.

Shaw could only stare coldly at him, realizing how badly he'd been duped.

"That's right, Shaw," Dorphin said. "I eased your gun out and unloaded it while you were off somewhere dancing with the angels." He stopped and stood back far enough to be out of the line of fire. "Doc emptied your rifle before he brought your horse over to you."

Shaw swung his cold stare toward Doc Penton, who only smiled slightly.

"Ready, Captain . . . ," Readling said, raising his right hand. He nodded, letting the captain and his men know to fire when he dropped his hand. Rifles' hammers cocked with a resounding metallic click.

Shaw saw the end coming; he slapped his horse's rump to send it out of the way, saving it, since he couldn't do anything to save either the senora or himself.

"Please, no, Howard!" the woman begged tearfully. She grabbed Readling and pressed herself to him. "I will do *anything* you want! I will do *everything* you ask of me! But don't kill him!"

"Anything *and* everything?" he said. Grinning, he stared tauntingly at Shaw as he spoke, using the woman's plea for his life as a means to further his control over her. "How can I say no to something like that?"

Instead of giving the signal to fire, Readling called out, "Captain, order their rifles down."

"Lower your weapons!" the captain called out to his men.

The woman relaxed, her fear and tension easing up. "Thank you, Howard," she sighed under her breath.

"Don't thank me yet, Rosa," said Readling. "I still want to know how Shaw knew about your father and brother in Mexico City." He stared at Shaw as he asked her.

"I—I told him," Rosa admitted hesitantly.

"Oh, did you, now?" Readling said slyly.

"Yes, I told him. I didn't mean to." She turned a scornful look to Shaw. "He has a way of making you tell him things. I was scared. I thought you might have ordered him to ask me. I—I wasn't thinking clearly. I made it sound like you were holding my father and brother against their will, even though I know it is not true." She looked at Shaw with fearful eyes.

"Shame on you, Rosa. Of course it isn't true," said Readling. He chuckled under his breath.

"I'll vouch for her in that regard," said Dorphin. "Shaw coerces you into saying whatever he wants to hear. Who's going to argue with some crazy man carrying a big Colt?" He stepped forward and knocked Shaw to the ground from behind with a hard, roundhouse swing of his pistol barrel.

"Damn, Big T!" Doc said to Dorphin, wincing as he heard the terrible sound of gun steel against Shaw's already injured skull.

"What?" Dorphin said. "The only reason this fool is still alive is that Mr. Readling said so. Otherwise I'd stake him down and skin him, Apache-style."

He'd snatched Shaw's big, empty Colt from his hand as he fell. "Here's a nice keepsake for me," he said, sticking the Colt down behind his gun belt. With a tight grin he looked down at Shaw, who lay groveling in the dirt, his mind desperately clinging to what ragged shreds of consciousness he had left.

"I'll—I'll take—" Shaw tried to speak, defiant even in his battered state. But though he could hear Dorphin through a dark wall of pain, he could not form the words to speak.

"Don't worry, Fast Larry," Dorphin taunted him. "If

you ever want this big Colt back, look me up. I'll be sleeping with it under my pillow." As he spoke he cocked back his boot and dealt Shaw a hard kick to the stomach. Shaw rolled into a ball in the dirt.

"That's enough, Big T," said Readling, feeling the woman's nails bite into his skin as she clenched his forearm. "I told her I wouldn't kill him," he said.

"I don't think you should let him live, Mr. Readling, sir," Dorphin replied, "if I might say so. This fool will get right back on our trail, crazy as he is."

Readling stared at Shaw sprawled out on the ground, then back at Dorphin with a look they both understood. Over his shoulder, he said to the *federale* leader, "Captain, leave a couple of men here. Have them see to it Shaw doesn't get back on our trail."

"*Sí*, but of course," said the captain. He summoned his sergeant over to him. As the sergeant arrived, sliding his horse to a halt, the captain lowered his voice and said, "Leave two men here. Have them kill this man after we are gone, but make sure they do it quietly. I do not want to hear any gunfire, *comprende*?" He studied the sergeant's face intently. "He must never be seen or heard from again."

"*Sí*, as you wish, *Capitan*," said the sergeant. He spun his horse and rode away toward two trail scouts who sat a little apart from the others. All of the soldiers sat watching Shaw scrape his boots in the dirt, still struggling to catch his breath after Dorphin's powerful kick.

As the sergeant approached the two scouts, he addressed them in a low, guarded tone, "You two stay behind with this man. After we are gone, cut his throat and roll his body off of the cliff, never to be found."

"*Sí*, Sergeant," said the older of the two men.

"Then continue scouting the trail ahead and join us at the mines," the sergeant instructed. "Do you understand?"

"*Sí*, Sergeant, we understand," the older of the two repeated, both of them nodding their heads in reply.

Dorphin stared down at Shaw, who lay curled up in a ball, his breath coming back in short painful gulps. For the sake of duping the woman, Dorphin said, "If this was my call, Shaw, I'd kill you. But Mr. Readling gave the order to let you live. So that's what I'm gonna do."

Shaw looked up at Dorphin, but was still unable to speak.

"Save your strength, Shaw. Don't try to talk," Dorphin said in a false display of mercy. He started to turn and walk away, but in afterthought he spun back around, sneering at Shaw. "Oh, and if I ever see you coming around bothering Mr. Readling again, you half-minded son of a bitch—" He drew back his boot and released another merciless kick at Shaw's ribs. "*Guess who I'm going to kill?*" he threatened, mimicking the very words Shaw had thrown at him the night before.

Shaw doubled up in pain again and struggled to catch his breath as the group gathered their horses, mounted and rode away, leaving the two young soldiers standing over him in the dirt. The older scout had picked up Shaw's repeating rifle and stuck it inside his bedroll across the back of his saddle.

"I have never killed a man in this manner," the younger of the two scouts whispered, staring down at the helpless gunman. "In fact, I have never seen the face of any man I killed in battle."

"Don't worry. Killing a man face-to-face is easier than you would think," the older scout said, reaching out a toe of his scuffed cavalry boot and nudging Shaw, as if he were some injured animal. "We only need to be careful not to get his blood all over us." He glanced appraisingly at the gap in the rock wall, and at the cliff edge beyond it.

Chapter 12

As the wagon had rolled away, the woman looked back over her shoulder, Dorphin beside her, handling the team of horses. Readling rode along ahead of the wagon on horseback, talking to the *federale* captain. The two scouts watched the empty trail for a few extra minutes after the others had ridden out of sight.

"Now we will kill you, Senor Fast Larry," the older of the two said down to Shaw, again nudging Shaw with the toe of his boot.

Shaw could hear the men, but he could only lay there, defenseless. He felt their hands grab him by his shoulders and drag him upward and away toward the cliff overhang. Unable to move, speak or make the slightest effort to save himself, Shaw hung limply between the two soldiers, his boot toes leaving long marks across the loose dirt and rocks.

At the edge of the cliff, the two soldiers pulled Shaw to his feet and held him upright from behind. The older scout pulled a knife from his belt and held its blade against Shaw's throat.

"When I slit his throat, give him a shove, and remember to watch out for the blood," he ordered.

The younger scout nodded. He held the limp gunman by the hair, an arm wrapped around his chest.

"Do it quickly," he said, struggling with Shaw's weight, "before I drop him."

The other man jerked the knife across the helpless gunman's throat, and the younger scout immediately turned Shaw loose. Blood flew as the blade swung away.

"It is done," said the older soldier, watching as his younger companion shoved Shaw into the crisp, thin air. He stepped back and ran the bloody knife blade across his palm, then stooped to rub his palm in the dirt.

"Holy Mother!" the younger soldier gasped, watching Shaw bounce, roll, slide and tumble end over end down the steep, rocky hillside. A steam of dust rose behind the limp, flailing gunman until he finally slid to a halt, spread eagle on the last few yards of loose, slippery gravel.

"He did not feel a thing," said the older scout with an air of sympathy. "When I go, I hope it's the same way."

"Really?" The younger scout gave him a strange look. "You would like to die, beaten senseless, your throat slashed, your body thrown off of a cliff?"

"That is not how I mean it," the older soldier said, staring down at Shaw, his body lying beneath the drifting rise of dust.

The young soldier looked back at Shaw's horse standing near the extinguished campfire. "We should take the horse."

"Take it, what do I care?" the older scout said with a shrug as they walked back toward their own horses.

But when the younger soldier walked toward Shaw's horse, the big bay lowered its arched head, chuffed and snorted and scraped its hoof.

"He is as *loco* as his owner, this one," the older soldier said with a short laugh.

As the younger scout ventured closer, the bay reared and pawed at the air.

"To hell with you, then, you *loco caballa*," the soldier said. "I will let the wolves and coyotes do with you as they please."

The two soldiers mounted their own horses and rode away on a thin path leading to the trail toward la Ciudad de Hombres Malos. As they galloped out of sight, Shaw's horse walked past the campsite, over through the gap in the rock wall and stood at the edge of the cliff, looking down at the still form lying sprawled on the hillside.

The animal shook its head back and forth vigorously, as if not accepting the sight lying below. Stepping back and forth on the edge of the cliff, the horse raised its head high and whinnied loud and long into the morning air.

"What was that?" Deputy Jedson Caldwell said, looking upward along the high ridges as he and Marshal Dawson rode on the lower switchback.

"It sounds like a wildcat must have a mustang trapped up there, getting ready for breakfast," Dawson said, tipping his broad hat brim for a better look along the higher ledges. The horse's long cry rolled and resounded, echoing out across the jagged hill lines.

"Still," Dawson said, "we best take a look."

The two lawmen nudged their horses, upping their

pace in the direction of the whinnying animal. Less than a thousand yards up the trail, they spotted the horse standing on the cliff above them. When they rounded a turn in the trail, Caldwell caught sight of a body lying limp and bloody on the steep hillside.

"My God, it's Shaw," he said, recognizing Shaw in spite of all the blood and dirt covering him. He jerked his horse to a halt and nudged it sidelong off the trail. Dawson stayed right beside him.

Caldwell dropped from his saddle and ran over to Shaw. Dawson moved a little slower behind him, taking time to check along the ridgeline and make sure this wasn't some sort of trap.

Caldwell stooped down over Shaw and rolled him over onto his back. "Shaw! Can you hear me?" Caldwell said frantically, wincing at the sight of Shaw's bloody, battered face. He saw the crusted deep gash running from Shaw's throat upward and across his chin, laying the meat open to the bone. "Jesus," he said.

"Is he alive, Deputy?" Dawson asked, still lagging back a little to keep an eye on the higher trail. Shaw's horse stood silent now that the two lawmen had arrived. The animal stared down at them with its big head lowered.

After a quick check, Caldwell stood up and called over to Dawson, "No, Marshal, he's gone."

"No . . ." The deputy's words caused a hard, tight knot to form in Dawson's stomach. He stepped down from his saddle and began leading his horse closer. Caldwell walked away from Shaw, toward Dawson through brush and rock.

"It looks like somebody tried to cut his throat and

missed," Caldwell said in a sorrowful tone. He'd taken off his battered, black derby hat and gripped it tightly in his hand.

"*Missed . . . ?*" Dawson looked skeptical.

Caldwell said, "It seems that somebody tried to cut his throat, and Shaw might've ducked his head at just the right second."

Dawson stood staring past Caldwell as the deputy walked toward his horse. "He's not dead, Deputy," Dawson said as if refusing to accept the fact.

"Make no mistake, Marshal—he's dead," Caldwell said grimly. "The fall alone would have been enough to kill him."

"Maybe it *would have been*," said Dawson, "but Shaw ain't dead." He gestured for Caldwell to look behind him. When the deputy turned around, he saw Shaw reach a bloody hand up over a knee-high rock and try to pull himself up.

Dropping from his saddle and grabbing his canteen, Dawson hurried in among the rocks and stooped down over Shaw as Caldwell cradled him in his arm. Even in his battered condition, Shaw awakened enough to claw at his empty holster with a bloody hand.

"It's all right, Shaw. It's us," Dawson said, watching him resist Caldwell's aid. Shaw managed to look up at Dawson, but the confused expression on his face showed that he was still uncertain who was standing over him.

"Us . . . ," Shaw murmured.

Caldwell said, "It's Crayton Dawson, and me, Jedson Caldwell."

"Undertaker . . . ," Shaw rasped, a faint trace of a smile coming to his cracked and bloody lips.

"Yes, that's me," Caldwell said. He looked Shaw up and down as Dawson held out the open canteen toward Shaw's mouth.

"Shaw, does anything feel broken?" Dawson asked. He let water trickle from the canteen onto Shaw's dry lips.

"Everything . . . feels . . . broken . . . ," Shaw said. "Where's my . . . horse?"

"He's up there, Shaw," Dawson said. "Don't worry. I'll go get him."

Shaw looked at Caldwell's hand, recognizing the familiar fingerless black leather gloves as the deputy opened his shirt and looked at his bruised and battered ribs.

"What happened, Shaw?" Dawson asked.

"A woman . . . ," Shaw managed to say, his eyes struggling to stay open, then giving in and closing.

"I might have guessed as much," Dawson said, taking the canteen back from the unconscious gunman's mouth.

"Help me get him into some shade somewhere," said Caldwell. "He's banged up something awful."

"How bad?" Dawson asked.

"As an undertaker, I've seen worse," Caldwell said, the two of them gathering Shaw between them. He looked down at Shaw, then back at Dawson and said, "But not *much* worse, come to think of it."

At the edge of the hill town, a wooden sign nailed to a post alongside the trail read BIENVENIDOS A LA CIUDAD DE HOMBRES MALOS.

"Welcome to the *City of Bad Men*," cousin Cervo translated out loud, the six riders sitting atop their horses in the morning light.

As Cervo spoke, Buck Collins eased his revolver up out of its holster. Almost before the words left Cervo's mouth, Buck fanned four quick shots into the brittle sun-bleached sign. Cervo and the others flinched as the four explosions resounded as one, catching them by surprise from less than four feet away.

"These people need to learn English for their own good," Buck said as a cloud of burned powder rose around him.

"Damn it!" shouted Matt Stewart, a serious-minded ex-railroad detective turned outlaw from Kansas. He had to settle his spooked horse.

Buck looked around at the others. "You best all get used to surprises when you ride with Ol' Buck," he said with a dark chuckle. "I'm plumb full of them."

"So much for going unnoticed. Everybody damn sure knows we're here now," said Russell Hogue in a critical tone.

"Good for them." Buck laughed, clicking his spent cartridges out onto the ground. "I say let them know right off, the *bad men* have arrived." He grinned and began reloading his revolver. "Hell, you could say we're the ones this pigsty town was named after."

Son of a bitch . . . Carlos Loonie turned away from Buck and looked at Ned Breck, who gave a slight shake of his head.

"Now, let's go make ourselves welcome—show these people what kind of *bad men* we are," Buck said. He jerked his horse around by its reins and heeled it onto the dirt street ahead. The five riders looked at each other.

"Santana ain't going to stand for this kinda behavior," Loonie said under his breath. They backed their horses, turned them and nudged them forward.

The riders drew closer to an iron hitch rail out in front of a sagging adobe cantina. The owner had heard the gunfire and seen the men coming. He'd hurriedly run from behind the bar, searching frantically for either his bartender or the six-inch-thick oak timber he used to cross-bolt the door from the inside. He saw neither, but finally, his dwarf bartender walked in through the rear door carrying a sloop bucket he'd just emptied.

"Rafael!" the cantina owner said to the dwarf. "We have trouble coming. Fetch the timber quickly!"

The dwarf had also heard the gunfire. Without hesitation, he dropped the bucket and hurried to a stockroom behind the bar.

"*Sante Madre!* Hurry!" the owner called out as the short man struggled back across the dirt floor, half carrying, half dragging the heavy oak timber.

Out front, Buck Collins slid down from his saddle and spun his reins around the hitch rail. Only a second behind, the others arrived and did the same.

"Looks like the place ain't open yet," said Matt Stewart, staring at the front of the ancient building.

"That's no problem." Collins grinned. He had seen the front doors swing shut from inside as they'd approached. "We know how to open a place, don't we?"

"Yeah, I expect we do," said Hogue. After many days and nights on the trail, none of the men had any reservations about kicking a door in and helping themselves until someone came running to tend the bar.

Inside the cantina, the owner and Rafael had managed to raise the oak timber and drop it into steel slots, one on either side of the wide door frame. With the timber in place, the owner breathed a sigh of relief. When he heard the pounding commence from the outside, he looked at the dwarf with satisfaction.

But the relief melted from his face as the pounding grew stronger and a gruff voice shouted, "Open this gawd-damn door! We saw you in there."

"We are closed, senors," the owner called out. "Please come back when we are open."

"Open the door! We'll burn this damn place to the ground!" another gruff voice called out.

The cantina owner leaned into the dwarf and whispered, "They always say this." He gave a tight, nervous grin.

Before the owner could stop him, Rafael pounded back on the door and shouted, "Get away from this door, you dirty sonsabitches! Or I'll—"

"No, no!" The owner grabbed the dwarf from behind and pressed a hand over his mouth, silencing him. "He didn't mean that," the owner called out through a barrage of curses and threats. The pounding grew more fierce. The owner let go of the dwarf and started running toward the back door. The dwarf saw the owner stop abruptly as Buck Collins stepped inside from the rear door, leaving it hanging open behind him.

"Who do I complain to about the service here?" Buck Collins said with a dark grin, his six-shooter out and cocked. "So far it leaves lots to be desired."

Chapter 13

————

By midmorning two armed townsmen lay dead in the dirt street. The few remaining residents of the ancient hill town had gathered enough food and supplies to last them a few days. They slipped away deeper into the shelter of the hillsides, the same way their ancestors had done in centuries past.

Atop an ancient adobe church, a concerned face stared out from under the hood of a black frock, toward the noise and commotion coming from the rollicking cantina. He murmured something dark under his breath, then looked away in disgust when he saw Buck Collins stagger out from the open cantina doors to relieve himself in the street.

Spotting a young Mexican trying to slip past the cantina along the side alleyway with a sack of supplies under his arm, Buck called out, "Hey, you! The hell you think you're going?"

The frightened young man stopped and froze in place for a second. Then he slowly turned his head toward Buck as the half-drunken gunman buttoned his fly.

"Me, senor?" the young man said, terrified.

"Hell, yes, *you*," Buck said, raising his gun from its holster as he took a sauntering step toward the frightened man. "What's in the bag?"

"Some food, senor," the man said, clutching the sack more securely under his arm. "Only food for *mi madre y mi*."

"Hunh-uh! No, no, no," Collins admonished the young man, wagging a finger at him, his six-shooter hanging loosely in his hand. "You started out all right, speaking English. Now try again."

The young man looked scared and confused. "My *mo*-ther and me, senor. . . ." he said in labored, broken English.

"That's more *hospitable*," Buck said with a satisfied grin. He reached his gun barrel out and poked it against the sack under the young man's arm. "Now show me what you've got there."

"*Es alimento*— I mean food, senor," the shaking young man said, quickly correcting himself. He started to hug the sack tighter, but Collins snatched it from under his arm.

"Don't be shy," Collins laughed. He pulled open the sack's drawstring and looked down at the butt of an old and battered pistol sticking up at him. "Oh, my!" Collins said in mock fear. "What have we here?"

"It was my father's before he died, senor," the young man said. "There are no bullets in it. He never shot it, except if he *haves* to."

"Good thing he never *haves* to," said Collins, chuckling at the young man's words and examining the gun in his free hand. "This old smoker would've blown up in his face."

From the door of the cantina, Hogue and Stewart stepped out and stood watching.

"*Sí*— I mean, *yes*, senor, you are right," the boy said, again correcting himself. He reached out as Collins held the gun butt back to him.

But just as Collins turned the gun butt loose, he raised the six-shooter at his side and cocked it an inch from the boy's forehead. He said angrily, "Pull a gun on me, you little snip? That'll get you killed straight-up!"

The young man stood frozen, his mouth agape, too frightened to move or reply.

"So long, little greaser," said Collins. He pulled the trigger; the boy's eyes clenched shut.

But Buck caught the hammer with his thumb a split second before it struck the cartridge. He let it down and gave a dark laugh.

"Let that be a lesson to you, kid," he said. "Never carry a gun unless you're prepared to use it to kill."

The boy's eyes snapped open as he realized that he was still alive, for the moment anyway. He stared at the open bore of Collins' pistol.

"Let me ask you this," Collins said, "now that we know each other better. Where's all your sisters?"

"I—I have no sisters, senor," the boy said, having a hard time keeping up with the gunman's English.

"I never said *older*." Collins grinned. "*Younger* will do, in a pinch." Seeing Hogue and Stewart watching, he gave them a knowing grin. The two only stared.

"I have *no* sisters, senor," the frightened boy said to Collins.

"I know better than that," Collins said, again cocking the gun inches from the young man's forehead. "Don't play me for a fool," he warned, and this time his voice sounded darker, deadlier. "I know all you snipes have a dozen or more sisters running around—every one of them hotter than a chili pepper, eh?" He managed a grim smile.

"No, no, senor, I have *solo hermanos*— I mean, *only brothers,*" he said, trembling. In truth he had neither brothers nor sisters. It was only him and his aging mother.

"What'd I tell you about talking *Mex* to me?" Collins warned. "I won't stand for it."

"Leave him alone, you *Tejas bastardo!*" the priest shouted, running toward Collins and the young man from the adobe church.

"What . . . ?" Collins turned, facing the priest with a dark glare. He called out to Hogue and Stewart, "Did he call me what I think he called me?"

"He called you a Texas *bastard,*" Hogue said, him and Stewart still staring, detached.

"That's what I thought," said Collins.

To buy the young man more time, the priest stared Collins down, enraged, his big, strong-looking fists clenched tightly at his sides.

"Yes—God forgive me—" he said, crossing himself quickly. "I called you a *Texas bastard!*" He glared back at the gunman boldly, fire in his eyes.

Stewart turned to Hogue and quietly mumbled under his breath, "I've got a gold twenty says this priest can kick his ass proper."

"I wish the padre would beat him into the ground, the stupid turd," Hogue whispered in reply. "Santana ain't going to like this at all."

"Yes, I called you a Texas bastard! Is my English good enough for you?" the padre said.

"Well, well," said Buck, slightly taken aback. "Are you sure you're a preacher? You don't talk like none I ever knew."

"I speak the language of those I'm talking with," the priest said. "You are a bastard, the son of nameless bitch dog and a scaly viper! The brother of snakes, and of slimy dung beetles—!"

"Hold it, Padre," said Collins. "I can see you've met all my kin." He grinned as he lowered his six-shooter a little, recognizing that the priest was challenging him to a fistfight. "But as a man of God, you ought to know that no family is perfect."

The priest started to say more, but he saw the cantina owner appear in the open doorway. He watched him stagger out into the street and collapse, landing with a solid thud. The priest ran to him, startled by the blood pouring down from a vicious welt on his forehead.

"What have they done to you, Javier?" he said, stooping down and helping the man try to stand.

"Help me, Padre," the owner pleaded in a weak, half-conscious voice.

"That's right, Padre. You take good care of your flock," Collins called out. He holstered his six-shooter and stuck the battered pistol he'd taken from the young Mexican down behind his gun belt. "This barkeeper might have just saved your life."

Hogue and Stewart watched the priest help the beaten

cantina owner stand up and wobble in place. Eventually letting their eyes wander from the scene, they noticed a rise of trail dust drift from the street leading into town. "Look what's coming here," Hogue said.

"I hope it's Santana," Stewart said. "Maybe he'll stop this fool, since the priest ain't going to do it." He grinned.

Buck Collins also spotted the rising dust, and watched the approaching horsemen come into sight. "Riders coming," he called out to the rest of the men inside the cantina.

Hogue and Stewart counted seven horses riding abreast toward them, spread across the empty street.

"Get ready to do some killing," Buck Collins called out, drawing his pistol again.

"Hold it, Buck," Stewart said, recognizing some of the men. "These men are Cut-Jaws. I've seen them before."

"If it's a fight they're looking for . . . ," Buck said, spreading his feet and starting to raise his pistol toward the riders.

"Damn it, Buck, it's some of the men we're trying to join up with!" Stewart said.

"Leave him be," Hogue said quietly. "Maybe they'll kill him."

"Yeah, and maybe they'll kill us too, just for being with him!" said Stewart.

But at the sight of a gun pointed at them, the riders drew rifles from their saddle boots, and Collins immediately lowered his six-shooter. "If you say you know them, that's good enough for me," Collins said.

"Easy, men," said Silver Bones to the riders on either

side of him. "I don't know who this crazy sumbitch is, but that's Carlos Loonie stepping out of the door over there."

Loonie walked out of the cantina and stood in front of Collins and the other men. He raised a hand toward Silver Bones.

As Bones and the others rode up, the priest and the cantina owner slinked away unnoticed. "But what about my cantina, Padre?" the owner asked. "You don't know how hard I worked to—"

"Don't tell me I do not know how hard it is to make a living," the priest admonished. "It is the same everywhere. Are you the only man who toils every day for his bread?"

"Forgive me, Padre," said the owner. "It's just that these men will trample all over Rafael."

"Rafael will flee when he feels it is the time to do so," the priest said, leading him away. "For now we must take care of your head."

As Silver Bones stepped down from his horse, he looked over suspiciously at Buck Collins, who stood with a dark, drunken grin across his face.

"Who's *this*," he asked Carlos Loonie, "and why is he pointing a gun at us?"

"He's one of the new men who came along with my cousin, Cervo," said Loonie.

"All right . . . if you say so," Bones said, still eying Collins as he spun his reins around the hitch rail.

"Have you heard anything out of Santana yet?" Bones asked. "By now he's usually sent somebody to round us all up."

"No," Loonie lied, "I've heard nothing." He stared at the arrivals as they stepped down from their horses. Spotting Aldo Barry, he said, "I see that you too have a new face riding with you. What happened to his nose?"

"Yeah, he's new," said Bones. "He rode in with Ruiz and Wilcox." He winced a little and said, "You'll be hearing all about his nose soon enough, I expect."

"What's to eat and drink in this town?" Bones asked.

"Plenty of mescal, whiskey, wine, hell, you name it," said Loonie. "As for food, we're getting ready to roast something, soon as we can catch it."

In the afternoon, the two *federale* trail scouts finally rode into the City of Bad Men and stepped out in front of the adobe church. They looked down the street at a large hog and two goats roasting above a roaring fire in the middle of the street out in front of the cantina. At the sight of so many horses, some hitched and others roaming freely in the dirt street, the two soldiers looked at each other.

"*Mandíbulas de corte*?" the younger scout asked the other, his hand on a holstered revolver. "The men the *capitan* warned us about?"

"*Sí, Cut-Jaws*," the older scout affirmed. He spat in contempt upon mentioning the name. "The *capitan* will want to hear about this pronto. If the Cut-Jaws are starting to gather here, they will soon be robbing and killing."

The two turned their horses around and kicked them up into a trot.

From the doorway of the cantina, Rafael the dwarf

walked out carrying a chicken in either hand. He looked down the street and saw the two soldiers leaving town. His left eye was black and blue, almost swollen shut.

"What's their hurry?" he said to no one in particular.

He twirled the birds around by their necks until their heads twisted off into his strong stubby hands.

"They were just in time for supper," said Loonie, staring after the two soldiers.

As the two headless birds flopped and batted their dying wings in the dirt, Rafael turned and walked back inside the cantina. As he made his way through the open cantina door, two half-naked young whores ran up to him. The two had appeared earlier, as if out of nowhere, along with an accordion player. The whores had mingled right in with the gunmen while the accordion player stood off to the side and played nonstop.

"Watch this!" one of the women called out to the men, some of them standing spread out along the bar, others seated at battered wooden tables scattered across the cantina's floor. She threw a leg up over Rafael's head and buried the dwarf beneath her loose peasant skirt. The men hooted and laughed as she grabbed Rafael by his head and ground her crotch into his face.

When she released Rafael and threw her skirt back from over his head, he spat and spluttered and wiped his eyes. But before he could collect himself, the other young whore bent over him and swung her large naked breasts back and forth, batting him across the top of his head. The drinkers roared and hooted.

The dwarf turned his face upward, welcoming the back and forth slap of warm flesh against his cheeks.

"Being small is not so bad!" he said in broken, muffled laughter as the swinging breasts pummeled his face.

He continued to laugh and squeal as the two women snatched him up, carried him behind the bar and stood him on a wooden crate he used to reach the bar top.

"All right! Who's ready for more, you Cut-Jaw sons-abitches!" he shouted in a fit of laughter, grabbing a bottle of rye in his stubby hand and shaking it toward the drinkers. "This is the best job an *hombre* like me ever had!"

In an alleyway behind the adobe church, Marshal Dawson and Deputy Caldwell heard the laughter and accordion music as they lifted Shaw from across the back of his horse and carried him between them to the church's rear door. They had long ago removed their badges and tucked them away in their pockets. But when they knocked on the thick door and saw the wooden peep-hole cover slide open, Dawson pulled his shiny badge out of hiding and held it up.

"We are lawmen," Dawson said to the curious eye looking out at them. "We are here under the authority of the Mexican government." He nodded at Shaw hanging limp, bloody and battered between him and Cald-well. "This man needs attention, bad."

"Is this man a prisoner?" the padre asked. Even as he spoke he pulled back a latch and swung the door open.

"No," said Dawson, "he's one of us." The two led Shaw inside.

The priest looked along the alley in the direction of

the cantina; then he gestured the lawmen to a small bed along a wall. From a wooden chair near the bed, the cantina owner looked up at the men. He was holding a wet cloth against the welt on his forehead. An empty wooden wine cup sat in front of him.

After the two had laid Shaw down and stepped back, the priest said, "I am Padre Timido, but do not let my name fool you. There is nothing *timid* about me. Welcome to God's house." As he spoke he pushed up the big sleeves of his robe and bent over Shaw.

"I would have beaten the face of one of those *hombres malos* into the dirt, had more of them not arrived when they did," he said. "Perhaps later I will do so. I was practiced in the art of fisticuffs before I came to do God's work."

"I see. Then it's good to have you on our side. I'm Marshal Crayton Dawson. This is Deputy Jedson Caldwell," Dawson said, watching the priest tend to Shaw.

"I have heard of you both," said Father Timido. He glanced at Caldwell, noting his derby hat and his black fingerless gloves. "You are the Undertaker, *sí*?"

"Well . . . I was once an undertaker," Caldwell said, turning bashful at the mention of his nickname.

"I understand," Padre Timido said, looking down at Shaw's bruised, sliced and beaten face. He touched a careful fingertip to the welt that Dorphin's pistol barrel had left on Shaw's head. He studied the older wound lying beneath it, and shook his head.

"What happened to this man?" he asked.

Dawson and Caldwell looked at each other.

"Which time?" Dawson asked, not sure where to start.

Chapter 14

As Father Timido worked on Shaw, Dawson explained how someone had tried to cut the unconscious gunman's throat before throwing him off a cliff. The cantina owner sat listening, wide-eyed, a wet cloth still pressed to his forehead.

"I know these hills you speak of," the priest said while he worked. "He could have fallen over a hundred feet or more, down between the switchback trails."

Caldwell said, "Luckily the rocks broke his fall."

Dawson gave him a look.

"Oh?" said the priest with condemnation. "You make jokes when this man lies injured?"

"No, Padre, this man is my friend," said Caldwell. "I only meant he was lucky he fell down a steep hill instead of a straight drop. He probably bounced a lot, and rolled and—"

"Leave it alone," Dawson said quietly between them.

The lawmen listened to the sound of music, gunfire, laughter and cursing coming from the cantina. The bar's owner groaned, shook his bowed head and kept the wet cloth against his injured brow. Shaw murmured mindlessly about the old witch and her sparrows.

Dawson had explained to the priest that the man lying with a fierce gash running from the side of his throat up across his chin was Lawrence Shaw.

"Ah, so this is Larry *Rápido* . . . ," Father Timido murmured under his breath, barely looking up while he held Shaw's chin wound closed with two fingers and sewed it snugly with coarse handspun thread.

The two lawmen exchanged glances. "Everybody's heard of *Fast Larry*, I suppose," Dawson said quietly.

Two gunshots exploded from out in front of the cantina, forcing its owner to cringe and let out a muffled sob. "I should not have left Rafael alone with those animals," he said with remorse.

"Rafael is in God's hands, as are we all," Father Timido said as he stitched. "Dawson, I hope you are here to do away with the Cut-Jaws Gang? They have killed two of our town already, and left their bodies lying in the street. The others must hide in the hills for safety."

"I'm sorry to hear that, Padre," Dawson said grudgingly. He didn't like to reveal what he and his deputy were up to. "We'd like to put them out of business. But it's always better to catch the leader of the gang."

"I see," Father Timido said bluntly. "You are waiting until Santana rides in. Then you will turn our modest town into a battlefield."

"We hope it's not going to be that way, Father," said Dawson.

"And this one, Larry *Rápido* . . . you said that he is with you?" asked the priest, gesturing at Shaw.

Dawson stalled for a second, not wanting to give

away too much about Shaw in front of strangers. "He's not with the Cut-Jaws," he said, sidestepping the question. "We found him along the trail like this."

"I see," said the priest. "I will ask nothing more about it." He sounded as if he understood the situation with the lawmen and Shaw. "Only by God's grace did you come along and find this one." He crossed himself quickly with bloody fingers.

"What do you think, Padre?" Caldwell asked. "Is he going to be all right?"

"*Sí*, he will be all right," said the priest. "I think it is a miracle we are witnessing here. He has no broken bones. He shows no bleeding inside. I have not seen a man injured so badly, yet still in such good condition . . . even with the *rocks breaking his fall*," he added, casting Caldwell a critical glance.

Caldwell looked away, a little red-faced.

Turning back to Shaw, the priest closely studied his face. "It troubles me that he is not yet conscious. He only barely awakened as I sewed his chin." As he spoke he brushed his fingers along the old bullet wound across Shaw's head.

"He was shot there, Padre," Dawson offered. "It hasn't been that long. I don't think he acts right yet because of it."

"I see," the priest said wryly. "I was afraid it was where he had horns removed."

Caldwell gave him a look.

But the priest gave a slight smile. "Forgive me, *mis hijos*," he said. "I should keep such dark jokes to myself— as should we all."

"I know this man is a gunman, Padre," Dawson said

on Shaw's behalf, "but I've known him for a long time. He's a good man."

The priest sighed as he stood from the side of the small bed and walked to a modest wooden cabinet. He took out a large bottle of wine and three wooden cups. "*Sí*, of course he is a good man," he said a bit wryly. "Why else would he be here in this, the *City of Bad Men*?"

"Not all men who come here are bad, Padre," Dawson said.

"No, they are not. Forgive me again." The priest sighed. He poured red wine into the wooden cups. "It has been a long and bloody day. Too much time has passed since my last cup of wine."

Dawson and Caldwell reached for the wooden cups that the priest handed them. He refilled the cantina owner's cup as well. The four raised their cups slightly in a toast and took a drink.

"*Gracias*, Padre," Dawson said for both himself and his deputy. He nodded toward Shaw. "What now?" he asked.

"Now we must let him rest," the priest said, "but only for a while. If he does not awaken soon, I will wake him. Perhaps with a few days' rest he will get over his old wound as well as his many new ones."

"*Gracias* again, Padre." This time it was Caldwell who spoke.

Dawson nodded his thanks. "About the City of Bad Men," he said, "how did this place ever get such a name?"

The priest looked back and forth between the two

lawmen and said, "It is not as one might think—that this was a place where bad men once came to consort. Nor was it ever a place of refuge for the kind of bad men it has come to attract these days." He gave a thin smile. "On the contrary. Bad men had to be brought here in chains, they dreaded this place so badly."

"So it was once a prison?" Caldwell inferred.

"No, Senor Undertaker," said the priest. "It was not a prison. It was a place much worse. The conquistadors brought bad men here, not to be shown the error of their ways and be rehabilitated. They brought them here only to be tortured and killed."

Dawson and Caldwell nodded and sipped their wine.

"It was a terrible place, la Ciudad de Hombres Malos," the priest said.

The cantina owner looked at the lawmen, then at the priest.

"What was so *terrible* about that?" he asked. "Do these men not deserve to die? They kill, they rob, they destroy. They are no better than wolves, I tell you."

The priest considered the man's words; then he looked at the lawmen and said, "So, tell me, what did you mean when you said you would like to put these men out of business? Do you plan to take them to jail?"

"No, Padre," Dawson said. "Men like these fight to the death once we get them cornered."

"I see," said the priest. "But you offer them the opportunity to go to jail, instead of dying?"

"No, Padre, I can't say that we do," Dawson said.

"We have taken prisoners—" Caldwell offered in their defense.

·"But hardly ever," Dawson interceded, cutting him short. He didn't feel the need to justify what they did in order to please the priest.

"Most times, we kill them," Caldwell said flatly. He gave Dawson a look that said the marshal hadn't allowed him to finish what he'd intended to say.

Father Timido gave a faint smile and said, "I like lawmen who speak the truth however brutal it may be." He raised his cup toward them as if in a toast and sipped his wine.

"Good," said Dawson. "I feel safe leaving our friend in your hands."

"I will watch over him until he is better able to ride," he said. "The two of you can stay here also and watch for Mingus Santana. I have a feeling he is not far from here."

Late in the night when the shooting, music and laughter had ceased, Loonie, Ned Breck and Matt Stewart remained awake, sitting at a table in the darkened cantina. On the floor surrounding them, all the gunmen except for Buck Collins lay sleeping, some with blankets, some without. The two young whores had gone from half naked to entirely naked. They lay sleeping in a corner, along with the dwarf and the accordion player, one ragged striped blanket pulled over all four of them.

"I don't trust him," Breck said. "I don't think he's got the sense to keep his mouth shut for long about what happened to the Fist and Tucker Cady."

The three studied each other's eyes in the dim light of a thin burning candle. "Buck Collins has got to go," Stewart whispered.

"And go tonight," Breck added, "for all our good."

"I say let's do it right now, while he's passed-out drunk by the fire," said Stewart. "We're never going to get a better chance." As he spoke he looked through the open front door toward the flickering campfire still burning in the street.

"Damn it," Loonie said, "all this over an accidental shooting."

"*Accident* don't cut nothing, Carlos," Breck said. "You know that as well as we do."

"Yeah, I know," Loonie said. With resolve he drew in a breath and said, "I'll do the cutting." He reached down, took a knife inside his boot well, tested its blade with his thumb and slid it back down.

Ned Breck picked up a bottle of mescal, uncorked it and filled Loonie's wooden cup. "Good man, Carlos," he said quietly. "We're all counting on you."

After a moment, Breck and Stewart looked at Loonie, who still sat studying the cup of mescal in his hand. Finally, Breck said, "Well . . . ?"

"Don't rush me," said Loonie, "I'm going. Let me finish my mescal and go relieve myself first." He raised his cup and downed his drink in a gulp. Then he stood up and walked to the back door. The other two watched.

"He's going the wrong way," Stewart whispered.

"He said he had to use the jake first," Breck whispered in reply.

Out back, on a long alleyway coming into town across a stretch of barren dirt and broken rock, two riders silently guided their horses through the dim moonlight toward the cantina. They saw Loonie's silhouette cross a well-worn path behind the cantina; they heard the creak of a privy door open and close. Careful not to be heard, they eased down from their saddles and crept forward, leading their horses.

Inside the outhouse, Carlos Loonie finished his business, buttoned his fly and slung his gun belt over his shoulder. But as he stepped out through the open door, the tip of a rifle barrel stuck into his ribs. He froze. What little affect the strong mescal had on him suddenly left.

"Easy there," he managed to say, before getting a look at the two faces in the purple night. "I don't know who you think I am, but—"

"You best be glad it's only us, Carlos," said a familiar gruff voice. The rifle barrel pulled away from his ribs.

Loonie let out a tense breath.

Another gruff voice said, "I hate it when he does that, don't you?"

Loonie looked back and forth beneath both men's low hat brims, finally recognizing the two shadowed faces. "I—I can't say it's real pleasant," he said to Thorpe.

"But I got you, didn't I?" Killer Cady said, his rifle still in hand.

"You got me sure enough," Loonie said under his breath.

"Is everybody here and ready to ride?" Morgan Thorpe asked.

Here was his chance to mention James Long, the Fist, without drawing suspicion, Loonie thought. "Everybody except for the Fist," he said. "I figured we'd see him before we heard from you or Santana."

"You should have," said Thorpe, sounding a little

concerned. "Him and Tucker was already supposed to be out here, rounding everybody up and getting ready."

"You mean you haven't seen my brother Tucker either?" Killer Cady asked.

"No, we haven't," said Loonie.

"Something ain't right," said Thorpe.

"It damn sure ain't," said Cady. He eyed Loonie closely.

"All I can tell you is what I know—" Loonie said with a shrug.

Thorpe cut him short. "We'll have to talk about it on the trail. We've come to gather everybody and slip out of here in the night without being noticed."

"Who all is here?" Cady asked, a hint of suspicion in his voice, as if he thought Loonie was hiding something from him.

"Did you find us any new, good men?" Thorpe asked before Loonie could answer Cady's question.

Loonie thought about Buck Collins lying out front, passed-out drunk, and he realized he'd lost the chance to kill him in his sleep.

"Yes, Bones and Ruiz brought along some new blood," said Loonie. All three men began walking toward the cantina's rear door. "I brought my cousin Cervo—he's itching to ride with us."

"Good," said Thorpe. "Where's your horses?"

"We tied them in an alley off the street," said Loonie.

"To keep them from burning?" Thorpe asked.

"*Burning . . . ?*" Loonie asked, confused.

"We saw the fire in the street from all the way up the trail," said Thorpe. "What the hell's the deal on that?"

Stopping at the rear door, Loonie said, "That's our cook fire from last night. I'll get it put out straightaway."

"No, leave it burning," said Cady. "It'll make it look like everybody's still here." He gave Thorpe a short, sly grin.

"Yeah, it's there anyway. Leave it burn," said Thorpe, he and Cady still leading their horses. "Get in there, get everybody up and out here without any noise or lantern light."

"I'm on my way," Loonie said, reaching for the door.

"It looks like we've got lots to talk about once we get on the trail," said Cady.

Loonie ignored the veiled suspicion in Cady's voice and walked inside the dark cantina.

Stewart and Breck stood at the table, just about ready to come looking for Loonie.

"Damn," said Stewart, "we started to think you must've dropped your pocket watch—"

Loonie cut him off in a whisper. "Thorpe and Killer Cady are here, right out back."

"Jesus, now what?" Breck asked.

"They're waiting for us to all slip out and ride off with them without being seen."

"What about this idiot?" asked Stewart, thumbing toward the fire out front where Collins lay in a drunken comma.

"Leave the sumbitch," said Loonie. "Nobody is going to miss him. Send everybody out the back door as you wake them up. I'll keep them from going out front—be sure to tell them it's how Thorpe wants it."

"I'd feel better if Collins was dead," Stewart whispered.

"So would I," said Loonie, "but this is how it is. So let's get going." He thought about how Buck had forced him to trade horses earlier. He smiled to himself.

It's time we trade back, you lousy bastard . . . , he said to himself.

PART 3

PART 3

Chapter 15

In the night, Caldwell stood watch from the church's short bell tower. He only had a partial view of the street out in front of the cantina, but it was enough to keep an eye on the fire. He also kept an eye on the edge of the alley beside the cantina, for in the shadowy darkness, he saw what he thought to be the first in a line of horses hitched along the alleyway.

But as dawn drew upward over the horizon, a sinking feeling came to him. He watched the sleeping man by the fire continue to lie with his mouth wide-open to the silver-gray sky. He quickly climbed down a ladder from the tower and shook the blanket Dawson slept under on the stone floor.

"Wake up, Marshal," he said. "I think we've been duped."

As Dawson rose beneath the blanket, the cantina owner's eyes snapped open. He still sat slumped at the wooden table where he'd fallen asleep.

"Duped?" Dawson said sleepily.

"There's only one down there," said Caldwell. "And
I believe he's dead."

Without another word, Dawson stood up, slung on
his gun belt and climbed the ladder to the bell tower.
As the two looked down over an edge toward the cantina, they saw a woman and a child emerge from an alley
with bundles of supplies and belongings under their
arms. They stood in the street a few feet from where
Buck Collins lay sprawled in the dirt.

"Yep, they've managed to slip past us," Dawson
concluded, turning back to the ladder. "Folks are already
returning from the hills. They must've heard their horses
leave in the night."

The two lawmen left the church and walked warily
up the alley behind the cantina. With their rifles in hand,
they stepped around into the side alley and saw only
one horse standing hitched in the first position by the
dirt street.

Dawson slumped against a crumbling adobe wall in
disappointment.

"I'm sorry, Marshal," said Caldwell.

"Forget it, Deputy," said Dawson. "I knew there was
a back door. I should have been watching it."

They walked, still with caution, to the front of the alley. When they stepped onto the street and looked over
at Buck Collins lying beside the fire, they saw the woman
and her child shy back away from them. The woman
gasped and crossed herself. The boy drew closer to her.

Father Timido called out to the woman and boy as
he came along the middle of the dirt street, the cantina
owner beside him.

"It is all right, these are lawmen," he said, walking

toward them, his arms spread as if to embrace the two frightened members of his flock.

The two lawmen approached Buck Collins and looked down. Caldwell poked his rifle barrel against the outlaw's leg.

"He's not dead," he said, noticing the slightest movement of Collins' scuffed boot.

"He's going to wish he was," Dawson said, noticing that the outlaw's left eyebrow and eyelash were missing, singed away, his face a deep glowing red from the prolonged exposure to the flames.

"Do you recognize him?" Caldwell asked.

"I believe it's Wayne Collins," said Dawson. "He's from near Somos Santos, where I grew up. They used to call him 'Wee-Wayne' as I recollect." He studied the singed face and shook his head. "He never had any sense—always rode the worst horse."

The two looked at the mousy misshapen horse standing at the edge of the alley. "Looks like he still does," said Caldwell.

The deputy stooped and pulled Collins' six-shooter from its holster, checked it and held it in his left hand. With his rifle barrel, he poked the outlaw in the belly.

"Wake up, *Wee-Wayne* Collins!" he said in a strong voice, loud enough to stir even the heaviest sleeper.

But Collins only grunted.

Caldwell poked him again, harder this time. Nothing.

"Wake up, you filthy pig!" Father Timido shouted, stepping and throwing half a bucket of water on the sleeping outlaw.

Collins spluttered and coughed; his eyes flew open

wide. His hands went to his face; then he let out a loud tortured scream as he writhed and rolled back and forth in the dirt.

"There . . . now he is awake," the priest said with a thin, tight smile of satisfaction.

"Holy God, my face! My face!" Collins screamed. "I'm roasted alive!" Shouting only worsened his condition, stretching his scorched face, causing him to roll harder, scream louder.

The deputy started to reach down and hold the gyrating outlaw in place on the ground, but Dawson stopped him, saying quietly, "Give him a second, Deputy. He's lit up something fierce."

"He is," said the priest with a sigh, standing beside Dawson, the half empty bucket in hand. "And that is too bad. I wanted so badly to beat his face into the ground with my bare hands." He clenched his fists tight just thinking about it.

When the gunman's screaming settled down into a terrible moan, Caldwell helped him to his feet and walked him inside the cantina. Seating the gunman at a table, the priest dipped a bar cloth into the remaining water in his wooden bucket. He handed the outlaw the wet cloth and guided it to his glowing red cheek.

"Whe-where is everybody?" Collins asked as the cool water soothed his throbbing face.

"They left you behind, *Wee-Wayne*," Caldwell said, wanting the outlaw to know that both lawmen knew his name.

"Wee-Wayne . . . ?" Collins looked at the two, not recognizing Dawson from his childhood. "I've killed men for calling me less than that. My name is *Buck* . . . Buck

Collins." He glared at Caldwell and continued. "And nobody left me behind. They know I'd kill them if they did."

"If they didn't leave you," said Caldwell, "where are they?"

Collins stared at Caldwell and Dawson. Without trying to answer Caldwell's question, he said, "Who the hell are you plug-uglies?"

"I'm Marshal Dawson . . . This is Deputy Caldwell," Dawson replied.

"Marshal . . . ? Deputy . . . ?" Collins said. He almost smiled, but then he realized what a mistake that would be, given the condition of his face. "You fellows must've made a wrong turn in El Paso. Don't you know where you are?"

"We know where we are," Caldwell said.

"Boys, this is *Mejico*," Collins chuckled in spite of the pain. "You shoulda carried a map." He looked at the priest and said, "Ain't that right, *preacher*?"

Staring at Collins, Father Timido clenched his fists and said to the two lawmen, "The other side of his face is not injured. I want to punch this one in the face so badly."

"Take it easy, Padre," said Dawson. "We need to talk to him some."

"Hey, I know who you are, *Marshal*," Buck said to Dawson. "You're the ol' boy from Somos Santos, where I grew up."

"That's right, Wayne. I am," said Dawson.

"Well, hell's fire, then, Marshal, you've got to let me go! Nobody from Somos Santos ever did harm to one of their own."

"We're not letting you go," Dawson said flatly.

"Well, you sure as hell can't take me back," said Collins. "You've got no jurisdiction here."

"We're not taking you back either," Caldwell said in the same flat tone.

Collins looked back and forth between the two and swallowed hard as understanding set in. "Holy Joe and Edna," he said, "you're the two lawmen everybody's been talking about, the ones working with the Mexican government cleaning up the border?"

"We are," said Caldwell. "Where's Mingus Santana? When are you supposed to meet him?"

Collins took a close look at Caldwell, noting his fingerless black gloves, his derby hat. "You must be the one they call The Undertaker."

"Answer him," Dawson said.

"And you," said Collins, "I remember now about you." He raised a finger toward Dawson. "You're the man who was bedding his best friend's wife while the fellow was off building himself a reputation with a six-gun—"

"That's enough," Dawson said, hoping to shut him up.

But Collins didn't stop.

"She got killed, didn't she?" Collins said with a sly, knowing grin. "Some gunmen came around looking for her husband and ended up killing—"

His words were cut short by a powerful left jab to the good side of his face. He flew sidelong from his chair. Caldwell caught him. Both lawmen looked stunned, seeing Father Timido in his fighting stance, his left fist still clenched. "The marshal told you that was *enough!*" the angry priest said, glaring at Collins.

Dazed by the punch, Collins slumped in the chair, his wet cloth hanging from his hand.

The priest settled himself instantly. He took the cloth and held it back gently to Collins' red face. "You must learn to listen when people are trying to tell you something," he said.

While the lawmen and Father Timido stood over Buck Collins, the cantina owner walked about the floor among broken bottles, damaged chairs, discarded cigar butts and other bracken from the night before.

"Look at my cantina," he said sadly, noting the empty shelves where fresh bottles of wine, whiskey and tequila had stood before the gunmen swooped down on the place.

He walked to the blanket in the corner and looked down. Beside the blanket lay a small pair of trousers, their pockets overflowing with money, both paper and coin. Holding the trousers, he flipped the blanket aside and gasped, *"Rafael!"*

The dwarf bartender lay naked, entwined among the sprawled arms and legs of the two young whores and the accordion player. But at the sound of the owner's voice, he awakened with a start and jumped to his tiny feet, looking all around, bleary-eyed.

"Oh, my God," he said, seeing the priest at the table with the two lawmen and the seated gunman. He made a grab for his trousers. "Give me those!" he said.

"No, I better keep them," said the owner, jerking the trousers out of Rafael's reach.

"They are my britches! Give them to me!" the dwarf demanded.

"They may be your trousers, but it is my money in them," said the owner.

"That's not your money," Rafael lied. "It's money I have been saving for a long time!"

"Then where is my whiskey, my wine, my—"

Before the owner could finish, the dwarf snatched the trousers from him and ran naked toward the rear door, money spilling in his wake.

The lawmen looked at the naked dwarf, then at the priest in surprise. But the priest did not turn an eye toward the incident. Instead, he pretended not to see a thing, even as the naked whores and accordion player began rising to their feet.

"If I do not *see* and *hear* such things, I am not called upon to *judge* such things," the priest said with a shrug. "I have learned this during my short time in this land of living perdition."

Dawson only nodded in understanding. He turned back to Collins as if no remark had been made regarding the fact that he had slept with Lawrence Shaw's deceased wife. He was certain Caldwell knew it; he was positive Shaw knew it. But it had not been openly mentioned or admitted to. It never would be, he told himself.

"Where's Santana, Wayne?" he asked forcefully, pushing all other matters out of mind.

"I told you my name is Buck!" he said.

"Where's Santana, *Buck*?" asked Caldwell.

"You can suck wind for it," said Collins, the wet cloth back against his red and glowing cheek. "I never *be-tray* my *pals-a*," he said in a mocking voice, a grin spreading across his face, even though the slightest movement nearly blinded him with pain.

The priest stepped forward, his left fist cocked.

"Whoa, now, let's hold on a minute, preacher!" said Collins. "Where do you get the right to hit an injured man like me? Is that what the Bible teaches you?"

"Where is Santana?" the priest asked, expressing no remorse for his action. "Tell them what they ask of you."

"All right, damn it," said Collins. "I've got the law and the church both down my shirt. All of Santana's regular men are wondering what's took him so long. We were waiting here for him. They say he usually sends one of his top men to get everybody gathered up."

Collins wasn't about to mention that he'd killed James "the Fist" Long. But he didn't have to.

"But you and the group you were riding with killed the Fist and left him off the side of the trail, along with Tucker Cady," said Dawson. "You thought it was us trailing you."

Collins looked stunned for a moment, then turned dead serious. "I don't know what you're talking about," he said.

"We were right behind you, Collins. We found their bodies," said Caldwell.

"Jesus . . . what a mama-kicking mess," said Collins. He shook his head slightly against the wet cloth. "I never should have hooked up with that idiot Loonie."

"Carlos Loonie . . . ," said Caldwell.

"Yeah, who else?" said Collins. "All right, here it is. Nobody knows for sure, but Carlos told his cousin, who ended up telling me that there's a big job about to get done. That's why Santana is taking in so many new men."

"How big are we talking?" Dawson asked.

Collins shrugged. "Beats me. But it must be awfully big. He's got men coming from all over to get in on it."

"Was it Santana who came here last night and got everybody to slip out of town?" Caldwell asked.

"I don't know. I was blind-down drunk, remember?" he said.

Dawson studied Collins' face for a moment, wondering what to do with him. The priest stepped forward from behind him, as if having read his thoughts.

"Leave this one here with me, Marshal," he said. "I will keep him until his face is well enough for him to ride."

"Hold on now," said Collins. "My face is well enough right now. I've broken no law and nobody has a right to hold me against my will. That's the law."

"You left the *law* at the border, Collins," said Caldwell. "Trust us, staying here is the best thing you can do. We're taking down Santana and his Cut-Jaws. We don't take prisoners. Do you understand what I mean by that?" He stared into Collins' eyes intently.

Collins looked up at the priest. "I hope you're a good cook."

"Yes, I am," said the priest. "I will bring you food three times a day."

"Bring me food . . . ?" Collins looked suspicious.

"Yes," said the priest. "There is a nice stone room beneath the church. It has a steel door on it, so you will not be disturbed." He offered a short smile. "I will teach you the most serious art of fisticuffs."

Chapter 16

Inside the office of the newly acquired Readling Mining and Excavation Enterprises, Howard Readling leafed through some papers given to him by a young French diplomat, Franc Labre. The diplomat had seen to it that everything was in order to make a smooth transition. He had greeted Readling and his party when they'd arrived the day before.

As soon as he'd seen the Mexican troops escorting Readling, Labre had immediately prepared to dispatch the remaining French soldiers to Mexico City. Now the troops were packed and ready for the trail. It appeared they couldn't leave quick enough.

"I trust everything meets with your approval, Monsieur Readling?" Labre said, his English nearly as good as his native tongue.

"Yes," Readling said, rising from behind a large but well-worn desk, "you have seen to everything. Thank you, sir."

"Good," said the Frenchman with a courteous nod and a smile of satisfaction. "If there is nothing more you require of me, I will be leaving with the soldiers this very day. They are assembled and ready to ride."

"That will be fine, sir," said Readling. "You and your government have been most cooperative. . . ."

Outside, on the front porch of a long barrack-style building, Captain Fuente arose from a cane-back chair, removed the thick black cigar from his mouth and watched his two trail scouts ride into sight past a guard shack overlooking the main trail. The two scouts looked all around at the French soldiers mounted and ready to depart from the hill country.

When the trail scouts stopped their dusty, sweat-streaked horses at the porch, they stepped down from their saddles and saluted the captain.

"Well, what did you find out in la Ciudad de Hombres Malos?" the captain asked both men, returning their salutes.

"Santana's men are there," said the oldest of the two soldiers.

"You are certain of this?" the captain asked, narrowing his brow.

"Yes, of this much we are certain," said the first soldier, "but we did not see Santana himself. We cannot say he is there with his men."

"I see," said the captain. He looked a little perplexed. "I wonder where he is." He stared off as if considering something of great importance. *Where are you, Santana . . . ?* he thought to himself.

"There is something else, *mi Capitan*," said the soldier.

"Oh . . . ? What is that?" the captain asked impatiently, sticking his cigar back between his teeth.

"At dawn, we looked back from atop the high trail and saw Santana's men crossing a valley," the scout said. "They are riding in this direction, even now."

"Are they indeed?" Something seemed to resolve itself in the captain's mind. He drew on the cigar and exhaled a long stream of smoke.

The younger scout put in without thinking, "Perhaps it would not be wise for the French soldiers to leave right now, *Capitan*?"

The captain looked at the young scout and stiffened in rage. "You are not yet a fully trained scout, and you think it is appropriate to give me advice?"

The older scout cut in quickly. "*Capitan*, if I may," he said. "This man is a young fool." He reached up and slapped the young soldier in the back of his head. The young man's hat fell to the dirt. "But he is learning. Let me take him away and have him beaten until he cannot walk straight. He will not offer his opinion again."

"Yes, you do that," said the captain, no longer interested in the young scout. He turned his eyes away and gazed off across the rugged hill terrain.

As the two scouts led their horses away toward a water trough, the older one scolded his younger partner, "What is wrong with you?" He started to smack him again in the back of his head, but he caught himself. "Don't you know better than to talk out of turn to a superior, especially a *capitan* like Fuente?"

"I spoke ahead of myself," the younger soldier replied. "It will not happen again." They walked on as the French diplomat emerged from the office shack and stepped into a waiting buggy.

On the porch, the captain stood with his cigar in hand.

He nodded cordially as the column of French soldiers turned and rode past him, out beyond the guard shack and onto the main trail. *Good riddance. . . .* He smiled privately, and stood watching until the entire column disappeared, leaving a rise of fine trail dust looming in the still hot air.

Inside the office shack, Willis Dorphin stepped through the rear door and closed it behind him. He stopped in front of Readling's desk and stood with his hat in one hand, his rifle in the other.

"Did you get it unloaded?" Readling asked in a lowered tone, even though there was no one else in the office.

"I did," said Dorphin. "We paid the miners for the week and sent them away for the weekend—told them that as new owners, we need to get settled in here. I had one of them stay behind. He helped me carry the crates down deep inside hole number three. He said they haven't worked the mine for two years, so nobody will be snooping around down there."

"What about him?" Readling asked pointedly.

Dorphin said without expression, "We don't have to worry about him. I left him lying down there too, once it was all hidden."

Readling breathed in relief. "Good work, Big T," he said. "I don't mind telling you, I've been on edge ever since we started this trip. I've never known gold to be such a burden."

"It's not all gold, sir," Dorphin reminded him.

"I realize there's more cash than gold," said Readling, "but the gold has been the problem, not the cash. I can explain having a few hundred thousand dollars on hand." He smiled. "Big business requires big dollars. Gold is different, especially gold with a U.S. Gold Depository stamp on it."

"Well, you can relax now . . . for a while anyway," said Dorphin.

"No," said Readling, "the Golden Circle appointed me to deliver and watch over their bank. I won't rest until I've been relieved of my appointment."

"The Golden Circle is a powerful bunch from all I've heard," Dorphin said.

"Oh . . . ?" said Readling. "What exactly is it that you've heard about *us*?"

Us . . . ? Dorphin weighed his words carefully before he replied. Then he said, "Back before the war, the Golden Circle was a group of powerful men dedicated to breaking away from the United States and forming their own nation. I've heard the Golden Circle and its ideas once swept all the way from Florida, across Texas, deep into Mexico and South America."

Readling looked impressed. "Bravo, Big T," he said. "I respect a man who keeps up on history as well as current events."

But Dorphin didn't stop there. "Had the war gone differently, the Circle might well have been running both Washington and Mexico City right now," he said.

"Yes, you're correct," said Readling. He raised a glass of whiskey sitting on his desk, offering a toast to the idea. "Just imagine," he said, "these two nations, the United States of America and Mexico, walking hand in hand into the future."

"Yes, sir, I can see that," Dorphin said, trying not to appear critical.

But Readling suddenly realized he was speaking with a man of lesser vision than himself. "At any rate," he said, pulling back a bit, "the finds of the Golden Circle now rest in my hands."

"I—I like to think that you'll have a place for me in all this, sir," Dorphin said humbly.

"You keep up the good work," Readling said, "I'll always have a place for you. I'll always need muscle to clear my path as I climb upward."

Muscle . . . ? Dorphin thought.

"Thank you, sir," he said, "but I was really thinking more along the line of—"

A heavy knock on the office door cut him off. Following the knock, a strong voice called out, "It is I, Captain Fuente. I must speak to you."

A nod from Readling sent Dorphin to the door. Dorphin opened it and stood to the side as the big Mexican captain walked in and across the floor, a short, stout sergeant right behind him. The sergeant veered away and stood by the wall at attention.

"What can I do for you, Captain Fuente?" Readling asked.

"My two trail scouts have returned from riding the higher trails," said the captain. "They spotted Mingus Santana and his Cut-Jaws Gang in la Ciudad de Hombres Malos," he lied.

"That's certainly good news. My compliments to your men, Captain," Readling replied.

"I must lead my men there right away," the captain said.

"Oh, really?" Readling raised his eyes slightly. "And why is that, Captain?"

"My orders from Mexico City are clear," said the captain. "Killing Santana and his men are my first and foremost priority."

Readling thought about the gold and cash hidden down inside the mine. "What about everyone here, Captain?"

"I saw your miners drew their pay, so there is no large amount of cash here," the captain said. "Santana will not be foolish enough to rob a payroll when it has already been distributed."

"How does Santana know the payroll has been distributed?" Readling asked.

"He has eyes everywhere," said the captain. "Believe me, he always knows when there is money on hand and when there is not."

"I don't like this," Readling said.

"Let me remind you, senor," the captain said, "Santana is in the City of Bad Men. My men and I will trap him there and kill him. He is not close enough to the mines to be of any danger to your new business here." He paused, then said, "I will leave some men here in case anything else comes up. But Santana will not be a problem for you, I can assure you."

Readling finally nodded and said, "All right, then. But make sure you understand, everything that goes on here will be discussed in Mexico City when I return there."

"Of course," said the captain. He gave a slight bow at the waist, then turned and walked out of the office, the sergeant following behind him.

Readling picked up his burning cigar from an ashtray and puffed on it as he leaned back against the edge of his desk in contemplation. "I don't know if I trust that man," he said. Then he gave a sly little grin.

Dorphin put in, "I don't trust any of these monkeys as far as I can spit, sir, if I may say so."

"And you're right not to," said Readling. After a moment of thought he added, "But this is Santana's country, and he's not going to rob a gold mine that he knows hasn't been working any big veins for the past year."

"No, sir," said Dorphin, "he wouldn't do that, I'm sure."

The captain was making his way back to the barracks where the soldiers where getting prepared for the trail, when the stout sergeant turned to him and said, "May I ask, *Capitan*, how much influence does this man have in Mexico City?"

"Will it matter?" the captain answered, without looking at him.

The sergeant thought about it. He gave a short smile as they walked on with deliberation. "No," he said, "it will not matter."

"When you pick some men to leave here, Sergeant," the captain said, "make sure it's none of my good men."

"*Sí, Capitan*," said the sergeant. "It only makes sense. We need our very best men to fight Santana's gang."

"Indeed," said the captain, "we are both thinking the same thing."

Shaw awakened slowly and torturously. He'd been dreaming of the old *bruja*'s weathered hands on his face. He had not been able to see her eyes, only the shadow of her face hidden inside her black hood. But it was her, he had reasoned in his sleep. Past her shrouded shoulder, he had seen the cage made of twigs and reeds.

Inside the cage, he'd watched the line of sparrows perched in a row, some picking at their feathers, others looking all around as if awaiting her command.

Oh, yes, it's her. . . .

He finally woke up completely, and quickly sat up in the small bed. Too quickly as it turned out. The pain in his head struck him so violently, so intensely, that for a moment the world before his eyes went blank, and he sat staring into a wall of blinding whiteness.

"Senor! Are you all right?" the young man seated in a wooden chair beside the bed asked.

Shaw gave himself a moment; then he opened his eyes warily, as if he knew he might have to close them again at any second should the pain demand it. But the throbbing had settled some.

He swallowed a dry knot in his throat and looked around with bleary eyes. He had no recollection of being found by Dawson and Caldwell, or of them bringing him to this place—this clean, modest room. Yet his memory struggled to come back as his senses slowly became better grounded.

"Where am I?" he asked the young man.

"You are *here*, senor," the boy said in earnest.

Shaw looked at him. "Is that the best I'll get from you?" he asked flatly.

The young man looked baffled for a moment until he realized that the injured *Americano* honestly had no idea where he was.

"Pardon me, senor," the boy said. "You are in la Ciudad de Hombres Malos. In Padre Timido's living quarters. He leaves me here to look after you while he sees to one of his other charges. . . ."

Padre Timido . . . ? The City of Bad Men . . . ?

Shaw sifted through his cloudy memory; but he came up empty. "How'd I get here?" he asked.

"The two *Americanos*—your two amigos brought you, senor," the boy said.

Shaw stared at him, drawing a blank.

"You know," the boy said, "the one who wears black gloves with their fingers missing—and a hat?"

"Caldwell . . . ," Shaw said. His memory seemed to churn and groan, beginning to draw itself together and move forward.

"No, he is the *Undertaker*," the boy corrected him. "The other is a quiet one. He seemed very concerned about you."

"Right," said Shaw, "my two amigos."

He pictured Caldwell and Dawson looming over him amid the rock and dirt on the hillside. He heard his horse whinnying down to him from the upper switchback. He felt his head pull back, the blade jerk across his throat. He winced as he raised his fingertips to the stitches running along his chin and down the side of his throat.

"Where are they?" he asked, still sitting upright, his gun belt hanging from the short bedpost at his right hand. His holster was empty.

"They left, senor," the young man said. "They asked Padre Timido to look after you until you are better, and able to ride."

He remembered Readling, and how he'd been set up,

how Dorphin and Doc Penton had unloaded his Colt and his rifle while he'd sat entirely blanked out, staring across the valley in the dark.

"Are you all right, senor?" the boy asked. "Should I go get the padre?"

"No," said Shaw, "I'm all right. Don't bring him to me." He pictured Dawson and Caldwell leading his big bay into town, his limp body lying over the horse's back.

His memory cleared some as he rubbed his throbbing head. Then he thought of the woman and pushed himself around onto the side of the bed. "But you can get my boots, help me go to him," he said. "Then you can get my horse for me."

"*Sí*, I will help you walk to the padre," the boy said, as if making mental notes. "I will get your horse for you."

He stood up, walked to where Shaw's boots stood on the floor and brought them back. Shaw reached around and pulled his gun belt from the bedpost and looked at his empty holster. He remembered Dorphin standing over him. He felt Dorphin's hard kick in his gut.

A nice keepsake . . . ? he heard Dorphin say, seeing him shove the Colt down behind his belt. *I don't think so*, he told himself. Again, he thought about the woman, and managed to pull together enough strength to push himself up and stand with his feet spread for support.

"What would you take for that old shooter?" he asked, nodding at the battered gun at the young man's waist.

"It is not for sale, senor," the young man said. "But you can borrow it." He slid the old pistol out and handed it to Shaw. "It is not so good, maybe?"

"I've gotten by with worse," Shaw said. *"Gracias."* He slid the pistol down into his holster, scrutinizing it now that its age and condition weren't hidden from sight.

"Let's go," he said to the young man. "I'm better enough to ride."

Chapter 17

Buck Collins slammed backward into the stone wall, slid down it and landed hard on the cellar floor. The unburned side of his face now looked as bad as the burned side. His jaw was bruised, and both eyes were almost swollen shut. His split lip bled down and dripped freely from his chin.

"Get up," the padre ordered. "I want to show you how affective a combination of short powerful lefts can be when an opponent is starting to wear out."

"Pl-please," said Buck Collins, trying to raise a hand toward the padre, who stood over him, his strong fists clenched and circling slowly in front of him.

"Oh? You are tired?" the priest said, as if in surprise. "You no longer feel as tough? You no longer want to push around the good people of my town like you did earlier?"

"I was . . . drunk. I must've been . . . out of my mind," Collins submitted, trying to lessen his beating. "I—I want to . . . tell them all how sorry I am."

"That would be good," the priest said. He shrugged

and dropped his fists. But then raised them again. "First, I think you must finish learning your fisticuffs lesson. After that, there is much more I need to teach you."

"Please . . . no!" said Collins. "I've learned my lesson. I swear I have!"

Father Timido's fists opened up. He reached down and helped the beaten outlaw to his feet. "I hope you have," he said in a serious voice. He dusted the front of Collins' shirt with his hand. "If not, I'll have to show you all over again. Do we understand each other?"

Buck Collins nodded, leaning back against the stone wall for support. "Can I—can I go now?" he asked.

"No," the priest said firmly. "You'll stay here until I say you can go. You will learn everything from table manners to not urinating in public—"

The priest stopped speaking when he saw Shaw step into the cellar from a stone hallway, his arm looped around the young Mexican's shoulders for support.

"I hope I'm not interrupting anything," Shaw said, looking at the blood on the battered outlaw's face, the red and brown front of his shirt.

"No," said the priest, "I have just been teaching this poor sinner fisticuffs, as well as a lesson in *humility*, something we must all learn at some point in our lives."

"He appears to be grasping it," Shaw said, looking Buck Collins up and down.

"I am a good teacher," the priest said. He raised his loosely clenched fists for exhibit and said, "There are men who will learn more from *these* than they will ever learn from the Bible," he said. He quickly crossed himself and added under his breath, "God forgive me for saying so."

"Whatever works," Shaw said, unconcerned. He took his arm from the Mexican youth and managed to stand on his own as the young man hurried away to get his horse ready to travel. "I came to tell you, obliged, Padre," he said.

"Do not thank me so soon, Larry *Rápido*," said the priest. "It is better that you thank me after you have been here a few more days. You must regain your strength and your . . ." His words trailed.

"My *senses*, Padre?" Shaw said, finishing the words the priest had started.

"*Sí*, your senses," the priest said. "There, I have said it. I am only being honest with you."

Shaw touched his fingers to the aching stitches on his chin and the side of his throat. "I appreciate honesty as much as the next fellow, Padre. But I've got to get moving."

"You must go now, to find Mingus Santana and his gang, and kill them, I hope?" he said.

"No, Padre," said Shaw. "The fact is, Mingus Santana has never done anything to me."

"*Who* did this to you?" the priest asked.

"Two soldiers," Shaw said, "acting under the orders of a rich American businessman."

"You must not hesitate to mention his name to me," said the priest. "After all, I am a man of the cloth. What you say to me is never repeated. Who knows, perhaps if you talked to me about this, you would be able to—"

"It would serve no purpose, Padre," Shaw said, stopping him from going any further. "He tried to have me killed. I've got to go."

"Why did he try to have you killed, my son?" the

priest asked. "Has there long been bad blood between the two of you?"

"No," said Shaw, "I hardly know the man. He has something of mine. I intend to take it from him."

"I see," said the priest. "It is something he stole from you?"

"No," Shaw said. "It's too hard to explain, but he has something that was once mine—something that's very precious to me." He pictured the woman in his mind, the fearful look she'd had as she'd pleaded with Readling for his life. "I'm taking it back."

"But what about your friends, the lawmen? They will come back for you. What shall I tell them?"

"Don't worry about it, Padre," said Shaw. "It's a sure bet we're headed in the same direction."

The priest watched him walk away, a little unsteadily, he thought. But he saw there was no point trying to reason with this man. He sighed, opening and closing his fists a few times. Then he turned to Buck Collins and said, almost gently, "Wash your face and clean yourself up some. I have sent a woman out to gather some plants to soothe your burn."

Moments later, in a shaded courtyard out in front of the church, Shaw met the young man hurrying to bring his horse to him. Shaw looked the big bay over good and stepped up in the saddle. The young man stepped forward.

"Senor, here is your sombrero. One of your amigos left it in your room."

Shaw took the broad-brimmed hat, examined it in his hands, seeing his bandana wadded up inside the crown. "*Gracias,*" said Shaw, taking the bandana and tying it around his sore and knotted head. He was surprised that the sombrero had made it through so much and was still with him. He set the big hat atop his head, drawing the string up in back against the base of his skull.

"Good as new," he said down to the young man, turning his horse to the street.

As he rode along the road, headed out of la Ciudad de Hombres Malos, he saw the faces of the townspeople studying him curiously. He watched an old woman walk along in a ragged black frock with the hood up to shield her weathered face from the glare of the sun. She carried a walking stave in one hand. Under her arm she carried a cage constructed of twigs and reeds interwoven with sinew, partly covered by a ragged cloth.

What the . . .

Without stopping, Shaw turned in his saddle and watched her slip around the corner of an alley. But before she disappeared from sight, she cast a fleeting backward glance at him. *Was it her . . . ? The old bruja . . . ?* he asked himself, or was his damaged mind still playing tricks on him?

He didn't know; and it didn't matter, he told himself, tapping his heels against the bay's sides with determination. All that mattered was the woman. His *Rosa . . .* , he told himself. He had to have her.

No sooner had the column of *federales* ridden away from the Readling Mining company than the two scouts cantered a thousand yards ahead and looked out across the lower hills and trails below.

Seeing a long cloud of dust reach up into a hillside

behind a group of riders, the older scout raised a badly scuffed telescope and stretched it out before his eye.

"Holy *Madre*," he murmured, looking at the same body of men they'd seen in La Cuidad de Hombres Malos. He lowered the telescope with a concerned look and bit his lip in contemplation.

"What is it?" the younger scout asked, seeing the look on his partner's face.

"It is *trouble*. That's what it is," said the other scout.

The younger scout could barely see the riders with his naked eye. "Let me look," he said, reaching for the telescope. While he studied the riders as they galloped out of sight deeper into the tree-covered hillside, the other scout looked back along the trail behind them.

"Their path will take them right to the mines," he said, puzzled.

The younger scout lowered the telescope. "Cleary it is so," he said. "We must warn the captain."

"After the way he jumped on you? I don't think so," the older scout said. "He thinks I had you beaten for speaking out of turn."

"I know," said the younger scout, "but it is our duty to report what we see."

"Report it, *sí*," said the older soldier, "but nothing more. You will keep you mouth shut as to what we should or should not do."

"I learned my lesson," the young scout said. He handed the telescope back to the older soldier. The two turned their horses and rode back along the trail to the column.

Seeing the scouts returning in a hurry, Captain Fuente let out a breath and addressed Sergeant Lopez, who was riding beside him, "Head these two off and hear what they have to say."

"*Sí, Capitan,*" the sergeant replied. He batted his heels on his horse's sides and met the two scouts a hundred yards ahead of the column.

"Sergeant," the older scout said, "we must tell the *capitan* that the Cut-Jaws we saw in town are heading for the mines!"

"Oh?" the sergeant said, appearing unaffected by the news. "How do you know these are the same men you saw in town? How do you know they are headed for the mines?"

The two scouts looked at each other.

"We watched them through the lens!" the young scout said, almost in disbelief.

"I see," the sergeant said calmly.

The older one began to understand. He shrugged, settling down, and said, "It looked like the same men, Sergeant. That's all we are saying."

"You have reported the information to me, that is good," the sergeant said. "Now continue on with your scouting. I will tell the captain what you saw as soon as I find time."

Find time . . . ? The two scouts looked at each other again, almost dumbfounded.

"But—" The younger scout began to speak, but the older scout cut him off before he could get started.

"*Sí*, Sergeant," the older scout said. "We will go now to further scout the trail."

The sergeant waited until the two had turned their horses and ridden away. Then he trotted his horse back to the column and fell in beside the captain.

"They said they have spotted the Cut-Jaws riding toward the mines, *Capitan*," he said.

The captain did not respond. He continued to stare straight ahead, as if the sergeant had not said a word.

The sergeant realized that his superior officer had just ensured that he could deny any wrongdoing by putting the sergeant between himself and the scouts. But that was as it should be, he reminded himself. When this was all over, he knew he would be taken care of for the part he played in keeping things running smoothly. The captain had promised him.

With no mention of the scouts or what they'd reported, the captain led the column on in silence for the next thousand yards.

Finally he broke the silence, saying, "We will continue down past the main trail toward la Ciudad de Hombres Malos until we are certain there are no outlaws lurking about."

"*Sí, Capitan*," Sergeant Lopez replied, going along with him.

Captain Fuente turned to him with a guarded, knowing smile. "This is what is expected of us, Sergeant," he said quietly.

An hour behind the Cut-Jaws, the two lawmen pushed on at the same strong, steady gallop they'd been riding at since they first began following the gang's fresh tracks. There was no doubt that the riders were headed for the old French mining complex, Dawson thought as they started across an open stretch of rocky ground leading up into the tree-covered hillside.

"There's no question now what they're getting ready to do," Caldwell said as they stopped at a blind turn in the trail to rest their horses. "Unless the French or the *federales* are there, the mines are sitting ducks for a big gang like the Cut-Jaws."

"Santana must've slipped in and joined them in the night at the cantina," Dawson said, staring at the hoofprints on the ground as if they held more secrets than he could discern.

"Maybe," said Caldwell. "We know James 'the Fist' Long is dead. But there's still Morgan Thorpe. Maybe Santana is sitting this one out and meeting up with the gang afterwards."

"Would he do that?" Dawson looked at him as he considered it.

Caldwell shrugged. "He's the boss," he said. "He can do whatever suits him."

Dawson thought about it. "I should have figured right off that it was the mines the gang would be after. There's nothing else around that big."

"Nobody robs mines," Caldwell reminded him. "Not like this anyway. It's too much work. It's like stealing a load of rocks until the gold is refined."

"Right," said Dawson, "and the Mexican government forbids refining gold anywhere except in Matamoros or Mexico City."

"They like to keep it close, where they keep their hands in the counting," Caldwell said wryly.

Dawson thought about the miners they'd seen earlier and throughout the day—two, three and four of them at a time traveling along the lower trails to town.

"It can't be a payroll robbery," he said. "It looks like everybody's gotten settled up and is headed out to spend it."

"What else could be there . . . ?" Caldwell mused.

"Big enough to make it worthwhile for a gang like the Cut-Jaws?" Dawson added for him.

Caldwell said, "On the way to town, Shaw woke up enough to say it was this new mine owner, Readling, who tried to have him killed."

"He also said it was all over a *woman* who's traveling with Howard Readling," Dawson reminded him. "I don't know anything about Readling except what I've come across in the newspaper now and then. But rich men don't like somebody getting too close to their womenfolk. Shaw is not the kind of man to back away quietly if he sees a woman he's stricken with."

"Yes, right . . . ," Caldwell said, letting out a troubled breath. "But none of this tells us what the Cut-Jaws are after at Readling's new mine project."

The two stood for a moment considering what Shaw had managed to tell them during his few hazy moments of consciousness on the way to town. Dawson shook his head slowly and came to a conclusion.

"Shaw's out of his head. We shouldn't pay a lot of attention to what he said. He sees witches and sparrows. He sees his dead wife . . ." He paused as the vision of Rosa came to his mind, then slowly drifted away.

"I hate to say it," Caldwell put in, "but I don't think we can put much stock in anything he tells us."

"Not until he gets better," the marshal was quick to reply.

"*If* he ever gets better," the deputy added, not liking his own words.

The two had started to turn their horses back to the trail when the sound of heavy gunfire resounded from the direction of the mines.

"Uh-oh," Dawson said, "it sounds like the party has started without us."

Chapter 18

When the two scouts heard the gunfire coming from the mines, they only stopped for a moment, long enough to listen to the intensity of the battle and shake their heads. Then they turned forward in their saddles and kicked their horses up into a trot in the direction of la Ciudad de Hombres Malos.

"The farther we are from the mines, the better," said the older scout.

"We were told to ride as far as town," said the younger soldier. "So, that is what we did, eh? If ever we are asked about it?"

"Yes, exactly," said the older scout. "It sounds like you are quickly learning what it takes to be a scout for the Mexican Army."

"*Sí*, I am learning to keep my mouth shut and my eyes straight ahead," said the young scout.

"At least we are out of any fighting," said the older scout. "I suppose we can be grateful to the *capitan* for that."

"*Sí*, what can happen to us now?" said the younger man. "All we have to do now is ride on to town and be careful not to fall off of the trail."

They both laughed and rode ahead at a faster pace, neither one of them interested in going back to the column now that they knew the captain, and possibly their sergeant as well, had some sort of deal cooking with the Cut-Jaws Gang.

They rode on as the battle continued in the hills behind them. . . .

At the mines, the few inexperienced soldiers Sergeant Lopez had left to stand guard lay dead in the dirt. They had been standing at the front entrance guard shack to keep an eye on the trail. But when the Cut-Jaws hit, they did so with such speed and ferocity that the soldiers offered almost no defense.

Inside the office shack, Dorphin, the Johnson brothers and Howard Readling had taken cover, piling furniture and equipment against the doors and in front of the windows. As the firing intensified, Readling crawled across the dusty wooden floor, ventured his face up to a window ledge and looked out, back and forth and all around the mine yard.

"Where the devil is Doc? And where's Rosa?" Readling said, dropping down quickly as a bullet whistled through the window past his head.

Dorphin and the Johnson brothers ducked down from the windows. They looked at each other. Dorphin crawled over beside Readling as he emptied the spent, smoking cartridge shells from his revolver and reloaded.

"It won't matter where either of them are if you get your head shot off," he said, speaking loud above the gunfire.

"Why are they robbing a damn mine project?" Readling asked loudly. "Don't they know this is all rough ore, still to be separated and refined?"

"You'll have to ask them that, sir," said Dorphin, getting a little put out by Readling's insistent questioning. "I'm busy keeping you covered and alive right now."

The shooting outside stopped short as Morgan Thorpe, who stood behind an empty freight wagon, shouted out loudly to his men, "Hold your fire, everybody. It's time I do some talking to this fine gentleman!"

Readling and Dorphin both ventured up and peeped out the window. "What do you suppose this is?" Readling whispered to Dorphin.

Before Dorphin could reply, Thorpe called out in an almost playful tone, "Howard Readling, I know who you are. I believe you're smart enough to see where this is going to go. You'll all die if you keep fighting."

"Who the blazes are you?" Readling shouted out across the window ledge. "Are you Mingus Santana?"

Thorpe smiled to the men beside him and called out in reply, "Yep, that's me, Mingus Santana."

"Well, Santana," Readling said with a bitter snap to his voice, "you've overplayed your hand this time. There's nothing here for you to rob unless you want to get your hands loading gold ore and hauling it somewhere to smelt it down."

"No, thanks, Readling," Thorpe called out. "I want to leave here traveling light as we can."

"Then I'm sorry to disappoint you, Santana," Readling said. "You've made the trip for nothing."

"Come on, now, Mr. Readling," Thorpe said knowingly, "don't make me turn ugly over this."

"It's the truth, Santana. There's no gold here," Dorphin called out. "Even the payroll's been made for the month. You've missed out on it. Now back away."

Readling turned to Dorphin and said, "Get a rifle and kill this son of a bitch, Big T."

Dorphin only stared at him for a moment.

"Do you hear me, Willis?" Readling asked in a sharp tone.

"Right, sir," Dorphin said.

He flagged Elvis Johnson to him, needing the rifle Elvis had in his hand. As Elvis crawled forward, Dorphin looked back and forth across the dusty yard.

Readling watched him. "I doubt very much that this is Santana speaking to us," he said to Dorphin. "But he must be the leader of these men. One good shot could change everything."

"Or it could make certain we all die here," Dorphin said.

"I want him dead all the same," said Readling.

"Whatever you say, sir," Dorphin replied.

"Back away . . . ?" Thorpe gave a dark chuckle as he called out to the shack.

"Dorphin, here's your chance," Readling said, easing to one side in order for Dorphin to slide the rifle barrel out over the window ledge and take aim.

"That's right. Back away," said Dorphin, "there's nothing for you here."

"What about that wagon you drove here all the way from the border?" Thorpe called out.

"Supplies, nothing else," Dorphin called out. He focused down the rifle sights and watched for the man to make himself the slightest bit more visible.

"I hope you're not lying," Thorpe called out, "else I'll have to kill every one of yas."

"We're not lying to you," Readling called out, giving Dorphin the opportunity to take his time and make his shot count.

Thorpe looked across the yard at Killer Cady and Carlos Loonie, who stood at the entrance of mine number three.

"What about it, Cady? Are they being honest with me?" Thorpe asked. "Or is there a load of cash and U.S. gold bars down inside that closed mine?"

Howard Readling stiffened at Thorpe's words. "How could they know?" He gave Dorphin an accusing stare.

"Don't ask me," Dorphin said. "How the hell could I have told them?" They both looked around at the Johnson brothers with questioning eyes.

"Don't neither one of yas say something you'll regret," said Witt Johnson. "Nobody accuses me and my brother of nothing unless they're ready to back it up with their lives." He levered a round into his rifle as he spoke.

"Doc Penton?" asked Readling.

"I don't think so," said Dorphin. "Doc most likely got caught short when this thing started, ran out of nerve and hightailed it while he could."

"Then how'd they know?" Readling demanded.

"What about the woman, Readling?" Dorphin asked,

dropping the *Mister*, now that everybody's life was on the line.

"She didn't know about it," Readling said. "I never told her."

Before they could discuss it further, Thorpe called out, "I bet you're saying to each other, *how's he think he's going to get that loot up outta there and loaded with us shooting at him? Right?*"

"It's something you better think about," Readling said in a threatening tone. As he spoke he saw the man claiming to be Santana take a step out past the protection of the wagon. "Get ready, Big T," he whispered down to Dorphin.

"Ready," Dorphin said. Yet, even with his finger on the rifle trigger and his focus down the rifle sights, he had no intention of shooting.

"I did think about it," Thorpe called out. "I figure you won't be shooting so long as I've got this beauty of yours in hand." He stepped farther out from behind the wagon with the woman pressed against his side, his arm snuggly around her waist.

"Jesus, no!" Readling whined, seeing the look of terror on Rosa Reyes' face. He cried, "Don't shoot!" as he grabbed Dorphin by his shoulder. But his sudden grip was enough to cause Dorphin to make a shot he'd otherwise decided against taking. The rifle bucked in his hands. At the wagon, Thorpe jumped back behind cover and slung the woman away from him. Breck caught her and kept her from falling.

"The fool shot me!" Thorpe said, leaning back against the wagon, his hands gripping his bleeding side.

From the shack, Readling called out, "Hold your fire

out there, *please*! That shot was an accident. It wasn't intentional! Don't hurt her!"

In spite of his wound, Thorpe called out, "Another accident like that and I'll gut her and let you watch her spill out on the ground! Am I clear on that?"

"Yes, you're clear!" Readling said quickly. "We understand! I give my word. No more shooting!"

Thorpe looked at the others with a pained smile and said, "That's how easy it is." He nodded toward where Killer Cady, Silver Bones and Carlos Loonie stood out in front of mine number three and said, "Some of yas get over there, get the loot up out of the mine."

"Man, you are shot bad," said Breck, turning the woman loose and stepping over to him for a closer look.

"Never mind me," said Thorpe. "Let's get done and get out of here." He jerked his bandana from around his neck, wadded it and pressed it against his bleeding side. "I'm going to have to . . . ride back to town." He grinned. "I hear that priest there . . . does good doctoring."

"Santana ain't going to like us riding there with all this swag," said Breck. "You said he wanted us to meet him at the canyon over at San Simon."

"Santana knows things don't always go the way we want them to," said Thorpe. "Now let's get busy and get it done, before I bleed to death."

When the Cut-Jaws had carried up the cash and the gold bars, they'd loaded it all back onto the wagon it had arrived on. Carlos Loonie pulled the wagon out of sight, locked its brake, jumped down from the seat and ran back to where Thorpe stood bleeding.

"Whoa!" said Loonie at the sight of blood. "What happened?"

"What does it look like?" said Thorpe. "I took a bullet." He nodded toward the loaded freight wagon. "I'll be having to leave here in a wagon until we get to town and get this wound dressed."

"Sure thing," said Loonie. "I'll drive you. Let's get out of here."

"One minute," said Thorpe. He turned toward the office shack and called out, "Readling, we're all loaded up out here."

Readling called out, "Then let the woman go, like you said you would."

"I never said I'd let the woman go when we got finished," Thorpe said. "I said I wouldn't kill her if you didn't fire on us while we loaded up."

"Damn it!" Readling said to Dorphin beside him.

"Just so you know, don't turn ugly and go blaming your men, Readling," Thorpe called out. "We found the swag by following the footprints into the closed-down mine."

Around the yard, the other Cut-Jaws laughed along with Thorpe.

Dorphin shook his bowed head and cursed under his breath. "The damn footprints. We didn't sweep them away."

"Damn it, Willis," said Readling. He rubbed his palm over his face to collect himself. Then he said, "Hell, I never thought of it either."

"Don't go easy on me," Dorphin said. "I failed you, sir. I'm going to have to live with that fact for the rest of my life."

Turning back to the window ledge, Readling called out to Thorpe, "Let the woman go! Show some honor here."

"Don't tell me about honor," said Thorpe. "She goes with us. If you come dogging us, she dies."

"I won't follow you," Readling said. "I give you my word."

"The word of a *big business tycoon*. Now, that is hard to resist," Thorpe said wryly. "But I'll have to pass. I need some insurance to keep you off my trail."

Readling started to say something, but Dorphin cut in ahead of him and called out, "Take me, leave the woman."

"He's not going to go for that," Readling said to Dorphin. "Thanks for trying."

But to everybody's surprise, the outlaw called out in reply, "Who are you, then?"

Readling took the cue. "He's my right-hand man, Willis Dorphin. He's more like family than hired help. He's the brother I never had. If anything happens to him, you won't be able to run fast enough or far enou—"

"Stop selling," shouted Thorpe. "Send him out. I'll trade the woman for him."

The Johnson brothers stood staring. "What kind of fool is this Santana anyway?"

"I don't know," said Readling, "but I'm not turning nothing down." He looked at Dorphin. "Are you sure you want to do this?"

"*Want to . . .* No," said Dorphin. "But I'll do it for you and for the woman. It'll make up for leaving those footprints."

Readling reached out and patted his shoulder. "Good

man, by God, sir," he said proudly. Then he called out to Thorpe, "I'm sending him out. What about the woman?"

"Soon as your man gets over here, I send the woman over there," Thorpe said, "plain and simple."

"All right," said Readling, "here he comes."

Chapter 19

The woman stood watching from her spot beside Ned Breck as Willis Dorphin walked out of the office shack and over to where his horse stood hitched to a post, just out of what had been the line of gunfire. The rest of the Cut-Jaws stood behind cover. They eyed him while he unhitched his horse and led it across the yard, his hands chest high, his revolver holstered—still carrying Shaw's big Colt shoved down behind his belt.

"Easy, everybody," said Thorpe with a faint smile on his face. "It's all going our way."

As soon as Dorphin arrived at the rear of the wagon, he stepped out of sight from the office shack and lowered his hands. He let out a breath and shoved his hair back up under his hat.

"That went better than I thought it would," he said to Thorpe. He smiled, but then he saw the blood on the outlaw's side. "Damn, what happened to you, Morgan?" he said.

"That *accidental* rifle shot nailed me good," said Thorpe. "Who fired it?"

"Beats me," Dorphin lied. "Both Johnson brothers have a rifle. Mine's still in my rifle boot. See?"

"Rifles don't know who they belong to," Ned Breck put in with a questioning glare.

"Who's the *mouth*?" Dorphin asked Thorpe, not about to start off taking any guff. He took a step toward Breck, his hand coming down close to the gun on his hip.

"This is Ned Breck," said Thorpe, his voice sounding strained.

Breck only glowered at Dorphin.

"Take it easy, Ned," Thorpe warned. "I've known Willis Dorphin since my gun-running days when he was decking for the railroad. You do not want to give him any shit." Just as soon as he'd spoken his coarse words, he turned toward Rosa Reyes and said sincerely, "Begging your pardon, ma'am."

Rosa looked away.

From the shack, Readling called out, "All right, where's the woman?"

"She's going with us," said Thorpe. "Says she likes us better." He ginned at Rosa as he pressed the bandana to his bleeding side. "Ain't that right, ma'am?" He wagged his gun barrel at her, forcing her to reply to Readling.

She took a step and called out, "I am going with them. I like them better."

Thorpe and the others chuckled.

"What about Willis Dorphin?" Readling called out, trying to hold down his rage.

"They said they'll kill me if you try to follow them, Mr. Readling," Dorphin cried out in mock terror.

"The question is, Readling," Thorpe called out, "who

do you want us to kill . . . the woman or this hired gun who's like a *brother* to you?"

Readling shouted a curse, then said, "If anything happens to the woman . . . !" His words trailed in his rage and frustration.

"I guess I see where *I* stand," Dorphin chuckled along with the others.

"Don't worry, ma'am," Thorpe said to Rosa Reyes. He looked her up and down, hungrily. But he clicked his cheek and said, almost as a warning to himself, "If anything happened to you, Santana himself would skin the lot of us."

Senora Rosa Reyes stood cool and calm. "I only want to get where I am going. I will get in no one's way," she replied.

"That's good, ma'am," said Thorpe. "I expect any of us here can say the same." He turned to Carlos Loonie and said, "Help me with the wagon. I'm bleeding too much to stand around here." To Ned Breck, Charlie Ruiz and Aldo Barry, he said, "You three hang back up in the rocks, just in case. If they make for their horses to follow us, shoot them down."

"You mean shoot *them* or shoot their horses?" Breck asked.

"Either one . . . Hell, shoot *both*," said Thorpe. "What the blazes do we care? Today, we've become rich men."

Atop a high cliff, Crayton Dawson stood in his stirrups with his telescope to his eye and gazed onto their back trail. He saw the *federales* riding upward at a good steady pace, less than an hour behind them. They had first spotted the soldiers earlier while the shooting still raged.

But now that the gunfire had stopped, it appeared the column was riding faster.

Turning in his saddle, Dawson looked out onto a trail ahead of them where he'd spotted dust stirring only a moment ago.

Beside him, Deputy Caldwell squinted his naked eyes, seeing with little success in the sun's glare.

"Sounds like the shooting's all over with at the mines," he said. "What can you see over in that direction?"

"It's the Cut-Jaws all right," Dawson said. "It looks like they've gotten their hands on a freight wagon. There's some small crates in its bed. There must've been something there worth stealing."

"Anybody from the mines on their trail?" Caldwell asked.

"No," Dawson said grimly. "That's a bad sign. We might find nothing but bodies at the mines."

As Dawson looked back and forth, seeing the faces of the Cut-Jaws as if they were only a few yards from him, he scanned back across the wagon bed, then back toward the front seat, where he saw the backs of two men and a woman seated between them.

"All right," he said to Caldwell, "I think I'm spotting Readling's woman, the one Shaw was telling us about."

A swirl of trail dust drifted across the circling lens view, then moved away. As it did, it revealed the woman's face as she turned and looked back into the wagon bed. Dawson got a good close look at her.

"My God . . ." He lowered the lens from his eye as if he'd been stricken in the heart.

"What is it?" Caldwell asked.

Without answering, Dawson raised the lens again,

looked through it and found her face for a second time, now only for a few seconds before more dust wafted in and she righted herself in the seat. Dawson let out a breath.

"Holy Mother," he said. He lowered the lens and rubbed his eye as if in disbelief. "I see why Shaw was so taken." He handed the lens sidelong to Caldwell as he spoke. "She looks so much like Rosa Shaw that I—"

He stopped himself short and shook his head.

Caldwell searched through the lens, seeing the streaking dust, the wagon, the backs of two men and a woman in the seat.

"I can only see the back of her head," he said sidelong as he continued looking. "I never saw his wife anyway. . . ."

"You have now," Dawson said in earnest, "as close as you ever will in this life."

When Caldwell lowered the lens, he looked at Dawson and saw the hurt look on his face, the wistful sadness in his eyes. He looked away for a moment as he collapsed the telescope between his palms and handed it back to him.

"Are you all right?" he asked finally.

"Yeah," Dawson said, but he drew a breath and let it out as he replied, "I wasn't ready for something like that," he said.

"So I see," Caldwell said. He continued looking off toward the stir of dust on the distant hillside, no longer able to see the faces of the men or the woman.

Dawson looked at him. "We lived in Somos Santos, within miles of each other. We were neighbors."

"I know," said Caldwell, turning his horse on the

trail. "I also know that there are things that are unresolved between you and Shaw over her."

Dawson turned his horse alongside him. "No, there's not," he said. "There are things Shaw and I have never discussed. There are things neither one of us wants to bring up. But there's nothing *unresolved.*"

"I understand," Caldwell said.

"It *resolved* itself somehow," Dawson said, "or else one of us would be dead." He nudged his horse forward with a tap of his boots.

They rode onto the trail leading toward the mining complex. But before they had made their way three miles closer, a series of quickly fired rifle shots exploded on the distant hillside. The sound caused the two lawmen to nudge their horses up into a trot even on the rocky, hazardous trail.

At the mines, Readling stood over the dead horses, gazing off along the trail, gripping his left arm where a bullet had grazed him.

"The sons of bitches," he said bitterly, a pistol hanging in his hand. "I'll get them for this even if it kills us all."

Elvis and Witt Johnson gave each other a look. Witt said, "Begging your pardon, Mr. Readling. But the woman sounded like she meant it when she said she liked them better than us."

"Don't be a damn fool, Witt!" Readling snapped at him angrily. "They told her what she had to say! What else could she have done but go along with them, under the circumstances?"

The Johnson brothers fell silent.

"Whatever the case, it's going to be a damn long walk to the City of Bad Men," Elvis said quietly. He held a wadded-up bandana pressed to a bullet graze along his left shoulder.

"What's this?" said Witt, jerking his rifle up at the sight of the two riders who appeared from around the front guard shack.

Elvis' rifle came up as well. "Jesus, there's more of them Cut-Jaws coming!" He levered a round into the chamber. The brothers flanked Readling on either side.

Readling raised his pistol with his good arm, cocked it and took aim.

"Hold your fire," Dawson shouted out loudly as he and Caldwell rode closer. "We're lawmen. We're not with the Cut-Jaws."

"Lawmen, eh?" Readling said skeptically. But he tipped his gun barrel up. "You look too much like us to be the law here in the Mexican hill country."

"We are the law all the same," Dawson said, speaking fast as he pulled his horse to a halt.

Following suit beside him, Caldwell said, "We heard shooting."

"Yes, you did," said Readling. "Now, who the devil are you?"

"I'm U.S. Marshal Crayton Dawson. This is my deputy, Jedson Caldwell," Dawson said. "We work here with the blessings of the Mexican government."

Readling let his gun down. "All right, I've heard of you fellows."

"So have I," said Elvis. He and his brother lowered their rifles as one.

"I sure wish to goodness you had extra horses, Mar-

shal," Readling said. "You see how they've left us here."
He gestured down at the dead horses lying sprawled
on the ground.

"Sorry we can't help you in that regard," Dawson
said firmly. "We're going after them, though. I caught
sight of them riding along the trail with a wagon."

"Yes, a wagon carrying crates of my gold and cash
on it," Readling said. "Which way do they appear to be
headed?"

"My guess would be they're going for the high trail
and south to San Simon first of all. There's water for
their horses there," Dawson said.

"I think one of them is wounded," Readling said.
"We found blood over by an empty wagon." He gestured to where Thorpe had stood.

"In that case they'll head north on the trail and cut
back to the City of Bad Men," Dawson said. "There's a
mission priest there who can patch up a bullet hole.
There's no one who can help them in San Simon."

"That settles it, then," said Readling, "they're headed
for la Ciudad de Hombres Malos." He rubbed the back
of his neck in frustration, then said, "I don't suppose
you'd sell us those horses, would you? I mean, for a *very
serious* amount of money?"

"Not a chance," said Dawson. "But we're going to
find the men who robbed you. With any luck, you'll be
getting your gold and your money back very soon."

Readling hated to think of a U.S. Marshal and his
deputy opening one of the crates and finding gold bars
bearing a U.S. Depository stamp on them. *Damn. . . .*

"All right," said Readling. He snapped his raised pistol
back toward the two lawmen. "What if I say we're tak-

ing those horses and leaving you here until help comes along for you?"

"*Jesus* . . . !" Elvis murmured. "He's lost his mind!"

Dawson's and Caldwell's rifles came up from across their laps as one. "You don't want this to happen, mister," Dawson said. "We'll leave you lying dead with your horses."

Readling's pistol tipped back up, some sense coming back to him. As if nothing had just happened, he said, "All right, Marshal, they're holding two hostages . . . a man who works for me and a woman who's traveling with me."

"We'll be careful not to get them hurt," Dawson said.

"What about us?" Readling asked. "How do we get out of here?"

"There's a column of *federales* riding up behind us," Dawson said. "You'll be able to get horses from them."

Readling saw the lawmen had nothing else for him. He nodded and said, "We'll be right behind you, then."

The two lawmen turned their horses and nudged them back onto the trail.

Chapter 20

As the two scouts rounded a turn in a winding switch-back, they both reined up hard at the sight of Shaw sitting his horse in the middle of the trail gazing coldly at them. Both scouts swallowed a hard knot and stared wide-eyed, stricken with fear.

"Just the two men I've been looking for," Shaw said quietly.

"Larry *Rápido*," the older scout whispered and crossed himself slowly, as if he'd witnessed a miracle. Shaw moved his horse forward and stopped less than four feet away as the soldiers continued to stare. He nodded down at his rifle, sticking up from the older scout's saddle boot. The soldier had swapped places with his own older rifle, which now lay shoved into his bedroll.

"I'll be taking my rifle back now," Shaw said in the same quiet but sinister tone.

"*Sí*, of course," said the older scout. "I—I want you to have it. I cleaned it real good, just in case we ever met again."

"You mean after you cut my throat and threw me off

the cliff?" Shaw said, watching closely as the scout drew the rifle up and handed it over to him, butt first.

"Yes, right after that," the scout said, nodding his head vigorously. "I felt so bad—as we both did, and I told my friend here, if by some chance you lived and we ever saw you again, I wanted to—"

The sound of Shaw levering a round into the rifle chamber cut him off. Shaw cocked the rifle and laid it across his lap, his hand around it, his finger inside the trigger guard. "What kind of six-shooters are you carrying?" he asked.

The two looked at the gun in Shaw's holster, seeing for the first time how battered and old it appeared. Realizing they had just been duped into arming the beaten-up gunman, the older scout shook his head in regret and said, "Mine is a Russian Smith & Wesson, senor."

"As is mine," said the younger scout.

"Raise them, and hand them over," Shaw said, feeling pain start to churn inside his head.

Both soldiers raised their holster flaps, lifted the big Smith & Wessons and held them out, butt first. Shaw pulled the battered relic from his holster and shoved it down beneath the flap of his saddlebag. The scouts stared in disgust at each other as he took both revolvers, cocked one and laid the other on his lap.

"Now, bullets," Shaw said.

"Bullets, senor . . . ?" the older scout said as if not understanding.

"These Russians shoot forty-fours. I carry forty-fives." He wagged the big pistol. "Give me some forty-four bullets."

"Of course, I forgot," the older scout said. He reached over, taking a black bandoleer of bullets from the younger scout's shoulder, and handed them over. Shaw hung it over his own shoulder.

"I'm happy to see that you are doing so well, senor," the older scout said. He gestured toward the stitches on Shaw's chin. "There will hardly be a scar, once you have healed—"

"Ride on," Shaw said, cutting him off, feeling the pain in his head growing more intense.

"You are not going to kill us, Larry *Rápido*?" the younger scout asked.

"No," Shaw said, "not unless you force me to. You're soldiers, you followed orders. Now get going." His head began to pound inside. Things began looking flat and gray in front of him. He could hardly distinguish the men from his surroundings.

"We go now," the older scout said as they both backed their horses a few steps. Before turning the animals, the soldiers noted the look on Shaw's face, seeing that he was having trouble staying upright in his saddle.

The younger scout gestured his eyes toward his rifle, still standing in its boot.

The older scout's eyes glittered, realizing Shaw had made a terrible oversight. Looking up at the young scout, the older soldier shouted, "*Ahora!*"

Acting on command, the young soldier snatched the rifle up from its boot as the older scout's hand went inside his tunic and came out swinging a double-action Colt Thunderer around toward Shaw.

The big Russian .44 snapped up from Shaw's lap and bucked twice in his hand, firing at little more than gray shadows. But Shaw's condition didn't hinder him any. The older scout flew backward from his saddle and landed dead on the ground. The younger scout went down only a second behind him. He lay groaning, writhing in the dirt, a gaping bullet hole in his chest.

Shaw's head cleared a little; so did his vision, as he batted his eyes and looked down at the big smoking revolver.

Nice gun. . . .

He held the revolver dangling down at his thigh as he nudged the bay over and looked down at the Mexican soldier lying on the ground.

"Larry *Rápido*! Larry *Rápido*!" the young scout said in a strained and sobbing voice. "Are you going to kill me?"

"Yep, I suppose so," Shaw said. The Russian bucked once more in his hand; the scout fell silent.

Shaw stepped down from his saddle and leaned against the bay's side for a moment, making sure that his head was clear and his vision was back to normal. When the world settled around him, he dragged the two bodies off the trail, dropped the saddles and bridles from their horses and shooed the animals away.

Back at his own horse, he stepped up and sat slumped in his saddle for a moment, as if he was trying to remember what to do next. He thought about the old woman he'd seen—or at least thought he had seen—on his way out of town.

"The *bruja* and her sparrows . . . ," he said quietly to himself. *How did she manage to train birds as wild and fast and headstrong as sparrows . . . ?*

Hell, he didn't know, he thought, and he put the

question out of his mind, tapped his boots to the bay's sides and rode on toward Readling's mines. He would find her if it meant his life. *Rosa . . .* , he told himself, *I'm not losing you again. . . .*

Ned Breck, Charlie Ruiz and Aldo Barry had hurried atop their horses and lit out as soon as they'd wounded Readling and Elvis Johnson. As they rode away, Aldo Barry had looked back and spoken with a nasal twang, his nose healing, but still purple and swollen.

"We should have finished them off," he said.

"To hell with them. They're hurt," said Ruiz. "That's all that matters."

"We killed their horses. They're not going anywhere, not for a while anyways," said Ned Breck in agreement.

"That's right," said Ruiz. "I don't want that money to stray too far out of my sight until I get my share of it."

"I don't give a damn about the money," said Aldo. "I just want to get my hands on Fast Larry, the son of a bitch who done this to me."

"Oh, boy, here we go again," Ruiz said between himself and Ned Breck. "We got to hear more about how he's going to *kill* Fast Larry."

"What'd you say?" Aldo asked in a stiff, angry tone.

"Nothing, forget it," said Ruiz. "If you ain't careful, you're going to catch up to Fast Larry. Then you're going to have to make good on all this tough talk you've been spewing out about him."

"Yeah," Breck put in with a dark laugh, "that's when you're going to wish you'd caught a wildcat by its ass instead."

"To hell with you both," Aldo said, his horse trotting

along beside them. "I'll kill him. Then you'll see!" His voice grew louder. "*Everybody* will see!" he raged.

Atop a cliff, they stopped long enough to look around and check their back trail. When they did, they saw two riders on their trail, gaining ground fast.

"Damn it, who's this?" Ruiz asked, staring beneath his hat brim, still squinting against the sun's glare.

"Figure they found some horses?" Breck asked, also staring.

"I don't know," said Ruiz. "It might be somebody else. But I ain't lagging back to find out." He kicked his horse forward. "Let's get caught up to the others. There's strength in numbers, you know."

Aldo Barry shook his head and looked away. His nose throbbed with his horse's pounding hooves.

The three rode on.

On the trail far behind them, Shaw stopped his bay and watched as the *federales* rode the last few hundred yards into Readling's mining operation. Easing down from his saddle, he led the bay onto the hillside and circled wide of the mines until he stood looking down on the yards from the shelter of brush and rock. Perched a hundred feet above the yards, he looked all around, searching for the woman as he watched the Mexican captain talk with Readling and his men.

"Damn it, Captain," Shaw heard Readling say, "you should have been here with your men."

"We turned and rode back as quickly as we could, as soon as we heard shooting," the captain replied, "even though we were supposed to ride to town."

Readling could sense that things weren't as they

should be, but this was no time to argue. He and the Johnson brothers needed horses in order to get on the Cut-Jaws' trail.

"All right, Captain," he said, "you got here as fast as you could," he relented. "But it's too late. What I need now are three good horses."

"But, Senor Readling," said the captain, "it is my job to run down these thieves. I'm taking my men immediately and getting your gold and the two hostages back. You can rely on it."

"We're coming too, Captain," Readling insisted.

"But we have no horses for you, senor," the captain said. "Where are the mules your workers use to haul the ore buggy from the mines?"

"Some of them belong to buggy men," said Readling. "They ride them to the towns on weekends. Apparently the French also took some of them," he added in disgust, "to eat, no doubt on their way to Mexico City."

"Then there is nothing I can do for you. We have no spare horses," the captain said.

"Tell three of your men to dismount, Captain. They can wait here. We're taking their horses," Readling ordered, utilizing the power he knew he had through his Golden Circle connections in Mexico City.

Shaw listened for a while; then, realizing the Cut-Jaws had taken the woman, he scooted back into the brush, rose into a crouch and crept back to where his bay stood hitched to a tree. The pain had eased up inside his head for a while, but as he moved it suddenly came back to him. He had to stop and lean against the bay for a moment before climbing up into his saddle.

The pain grew more intense as he turned his horse

and rode it away, back toward the trail. He planned to move around the *federales* and get back on the trail ahead of them. But before he could get on his way, he caught sight of someone hiding in the brush to his right. He swung the big Russian .44 around, cocking it.

"You, in there," Shaw called out, "stand up, hands good and high."

As he called out, his head pounding insistently, everything began to take on the grayness he'd seen earlier. He struggled to remain upright in his saddle.

In the brush, Doc Penton stood up with his hands above his head. "Don't shoot, Shaw," he said. "I'm not going to cause you any trouble."

Shaw had a hard time focusing, but he managed to recognize Penton and said in a thick voice, "What are you doing out here, Doc?"

"Damn, Shaw, I thought for sure you were dead," Penton said, taking a step forward. "Didn't those soldiers cut your throat and leave you bleeding out?"

"They did," Shaw said, "and that wasn't but half of all they did. But they didn't get the job done." He paused before saying, "You did your part, Doc, unloading my rifle for Dorphin."

"I know," Doc said, "and I'm sorry." He sounded sincere, but so had the two soldiers until they'd decided to make a move on him.

"I bet you are," Shaw said, managing to keep himself sitting straight even though the image of Doc Penton moved in and out of the dim grayness before him. "Are those your horses?" He gestured toward two horses standing hitched to a tree a few yards deeper into the brush and rock.

"Yeah," Doc said, "they are now."

"You still haven't told me what you're doing out here," Shaw said.

Doc looked ashamed as he stalled for a second. Finally he said, "I'm hiding, Shaw . . . all right?" He tilted his chin up. "I ran, grabbed the horses and hid out here when the Cut-Jaws rode in, because I didn't want to get myself shot."

Shaw just stared at him. "All this time you've been hiding?"

"That's right," said Doc. "I'd screwed myself up enough guts to go back, but then the soldiers came riding in and I stayed here. Now I don't think I can go back and face Readling and the Johnson brothers."

Shaw started to sway in the saddle, but he caught himself. He couldn't put off shooting Penton. He had no idea how long he'd remain upright. The grayness closed in deeper around him.

"Do you know what I did with those soldiers, Doc?" he asked, cocking the big Russian.

"Knowing that's the kind of guns they carry," Doc said, referring to the big Russian Smith & Wesson in Shaw's hand, "I've got a pretty good idea."

"You're right. They're dead," Shaw said, feeling his voice sound farther away. "Now you're going to die too," he added.

"This close to the yard and to the *federales*?" Penton asked.

But Shaw could no longer make out what Penton was saying. He only saw his lips moving. "So . . . long, Doc," he said, barely staying conscious enough to keep the big revolver steady.

Penton squeezed his eyes shut, waiting for the bullet to hit him. But instead of hearing a shot explode, he heard Shaw topple from the saddle and land at the bay's hooves. The bay chuffed, reached down and sniffed at its rider lying in the dirt.

"Huh . . . ," Doc said in surprise. He stepped forward with his hands still up and said down to Shaw, "Are you hit somewhere, Shaw?"

When Shaw didn't answer, Doc shrugged to himself and said, "Damn, this has been a strange day for me."

He stepped over to the bay, took down Shaw's canteen, uncapped it with a shaky hand and took a gulp of tepid water. With his own gun in its holster, he stooped down, picked up the big Russian .44 lying cocked and ready to fire. He plucked a twig from its cylinder and dusted some dirt from it.

"After all this, I'm the one who ends up killing 'the fastest gun alive'?" He shook his head. "It can't get no stranger than this."

He held the tip of the gun barrel down close to Shaw's head. "This time it'll *get done*, Fast Larry," he said to the unconscious gunman.

Chapter 21

━━━◆━━━

In the middle of the night, Marshal Dawson and Deputy Caldwell were perched on a hillside, staring down onto glowing firelight radiating from the trail below them. They had slipped down within thirty yards of the camp, close enough to see the faces of the men sitting around a low fire sipping coffee. Dorphin sat amid the men, talking freely, a rifle across his lap, a pistol standing in his holster. The two lawmen had heard one of the other gunmen call Dorphin by name only a moment earlier.

"He doesn't appear to need much saving," Caldwell whispered to the marshal.

"It's good to find out now, instead of later," Dawson replied.

The woman sat off to the side; she wasn't tied up, but Silver Bones stood nearby, watching over her with a rifle in his hands. His mouth was still bruised and misshapen from the slam of Shaw's rifle butt.

"We haven't seen or heard anything yet to make us

believe Mingus Santana is with this bunch," Caldwell reasoned.

"True," said Dawson. "We don't want to go charging in there and risk getting the woman hurt." He thought about the blood they'd found in the mining yard. "We know at least one of these men needs tending to in the City of Bad Men. We can hang back and trail them there."

Caldwell nodded in agreement.

"All right, let's slip in and get her out of there without a fight," Dawson said. "We can deal with them anytime."

"Right," said Caldwell. "They seem to be treating her good enough right now, but that can change with any turn of a card."

The two left their horses hitched to a stand of short rocks and moved away in a crouch, circling wide of the outlaws' campfire in the purple moonlight. When they'd found a safe place behind Silver Bones and the woman, Dawson made a gesture that told Caldwell to wait there. The deputy stopped and gripped his rifle in both hands, ready to provide the marshal cover fire if he needed it.

Dawson slipped along silently, as far as he could in a crouch. Then he dropped down onto his belly and crawled the last few yards until he stopped behind a rock only six feet behind Silver Bones. The woman still sat to the side, suspecting nothing, gazing over toward the flickering campfire ten yards away.

Here goes. . . .

Dawson stood up and moved forward fast, holding his rifle high. Seeing the back of Silver Bones' head, he made a powerful short jab with the rifle butt and sent the outlaw tumbling to the ground. The woman heard a sound, no different than a sack of grain falling. But when she turned toward the noise, Dawson had already crossed the few feet to her.

Seeing the look of fright and surprise on her face, the marshal threw his gloved hand over her mouth to keep her from screaming. "It's all right. We're lawmen. We've come for you." He pulled her against him.

Her eyes darted wildly back and forth above the edge of his glove, looking for the other lawmen.

"Do you understand me?" he whispered. "We're here to save you."

She nodded vigorously, wild-eyed, yet she still hesitated until Dawson took his hand from her mouth and pulled her away with him toward the cover of brush and rock. Once they were safely hidden, she jerked free of him and spoke in a whisper, suspicion in her voice.

"*Americano* lawmen? Out here, in the hill country? Who are you?" she demanded. She saw Caldwell appear out of the darkness.

"Not now, ma'am," Dawson whispered. "We've got to get you out of here, before they find the rifleman knocked out."

The three hurried away toward the horses, the woman being helped along by the lawmen on either side of her. When they reached the animals and unhitched them from the rock, Dawson swung her up onto the saddle and pulled himself up behind her. They rode away without incident, looking back onto the flickering campfire glowing peaceably in the night.

"We were lucky, getting out of there without firing a shot," Dawson said, his face close enough to the woman's hair to catch its soft, flowery fragrance.

Jesus. . . . Shaw was right, he thought, closing his eyes for a moment as if feeling Rosa Shaw's hair once again caress his cheek. Head injury or not, he could see that the two women were almost identical.

Stop it . . . , he had to tell himself. He'd had to do the same many times since Rosa's death, as he often found himself lost in his memories of his best friend's wife.

"Who are you? Where are you taking me?" Rosa Reyes asked over her shoulder.

Beside them, Caldwell offered a response, as if he realized Dawson needed a second to collect himself.

"La Ciudad de Hombres Malos," Caldwell said in Spanish, in respect of her native tongue.

"The City of Bad Men," she translated back to him with a snap. "My English is good, senor," she said. "You do not need to make concessions for my benefit."

"No, senora," said Caldwell, "I understand that, and I apologize."

Dawson reached past her knee, feeling the heat of her bare skin, her skirt hiked up for riding. He picked up his canteen by its strap and uncapped it. He had to keep himself in close check with this woman, he realized.

"This is my deputy, Jedson Caldwell, senora," he said quietly. "I'm Marshal Crayton Dawson."

"I am Senora Rosa Reyes," she said, nodding first at Caldwell in the moonlight, then turning her words back over her shoulder to the marshal. She paused in reflection for a moment, then said, "I have heard of you both . . . from my father. Thank God you came along when you did."

"You appeared safe enough for the time being, senora," Caldwell said.

"Yes," said Rosa Reyes in a brittle, prickly tone, "for a defenseless kidnapped woman, in the company of several armed thieves and killers who are on the run, I should never have felt safer in my life."

"Again, I apologize, senora. I'm an idiot," Caldwell said flatly, apparently unable to converse with the woman on any intelligent level without his words tangling into a mess.

To get the deputy out of the spot he'd stumbled into, Dawson cut in, saying, "What about the man, Dorphin? It looks like he's part of the Cut-Jaws."

"Yes," said the woman. "It was he who told the Cut-Jaws about Readling's plan to hide all the cash and the gold at the mines."

"Do you know why a man like Readling would do such a thing—bring such a valuable cargo to a place like this?" Dawson asked, handing the canteen around to her.

"Yes, I know why," she said. "Because he is a pig and an outlaw himself, only of a different sort." Her voice became stronger as she spoke. "The gold and the cash belong to a group he's part of called the Golden Circle. Have you heard of them?"

Dawson looked at Caldwell in the moonlight.

"Oh, yes, senora," Dawson said. "The Golden Circle has been around for a long time. If Readling is a member, you're right, he's an outlaw himself, only a more polished and refined one."

The woman sipped the tepid water, then handed the canteen back to Dawson.

"I can tell you many things about the celebrated Mr. Howard Readling," she said in a bitter tone. "He had my father and my brother killed." She paused for a second, then continued. "I was told as much by the gunman, Lawrence Shaw. Readling then had soldiers kill Shaw, I'm certain of it. He told me he would not . . . but he did."

"Good news, Senora Reyes," Dawson said, recapping the canteen. "Lawrence Shaw is not dead. We found him and took him to a church in the City of Bad Men. He's there now recuperating," he added.

"Thank God," she said, crossing herself, appearing stunned by the news. "But how can it be that they did not kill him. He was so helpless, and out of his senses?"

Helpless . . . ?

"Senora, I could tell you stories about that one . . . ," Dawson said, nudging his horse forward.

Near dawn, Shaw awakened and looked off across the purple hill country surrounding him. He remembered the last time he'd drifted off into the grayness and awakened with his gun standing unloaded in his holster. Instinctively, he reached his hand down his side and he felt the empty holster on his hip.

A small fire flickered between him and Doc Penton.

"I've got both the Russians, Shaw," Doc said quietly, sitting a few feet away, facing him across the fire. One of the big .44s hung loosely in his hand.

"You should have killed me when you had the chance, Doc," Shaw said. He was still foggy, but the pain in his head had eased off.

"Not with the *federales* so close," Doc said. "But who says I don't still have the chance?" The big revolver flipped upward in his hand, his thumb cocking the hammer as he leveled it in Shaw's face.

Shaw didn't flinch. "Do it, Doc," he said calmly, his eyes level on Penton's. Make yourself the *fastest gun alive*. I'm through with it."

"The fastest gun alive . . . ?" Doc said. He let the hammer down with his thumb, flipped the gun around in his hand and laid it on Shaw's lap, butt first. "I already considered it, when you were lying knocked out on the ground." He nodded at the revolver and said, "I only took the guns because I didn't know what kind of mood you'd come back in."

Shaw stared at him.

Doc shook his head. "Fastest gun alive sounded like a lot of work to me." He gave a thin smile.

"A wise observation," Shaw said. He picked up the Russian and slipped it into his holster.

Doc handed him the other one and Shaw slid it down into his belt. "Besides, my gunning days are over. I've run out of nerve."

"That's hard to believe," Shaw said.

"I know," Doc said. "I started hiring out my gun when I was sixteen . . . charged a cousin of mine two dollars, and as much time as I wanted rolling in the hay with her, to kill her husband, Blaine."

"Everybody has to start somewhere," Shaw said.

"Yep, that's what I told myself back then," said Doc. "But I spent the two dollars on whiskey and more bullets. And I got so tired of rolling in the hay with her, I contracted a rash."

"What can I say?" Shaw shook his head slowly.

"I've lived by the gun ever since," said Doc. "Now look at me. I've run out of guts and I can't keep from shaking every time I think about dying. Hell of a note, ain't it?"

Shaw stared at him. "Seeing Blaine's face more clearly these days, I expect?" Shaw offered.

"Him, and every other son of a bitch I sent to hell," Doc reflected. "But that's not so new. I've been seeing them for years."

"I know the feeling," Shaw said.

They sat quietly until Doc asked, "What got into you anyway, Shaw? You could have had it made hands down with Howard Readling. He liked you—I mean, he respected you, that is . . . leastwise as much as a man like him could respect anybody."

"The woman is what got into me, Doc," Shaw said. "I was married to a woman who looked enough like Rosa Reyes to be her twin—even had the same name, *Rosa.*"

"Damn," Doc said. "No wonder she had you acting about half, you know . . ." His words trailed as he touched his fingers to the side of his head.

"Half *crazy*, you mean?" Shaw said, finishing his words for him. He touched his fingers to his head too. "Yeah, I suppose so . . . her, and taking a bullet in the head," he offered.

"A bullet in the head never helped anybody," Doc said with a wince.

Shaw nodded and continued, saying, "The life I live got my wife killed. When I met Rosa Reyes, I knew it was my own wife, Rosa Shaw, come back to me to give me another chance."

Doc Penton stared at him.

"I know how all this sounds, Doc," Shaw said, not even stopping to question why he was telling Penton any of it. "But this woman *is* my Rosa, no ifs, ands or buts about it."

"A head wound can knock a man plumb off his fences for a long time, Shaw," Doc Penton said.

"I know," Shaw said, "and the crazier it makes a man, the least likely he is to see it."

"Yep," Doc said. "I'm glad you understand that."

"Only this is not *crazy* talk," Shaw said, as if he hadn't heard him. "I don't how things like this work, but Rosa has come back to me somehow, and I'm never going to let her go."

"Shaw, listen to me—"

But Shaw stopped Doc Penton with a raised hand, already recognizing that Doc was going to try to reason with him and change his mind.

"No, Doc, *you* listen to *me*," he said. "We've been getting along real good, you and me, sitting here, neither one of us trying to kill the other. Don't go telling me what I don't want to hear."

Doc fell silent. After a moment, he said, "Well, why don't I boil us some coffee?"

"Yeah, good idea," Shaw said.

"What do you think of me riding with you anyways?" Doc asked.

"Suit yourself," Shaw said, "but keep your hands off my rifle."

"I told you I was sorry for what I did," said Doc.

"And I heard you," Shaw replied.

Chapter 22

Gazing down from the bell tower above the church, the young Mexican saw a wagon roll into sight ahead of a billowing cloud of dust. He turned, hurried down the ladder and raced through the hallway to where the priest stood before a cracked and tarnished mirror.

"What is it, Julio?" the priest questioned over his shoulder. He was in a fighting stance, shooting his fists out in fast short punches at an imaginary opponent.

"Riders are coming. They bring a wagon, Padre," said the boy. "It looks like the same men who were here before."

"The Cut-Jaws?" Father Timido asked, looking surprised.

"*Sí, Las Mandíbulas de corte,*" Julio said quickly, repeating the priest's words in Spanish.

"I see," said the priest. He stopped punching, straightened his loose sleeves and adjusted the front of his black robe. "Perhaps the time has come for me to chase them away for good."

The young man stared in amazement. "Can you do such a thing, Padre?" he asked.

"Of course," Father Timido said proudly, jutting his chin. "I am a man of God. I can do many things. I can tell these men to go, and they must go. I can beat in their faces if they disobey me." He smiled a little as he opened and closed his tight fists. "This is the power I have."

The padre and the young man hurried to the ladder and climbed up to the bell tower. Father Timido looked out at the riders and the freight wagon, which were now drawing closer, leaving a swirl of dust behind them.

"I sense that they are coming here, to our humble church," he murmured.

"Then what must we do, Padre?" the boy asked.

"I know what I must do," Father Timido said. "But as for you, Julio, I think it is time for you to go join your family."

"I cannot leave you here alone with them, Padre," the young man said, concerned, in spite of all the priest's bold talk.

On the street below, many of the townspeople had already seen the rising dust and were once again frantically preparing to leave.

"The best thing you can do for me, Julio, is to go, take your family back to the hillsides and stay there until these men are gone," Father Timido said.

The young boy submitted. "I will do as you tell me to do, Padre, but I do not like it. I want to stay here with you."

Father Timido turned and looked at the boy. He smiled. "Julio," he said, "I have been here almost three years, and always you have been at my heels. If I stop too quickly, I know you will bump into me."

The boy stared at the approaching riders and said bitterly, "If I only had a gun—"

"*Shhh!* Stop that kind of talk," the padre said. "You had a gun. You lent it to Larry *Rápido*, remember?"

"*Sí*," Julio said, "and that was a mistake. If I had it now—"

"Stop it," the priest said, cutting him off again. He turned and laid a hand on the boy's shoulder. "You are a good boy. But I am sorry to say, this is not a day for *good boys*. This is a day for *bad men*." He gestured a hand around the town below them. "What better place for *bad men* than this *City of Bad Men*?"

Julio stood quietly.

The priest patted his cheek. "No, you go and do as I tell you. You must grow to be strong of both mind and body, so that when you are a man, you will be a *good* man. You will be the kind of man who will put himself between outlaws and this beloved country of ours. Knowing you have done that with your life is all I care about."

The boy looked frightened. "Padre," he said, "you talk as if this will be your last day here."

"We never know what day will be out last, my son," the padre said. "Now go. See to your family."

When the boy had descended the ladder, Father Timido stood watching. He saw the boy cross the dusty street and disappear into a small adobe house. A moment later, he saw the boy and his mother leave through a back door with a bundle of belongings and supplies, which the boy carried on his thin shoulder.

"Now, my bold *desperadoes*," he murmured toward the rising swirl of dust that trailed the horsemen and wagon as they closed in on the town. "Welcome back to the *City of Bad Men*. Let us see what this day holds in store for us." He stood straight and tall, making sure the outlaws could see him clearly.

On the seat of the wagon, Morgan Thorpe sat slumped, the bandana pressed to his side now blackened and crusted with dried blood. Beside him Carlos Loonie drove the team of horses hard. The wagon bucked and bounced and rumbled forward.

Raising his head slightly, Thorpe saw the lone figure in his black robe staring out toward them from the bell tower.

"There's the good Padre now," he said to Loonie in a weak voice, managing a thin smile. "I feel better already."

Loonie spat sidelong from the wagon seat. "Our Father Timido should have been a doctor. He's certainly had to cut a lot of bullets out of folks."

As Loonie and Thorpe watched, the padre left the bell tower. Now that he saw the boy and his mother were safely out of town, he climbed down the ladder and walked to his sleeping chambers.

He knelt and slid a small ironclad box from beneath his bed, unlocked it and took out a gun belt wrapped around a slim-jim holster that housed a big Colt Dragoon. Knowing the gun belt would show too clearly under his robe, he slipped the gun from the holster, placed the empty holster in the box and slid the box back under the bed.

From the wagon, Loonie and Thorpe saw the priest reappear at the open side door of the mission church's adobe-walled courtyard.

From the path up the rocky tree-covered hillside, the boy Julio looked back and saw the padre step out of the churchyard as the wagon and riders came to a halt in a stir of dust.

The boy said a quick prayer for the padre. Then he crossed himself, turned and climbed the hill path, taking his mother's hand in his. "When I *do* become a man, I will be like Padre Timido," he vowed in a whisper. "Because of him I will be a *good man* . . . in spite of this place where I come from."

At the church, Carlos Loonie and Matt Stewart helped Thorpe down from the wagon and through the door into the courtyard. Once they were inside, Killer Cady looked all around at the others, who had stepped down from their saddles. They gazed back in the direction of the trail as if in dark anticipation.

"We don't want to stay bunched up here," Cady said. "Some of you go water your horses and get yourself some grub and something to drink at the cantina."

"You don't have to tell me twice," said Hogue. He looked at Silver Bones' battered face and said, "Do you feel like a shot or two would help that mouth of yours?"

"Yes, I do," said Bones, standing with his horse's reins in hand. He wasted no time turning the animal around and leading it away along the dirt street, Hogue walking alongside him.

"I expect it's no secret Santana's going to shit a squealing worm when he learns that we lost the woman," Hogue said sidelong to Bones.

"A squealing worm . . . ?" Bones questioned, giving him a strange look.

"It's an old expression, is all," Hogue said.

"I sure as hell never heard it before," Bones said in his new toothless voice.

"He'll throw a fit, is what I meant by it," Hogue said.

"I don't know," said Bones. "Look at all the money we made . . . and hardly anybody hurt on our side. Santana has to look at it as a job well done, woman or no woman."

As they walked on to the cantina, Killer Cady, standing at the wagon, saw Ned Breck, Charlie Ruiz and Aldo Barry come into view on the trail.

"Here comes the three you left to take care of Readling and his men," Dorphin said, still standing near the wagon bed as if guarding its cargo.

"Good," said Kale, standing nearby. "The sooner we're all back together, the better."

"Yeah," said Killer Cady, looking back contemplatively across the hill country. "If we ain't careful, this town could fill up awful fast."

At the bottom of a thin path Shaw and Doc Penton had taken down from the switchbacks, the two sat atop their horses watching Dawson ride up into sight, someone seated behind his saddle. Shaw stared ahead, waiting to see Caldwell ride into sight as well. But when he didn't see the deputy ride up, he looked closer and realized it was Caldwell riding double with Dawson.

"Here comes a story if I ever seen one," Shaw said quietly.

When Dawson spotted Shaw and Doc Penton, he rode straight to them. A few feet away, Caldwell dropped from behind Dawson's saddle and stood with his rifle in hand.

"What happened?" Shaw asked Caldwell. "Did your horse go lame on you?"

"No," Caldwell said.

"Senora Rosa Reyes stole his horse last night," Dawson cut in.

"She just slipped away into the night," Caldwell said in a bitter tone. As he spoke, he eyed the spare horse standing beside Doc, its reins in Doc's gloved hands.

"We saved her from the Cut-Jaws," Dawson said. "Then she turned around and did this to us."

"She must've been scared," Shaw said in the woman's defense.

Dawson and Caldwell just stared at him.

"I don't think the woman is afraid of anything," Doc Penton said.

"Who's this?" Dawson asked Shaw.

"This is Doc Penton," Shaw said. He introduced the three, then said, "Doc was with Readling when the Cut-Jaws hit the mines. Says they stole crates of gold and U.S. currency from Readling."

"We know," said Dawson. "The woman told us the same thing."

"It's gold and cash that belongs to the Golden Circle," Caldwell said.

"All of it stolen from the U.S. government over a long period of time, no doubt," Dawson put in. "Do you realize what this means, Shaw?" he asked, noticing that Shaw looked better than the last time he'd seen him—his senses seemingly clearer as well.

But then Shaw said, "I don't care what it means. I don't care about the Golden Circle. Where do you think she went?"

Dawson let out a breath and said, "Look, Shaw, I saw her. I know how much she reminds you of—"

"Where do you think she went?" he repeated, his tone more pressing this time.

"I figure she's heading for the same place we're headed," Dawson said. "That's the direction the Cut-Jaws and their wagon is headed in too."

"Here's a question for you, Marshal," Doc said. "If you take the wagon from the Cut-Jaws, do you give it back to Readling, knowing it's going to the Golden Circle?"

"That's a good question, Doc," Dawson said. "Are you still working for Readling?"

"No," said Penton, "I expect I'm not, anymore." He looked at Shaw, wondering if Shaw was going mention what Penton had admitted earlier. When Penton realized that Shaw wasn't going to reveal anything they'd talked about, he spoke for himself, no longer ashamed of his actions.

"I told Shaw I lost my nerve back there, Marshal," he said. "But the more I think about it, the more I recognize that's not what happened. I believe it was just the first time in my life I realized how bad it would be to get myself killed saving some lousy rich bastard like Howard Readling. It spooked me."

Shaw looked off in the direction of the City of Bad Men and said, "Doc, unless you want to ride into town with me, this might be a good place for you to split off."

"Are you telling me to leave, or giving me the choice?" Doc asked.

Shaw only shrugged.

"Then I think I'll ride along with you. I hate the idea of getting this close to la Ciudad de Hombres Malos without stopping in and saying howdy."

Caldwell cut in and said, "Any chance of me riding your spare?" As he spoke he stepped closer in hopeful anticipation.

"Help yourself," Doc said. He handed the deputy the horse's reins.

"Obliged," said Caldwell. He swung up atop the roan's saddle and reined it back and forth in place to get a feel for it.

In a moment, the four men had turned the horses and trotted them toward the thin trail.

Chapter 23

When Howard Readling looked back and saw that Captain Fuente had brought his column to a halt, he cursed and swung his horse around, riding back toward the captain, the Johnson brothers right behind him. The captain sat waiting. Beside him, his sergeant raised a hand to steady the men as Readling slid his horse sidelong to a halt and glared at the captain.

"What the blazes is the holdup, Captain?" Readling demanded.

Captain Fuente stared at him stone-faced and said calmly, "Nothing is holding us, senor. I said we would find the men who robbed you, and we have." He nodded ahead toward the dirt street running the length of the dusty, seemingly deserted town. "Now it is up to you to take back what is yours."

"Damn it!" said Readling. "You're supposed to be guarding my property! You said I'd be getting my property back very soon!"

"*Sí*, that is what I told you," said Fuente. "But that

did not suit you, senor. You insisted on coming with us, as if we are not capable of doing the job without you overseeing us." He shrugged. "So, there is your property. Now do with it as you wish. I will not endanger my men by sending them to do something you and your men can do for yourselves." He sat firmly, his big wrists crossed on his saddle horn.

"I get it," Readling said in an angry tone. "You had no idea we would track these men to town. You thought you were leading us on a wild-goose chase. But something brought them here instead of where you thought they would go."

"Be very careful what you say, Senor Readling," the captain warned. "You are not in New England anymore. I take your accusations most personally."

"I had a deal with Mexico City for a column of men to be here until I got settled and brought in my own security," Readling said.

Captain Fuente gave a thin, smug grin. "Everybody in the Mexican hill country has a *deal* with someone." He chuckled. "Sometimes there are deals inside deals. But I need not explain how such things work, not to a businessman like yourself, eh?"

"I'll have your hide for this," Readling growled, as the captain backed his horse a step and nodded toward the sergeant, giving the signal to turn the column away from town.

"Senor, do not make foolish threats," the captain said, wagging a finger at him. "You are in no position to be doing so."

Readling and the Johnson brothers watched as the

column circled, completed a turn on the trail and rode away.

Elvis turned and looked down the long dirt street at the wagon sitting alone out in front of the adobe mission church. The doors of the cantina were wide-open; a line of horses stood in the side alleyway, and at the iron hitch rail out front.

"Brother Witt, am I a damn fool, or does it appear that these Cut-Jaws are just daring somebody to come take the wagon?"

Witt Johnson stared long with his brother, studying the situation, looking along the roofline to see if anyone was there waiting to pull an ambush.

"It does seem like it will be awfully easy to take back, considering all the trouble they went through to steal it," he said under his breath.

"Yes, it does," Readling put in, sitting in his saddle with a rifle across his lap. He had no idea where the woman might be. But he knew how important the gold and the cash were to the Golden Circle. He also realized how little his life would be worth if he allowed them to be taken from him without making every attempt to get them back.

While Readling considered this, Elvis Johnson said quietly, "What sort of bonus is in the deal if me and brother Witt ride in there with you, take that wagon and roll away with it?"

"Five hundred dollars," Readling said without hesitation. "But the two of you ride in alone and bring it out."

Elvis and Witt stifled a laugh. "Hell, it's worth five

hundred dollars just to sit and watch you try to ride in there and get it by yourself."

"That's five hundred *apiece*," Readling pointed out quickly.

"No, it's not," said Elvis. "It's *five thousand* apiece, and you're right here with us. Else you can ride away empty-handed and go explain to whoever's running the Golden Circle how you let their bank get away."

"You men are supposed to be working for me. This is robbery," said Readling with anger and disgust.

"No," said Witt, "that was robbery." He nodded toward the lone wagon. "This is *recuperation*."

"As far as working for you goes, we've both quit," Elvis said.

"For all we know, there might be no one around guarding the wagon," Readling said. "The sight of the approaching *federales* might have scared them away."

"Yeah, right," said Witt, "and if you thought that was the case, we wouldn't be sitting here talking about it. You'd be in the wagon seat right now, *yee-hiiing* them horses on down the trail."

"Damn it," Readling said, looking all along the empty street.

"Whatever you decide, you best do it fast, Mr. Readling," Elvis said. "Once us Johnsons lose interest in a thing, it's hard to get us back on task."

Readling looked down and checked his rifle. "All right, damn it. Let's get the wagon."

The three dismounted and slowly led their horses onto the dirt street toward the adobe church.

"Spread out," Witt said as they walked past the cantina. They felt eyes on them from inside the open doorway, but they continued on toward the freight wagon, rifles in hand.

Arriving at the wagon without incident, the Johnson brothers stood a few feet away on either side, looking back and forth warily along the street. Readling hitched his horse to the rear of the wagon and climbed up among the small wooden crates stacked in its bed.

"Let's go, Mr. Readling," Witt called out in a hushed tone, seeing Readling rummage among the crates. "You can count it once we get out of here."

"It's gone!" Readling said.

"Gone?" Witt and Elvis looked up at him as he jerked a second crate lid open on its hinges. He slung the empty crate into the dirt street and stood fuming.

"All right, you sonsabitches!" Readling ranted toward the cantina, turning in a slow circle to take in every possible watching eye. "Where's my damn *gold*? Where's my *money*?"

"Okay, now," Witt said. "We might want to back away from here, easylike." He gestured toward five gunmen who filed out of the cantina and onto the street, slowly walking abreast toward them.

Twenty feet away, the door to the courtyard of the church opened with a creaking sound and Willis Dorphin stepped out.

"When did this become *your* gold and *your* money, Readling?" Dorphin asked, his hand poised beside the gun on his hip. He still carried Shaw's big Colt stuck down into his belt.

"Willis . . . ?" Readling looked at him, stunned.

"I thought the gold and the cash were property of the Golden Circle, Readling," Dorphin said with a flat expression.

"It was—I mean, it *is*," Readling said. Realizing that Dorphin was in on whatever treachery was at hand, he said quickly, "You and I have a wonderful opportunity here, Big T, if we play our cards right."

"Yeah, us too," Elvis Johnson put in, seeing the gunmen walking closer.

"Where is all the gold, the cash?" Readling asked quickly.

"It's somewhere safe, not too far off, Readling," Dorphin said. "When the Golden Circle comes for it, Santana is going to make a deal . . . they get back the money they need to finance *their cause*, he gets their support in raising his own army."

"Listen to me, Big T," said Readling, starting to sweat, "it's not too late for the two of us to get the money and claim it for ourselves. Just lead me to it."

"You had no intention of ever putting all that money back into the hands of the Golden Circle, Readling, and I know it," Dorphin said with a sly, tight grin. "That's why I threw in with Santana. If it was going to get stolen anyways, I figured I needed to grab myself a piece of it before it all got away."

"You're being deceived!" Readlng said, growing more worried as the gunmen drew closer. "Take me to it, before it's too late!"

"It already is," said Dorphin.

Readling saw the look on his face, saw his hand go to the gun on his hip. He swung the rifle up toward Dorphin, but before he got it leveled, Dorphin's gun streaked up from its holster and fired. Readling caught the bullet in his chest. He rocked up onto his toes and staggered backward with the impact of the shot. Then he sank to his knees and pitched forward onto his face.

Witt and Elvis Johnson spun back and forth, not knowing which way to direct their fight as the gunmen advanced on them. "You didn't have to cut us out. You could have brought us in on this, Dorphin!" Witt shouted.

"No, I couldn't," said Dorphin.

"And why not?" Elvis demanded. He stood with his rifle already leveled, cocked and ready to fire.

"I've watched you two. You've both got a streak of *good* in you that can't be trusted," Dorphin said.

"A little *good* never hurt nobody," Witt said.

"See what I'm talking about . . . ?" Dorphin said to Elvis. "You're both too stupid to live."

Elvis let out a rebel yell as he pulled the trigger on his rifle. A few feet away, his brother, Witt, did the same thing.

But Dorphin was cool, confident, seeing the outcome in his mind before it even started.

From the church bell tower Morgan Thorpe looked down, standing beside the priest, his side wrapped and bandaged with fresh white gauze.

The two watched the barrage of bullets slice through the Johnson brothers so quickly that the wagon horses only spooked for a second. They jerked once against the wagon brake, then settled on the ground as a ringing silence set in beneath a drifting swirl of burned gun powder.

"I'm sorry to bring all this trouble here," Thorpe

said in a weak voice. "But I was shot and I knew I couldn't make it very far—"

"Save your breath, *por favor*," said the priest, cutting him off. "You say the money and the gold is safe. That is the main thing."

"Yes, it's safe," said Thorpe, "right where we were planning to hide it all along. I even left three men to watch over it until we get there."

The priest nodded in approval, then climbed down the ladder and walked along the hallway. Thorpe came down the ladder much slower, only catching up to the priest at the stairs leading to the stone-lined cellar.

When Thorpe heard muffled groaning from down in the cellar, he asked, "What is that?"

"That is Wayne Collins, formerly known as 'Buck' Collins. He is shackled to the cellar wall. He's the man you left lying by the fire because he was such a drunk and a fool and a bully."

Thorpe eyed him and said, "I didn't leave him here. I don't know what you're talking about."

The priest thought it out in the space of a second, and then said with a shrug, "*Someone* left him here." He showed Thorpe his bruised and scuffed knuckles.

Thorpe gave a low whistle. "He must really be a hardhead."

"Yes," said the priest. "I have been beating him sense-less every few hours, hoping to teach him things he needs to know about getting along with others. But so far, it has done little good."

"Does he know who you are?" Thorpe asked.

"He knows that I am the mission priest here in la Ciudad de Hombres Malos."

"But does he think you are Padre Timido," Thorpe asked, "or does he realize you're Mingus Santana, the man he rides for?"

The priest shot a glance all around out of habit, making sure no one could hear them. "No one but you and Reilly Cady know who I am." He smiled. "To everyone else I am still the poor mission padre who does God's work in a place where no one else wants to serve."

"What about the Fist? He knows, doesn't he?" Thorpe asked.

"I am afraid James Long—the Fist—is dead," the priest said, not wanting to tell Thorpe that Collins had confessed everything to him, hoping to make the beatings stop. Any time he wanted to end Collins' life, he only had to tell Reilly Cady who killed his brother, Tucker. But for now, he might yet be able to save Collins—with enough beatings—and turn him into a follower. He'd wait and see, he thought.

"Should Cady and I be worried, Padre, knowing who you are?" Thorpe asked, only half joking. "None of the new men have any idea you're actually Padre Mingus Santana."

The priest deliberately ignored his question, preferring to keep Thorpe a little cautious around him.

"Who I am has been a secret for three years," the priest said. "But soon, with the Golden Circle's riches and support, we will win over more and more followers until I can let the people know who I am . . . and what I will do for them."

"Can we ever count on the Golden Circle's support, Padre?" Thorpe asked. "They're a tightly closed bunch, have been since back before the war. Their goal is to make Mexico and the Caribbean slave ports—a source of cheap labor for their future expansion."

"I *will* have their support, now that I possess the main source of their wealth," said the priest. "As for slaves, only the future will decide who is to become slaves and who is to become masters."

Thorpe didn't comment; he decided to let the matter pass. Instead he said, "What about the woman, Rosa Reyes? I'm surprised you're not more upset that she's missing."

"These things always have a way of working themselves out," the priest said. "Rosa will always do what needs to be done, and she always knows what needs to be done. That is why she is with me." He smiled and continued walking toward the rear of the church. "Now you must go and get some rest. It will not be long before we have to—"

He stopped and turned midsentence as he heard a door slam and saw Silver Bones come running down the hallway toward them.

"Thorpe, we've got more riders coming," Bones said, his mouth still stiff, swollen and sore from Shaw's blow. "It looks like one of them is Larry Shaw."

"Shaw? I don't think so," said Thorpe. "Willis Dorphin had two soldiers kill him."

"They failed to kill him," the priest cut in. "Shaw was here. I cared for him, sewed up his chin where the soldiers tried to cut his throat."

"Damn," Thorpe said. "Having a man like Shaw around is never good, unless he's on our side."

"He won't be around long," said Silver Bones. "I'm going to kill the rotten son of a bitch as soon as he gets here." Just as he finished speaking, he caught himself and said, "Begging your pardon for the coarse language, Padre."

The priest and Thorpe looked at each other. "Come with me, Bones," Thorpe said. "Let's not bother the good padre with our worldy problems."

Chapter 24

Dawson and Caldwell had stopped on the trail at the sound of gunfire coming from the City of Bad Men. Behind them, Doc Penton and Shaw nudged their horses until the four men sat abreast, staring toward the town. Not another sound was heard save for a low rush of wind from the surrounding hills.

"That didn't take long," Shaw said, noting that the shooting had lasted only a few seconds.

"I figure that was Readling and the Johnsons," Doc Penton remarked. He shook his head and said, "I can say this for Elvis and Witt, they stick 'til the end."

The other three made no reply.

Dawson heeled his horse forward slowly toward the beginning of the wide, dirt street, his rifle up, the butt of it resting on his thigh. The other three rode right beside him, spreading out as they went.

When the Cut-Jaws had spotted them only moments earlier, the outlaws had scattered, taking position in alleyways and up along the rooflines.

"Looks like we'll have to hunt them down from one spot to the next," Caldwell said.

"Maybe not . . . ," Shaw murmured to himself.

As Dawson, Caldwell and Doc Penton nudged their horses over to the iron hitch rail out in front of the cantina, Shaw stopped his bay in the street and sat staring straight ahead like a man in a trance. He held a Winchester rifle propped up in his right hand. The butt of one big Russian Smith & Wesson stuck up from his holster; the other was shoved behind his belt.

Not a living person could be seen on the street ahead of him, only the bodies of Readling and the Johnson brothers lying bloody on the ground out in front of the adobe church.

From inside the cantina, Rafael the dwarf walked out wearing a new white linen suit, already soiled and stained from the day's events. His left eye was black, an injury he'd received while reconciling matters with the cantina owner—the *former* owner now. A large cigar rode between his short fingers.

"Good day, gentlemen," he said in English to Dawson, Caldwell and Penton as the three swung down from their saddles. "I'm Rafael, the owner here." He spread a hand proudly toward the crumbling adobe walls and the darkened interior of his newly acquired enterprise.

"You know why we're here," Dawson said, not feeling like mincing words.

"I do," said Rafael, "and I'm instructed to tell you that if you'll ride on, no harm will come to you." He gestured up the street with his cigar. "You may even take the wagon if you like."

Knowing that only meant that the wagon was empty, Dawson gave the man a look. "We didn't come here for empty wagons," he said.

The dwarf shot a quick glance back and forth along the street. "They will kill you, senors," he said in a guarded tone. "These men are not to be taken lightly."

"Obliged for the advice," Dawson said.

From the window of a closed-down saddle shop, Aldo Barry stood seething, staring out at Shaw.

"Look at the son of a bitch," he said to Hogue, who was standing with him, his nasal twang still ringing. "Thorpe is asking a lot, not letting me kill Shaw, after what he did to me."

"Maybe you was lucky he only mashed your snout. He's the fastest gun alive. He could have killed you," Hogue said to the young surly gunman.

"No, he couldn't, not straight up," Barry said. "If it wasn't for Thorpe telling me not to, I'd kill Shaw right there where he's sitting."

Hogue said, "If I had that hard of a grudge boiling, I wouldn't let anything Thorpe said stop me."

Barry looked at him. "Are you saying I'm scared? Of him?"

Hogue didn't reply. Instead he nodded toward Shaw and said, "There *he* is . . . Here *you* are. I can't see you ever getting a better chance to make good on all your talk."

Across the street, Silver Bones stood behind a pile of firewood alongside an abandoned blacksmith forge. He rubbed his pained and swollen lips, feeling the gap where his front teeth had been before Shaw knocked them out with his rifle butt. He stared at Shaw and cursed under his breath.

Hearing his anger, Willis Dorphin looked at Bones and said, "I'd like to kill him myself. I know he'll never forget what I done to him. I'll have to watch over my shoulder the rest of my life, so long as the sumbitch is alive."

At the hitch rail out in front of the cantina, Dawson had just started to say something to the dwarf owner when a loud thud caused Caldwell, Doc and him to spin around toward the street.

"Christ, he fell off his damn horse!" said Doc Penton, staring at Shaw, who lay in the dirt at the big bay's hooves.

"Oh, man!" said Caldwell.

"Jesus! Not now, Shaw, of all times . . . ," Dawson murmured to himself.

Dawson and Caldwell both hurried to Shaw, who was now pushing himself up with both palms. Doc Penton stayed at the hitch rail, his gun drawn, watching the street in both directions, knowing that something like this was all it took to spark a simmering gunfight into full flame.

"I'm all right," Shaw said, struggling up as the two lawmen arrived at his side. He swiped them away with his dust-covered hand, turned and leaned against the bay's side.

"You're not all right," said Caldwell. "You just fell off your horse."

"With every Cut-Jaw in town watching," Dawson added, looking all around. "These men are like wolves. If they smell blood or see a weak spot . . ."

"Back away from me," Shaw said. "I won't be a *weak spot*."

"That's not how I meant it," Dawson said. He and Caldwell stepped back and gave Shaw room.

Without raising his lowered face, Shaw looked along the street, his eyes darting from one adobe storefront to the next.

At the saddle shop window, Aldo Barry watched Shaw struggling to stand upright, a hand on the bay's side to steady himself.

"Maybe you're right," he said. "I might never get a better chance. He looked toward the church bell tower, where he knew Thorpe was watching. What could Thorpe really say to him, after he'd just killed the fastest gun alive? *Not much . . .* , he thought, smiling to himself.

Across the street, Silver Bones saw Aldo Barry step out into the sunlight. He knew what the vengeful gunman had in mind. Bones also looked toward the bell tower. Then he looked back at Shaw, the weak gunman appearing to have a hard time staying on his feet.

"What the hell, there's a gunfight coming anyways," he said, his toothless mouth causing a whistle in his voice.

"Where are you going?" Dorphin asked, seeing Bones walk toward the middle of the street.

"Where do you *think*?" Bones said through his blue-purple lips. "I'm killing him while I can."

"Not without me, you're not," Dorphin said, stepping out behind him.

"What the hell's this?" another gunman asked the two men standing near him.

"It's starting. That's what," one of the gunmen answered. "Let's go."

Dawson and Caldwell had already stepped back away from Shaw. But seeing the Cut-Jaw gunmen appear from both sides of the street, the lawmen stopped and stood firm.

"Did he do this on purpose?" Caldwell asked Dawson in a tense whisper.

"I can't even guess," said Dawson.

Doc Penton stepped forward, taking position a few feet from the two lawmen.

In the church bell tower, out of sight behind its thick adobe housing, Thorpe whispered toward the ladder as he heard footsteps climbing up.

"Stay back, Santana! It's commencing," he said.

The priest stuck his head up anyway and said in a harsh tone, "I warned you never to call me that. It's *Padre Timido*, you fool."

"I'm sorry, Padre," said Thorpe, a gun in his hand, his free hand pressed to his wounded side.

"I gave you the order to not kill them if you can keep from it," the padre said. As he stepped up off the ladder, he reached back, took Rosa Reyes' hand and assisted her into the tower.

"I know, Padre, and I respect it," said Thorpe, "but some of these men want Shaw dead so bad that they can't even think straight. They don't give a damn about any order."

The priest turned and looked down on the street without being seen. He shook his head. "This man, Larry *Rápido* . . . if only I had a hundred like him."

"Take a good look, Padre," said Thorpe. "After today there will no more Larry *Rápido*." He gave a smirk.

The priest let out a breath and said, "All right, it was

coming. There was no stopping it." He turned to Rosa
Reyes and said, "We must go now, while everyone is
busy killing each other."

But the woman had looked down and seen Shaw
standing there, and she couldn't shake the feeling that
he had come there for her. Oddly, since the day she had
spoken with him in the wagon, she'd felt as if something was constantly drawing her toward him, wherever he was. The feeling made no sense, and yet she
could not—*would not*—dismiss it. *Why do you come to
me . . . ?* she asked him silently, as if he could somehow
hear her.

"*Uno momento,*" she said to the priest, staring down
onto the dusty street, where men were about to kill each
other.

One moment . . . ? The padre was not used to having
his orders ignored. He took her by her forearm. "Come
with me, Sister Rosa. This is not a place for a *sacerdote y
una monja*. We must go."

"I am no longer a nun," she reminded him, "not
after the things I have done. It is also highly question-
able that you are still a priest." She rounded her forearm
away from him. "I said *one moment,*" she repeated coldly,
this time in English.

Shaw looked from Aldo Barry on one side of the street
to Silver Bones and Willis Dorphin on the other side,
then spoke quietly to Dawson.

"The three of you keep out of this," he said.

"You know we can't do that, Shaw," Dawson replied
in the same quiet tone. "Even if this wasn't my job, I

couldn't turn back on you. Not with the shape you're in. You and I have been friends too long."

"Me neither," said Caldwell.

"That's real touching," Shaw said wryly. "But I brought them all out here. The least I can do is shoot them for you."

"I knew it . . . ," Caldwell said under his breath. "He fell on purpose, didn't he?"

Dawson didn't answer.

"What about you, Doc?" Shaw asked. "Are you here out of friendship?"

"No," Doc said, one hand poised near his gun butt, his other clenching a rifle, "I just want to fight."

Shaw gave a short grin. "That's me all over," he said. "As for the shape I'm in . . ." He raised his voice for the gunmen to hear. "I'm feeling *good* today."

That does it . . . !

Aldo Barry was the first to snap, hearing Shaw's taunt.

"I'll *kill you*!" he bellowed, his broken nose causing his voice to sound like the honking of an angry goose.

But Silver Bones was not going to let Aldo Barry beat him to Shaw. He walked faster toward Shaw in the middle of the dirt street, his revolver raised arm's length. A few feet behind and to Bones' left, Dorphin hurried along, raising his rifle to his shoulder, wanting to get a shot at Shaw from as far away as he could manage. Shaw stepped away from the bay, giving it a shove on its rump. The animal hurried off and stopped a few yards away.

Aldo bellowed, "I can't tell you how bad I've wanted to kill you, Sha—"

His words stopped as the big Russian bucked in Shaw's hand and the bullet from its fiery barrel picked Aldo up and flung him backward onto the dirt street. The impact was too great to turn him loose. He hit the ground, rolled a back flip and almost came back onto his feet. But his legs had gone limp and he melted to his knees for a second, then fell to the ground. Blood splattered through the air around him from the large hole in his heart.

Silver Bones wasted no time. He began firing as Shaw's bullet nailed Aldo. But Shaw spun toward him as Bones' third shot sliced through the air past his head.

Shaw made his shot count. The big Russian bucked in his hand again. This time Bones flew backward, twisting as he left his feet, like some sort of ballet move gone terribly wrong.

"I've got him, everybody stay out of it!" Dorphin shouted, seeing Bones hit the ground out of the corner of his eye. It didn't matter; he had Shaw. One pull of the trigger was all it took. He had his sights locked dead on him, Shaw standing there, the big Russian hanging at his side, smoke from its barrel curling up his hand, his forearm.

Along the main street of the City of Bad Men, the Cut-Jaw gunmen stood staring.

"All right, then, have it your way . . . ," Carlos Loonie said to himself on everybody's behalf.

But before Dorphin could pull the trigger of his rifle, he saw Shaw swing the big Russian up at him so fast, it caused him to freeze for just a second.

Shaw called out to him from behind the cocked and leveled Russian. "Remember what I said, Big T? If you told Readling what I said, guess who I was going to kill?"

"You can go straight to hell, Shaw," Dorphin raged, realizing in a flash that he'd failed in saving his own life.

"Guess who's going first?" said Shaw. The big Russian bucked in his hand for the third time.

Chapter 25

The Cut-Jaws gunmen did as Dorphin had asked them to do and stayed out of the fight. They'd watched as if none of it had anything to do with them. But the second that Willis Dorphin hit the dirt with a bullet hole through the center of his forehead, the outlaws seemed to snap back to life, as one.

Bobby Flukes turned toward Dawson, Caldwell and Doc Penton with his rifle up. "Kill them," he shouted as he pulled the trigger. He got off a shot that nipped Doc across his shoulder. But before he could lever another round into the rifle chamber, a bullet from Caldwell's Colt nailed him in the chest.

Next to where Flukes stood, Rady Kale fired on Dawson with a big Dance Brothers pistol. His first shot knocked Dawson's hat from his head; his second shot went wild as Shaw fired the big Russian in Kale's direction.

"Kill Shaw, damn it!" shouted Carlos Loonie, seeing the bullet hurl Kale backward in a spray of blood.

Crouched down low, Shaw shifted his aim, following the path of the fighting. Out of the corner of his eye he saw the woman standing in the church bell tower looking down at him. Even from that distance, he felt as if their eyes met just for a second before he looked away. But when he swung his eyes back to the tower, she was gone.

Enough of this. . . . He shook his head as if to clear it, not even certain he'd really seen her there. But he had no time to consider it.

Matt Stewart and Russell Hogue fired on him as one. A bullet streaked through his duster sleeve, and another screamed across this left ear. But as the two fired on Shaw, Loonie himself ran to cover behind the stack of firewood out in front of the blacksmith shop.

Dawson Caldwell spun backward and went down to his knees when a bullet Stewart fired at Shaw went wild and nailed him in his left shoulder.

Dawson fired quickly at Stewart. So did Shaw. Both of their bullets hit their target. Stewart stiffened upward onto his toes as the bullets sliced through him. He almost managed to recover and throw his gun out at arm's reach. But Penton fired his rifle as bullets whistled past him. His shot went through Stewart's heart and dropped him to the dirt.

Recognizing that the lawmen, Doc and Shaw weren't going to be easy to kill, Carlos slipped away from the woodpile and ran toward the church. Shots exploded back and forth behind him. Seeing Loonie retreat, Charlie Ruiz and Ned Breck did the same.

Russell Hogue was left standing alone in the street

on wobbly legs. He'd taken a bullet to his right side—several other stray bullets had nicked and grazed his body.

"Sonsabitches!" he shouted at both the Cut-Jaws who'd abandoned him and the lawmen who'd shot him. "All of yas. Every damn motherless ones of yas!"

"Drop the gun," Doc Penton called out, not realizing that Dawson and Caldwell had come here with no intention of taking the Cut-Jaws prisoner.

"You too, mister!" Hogue called out to Doc, his pistol hanging in his bloody hand. "You're a motherless son of a bitch too."

"Drop it," Doc insisted.

Shaw and Dawson gave Doc a questioning look. The two had hurried to where Caldwell had fallen to the ground, blood gushing from his shoulder in a braided stream.

"Shoot him, Doc," Shaw said flatly.

Hearing Shaw, the bloody swaying gunman turned toward him. "*City of Bad Men*, my ass," Russell Hogue shouted in disgust. "Look at me!" He spread his arms to show that he was still standing, despite how many times he'd been shot. "There ain't a *bad man* amongst yas—"

Before his words had fully made it out of his mouth, Shaw's first bullet hit him. Then the second bullet. Then the third. Shaw had dropped his rifle in the dirt beside Dawson and Caldwell and started walking toward Hogue with both of the big Russians bucking in his hands.

When the sixth shot struck Hogue, he finally left his feet and sank down onto his knees, his gun still in hand.

"Now . . . that's more . . . like it," he said as a strange, pained grin spread across his bloody face.

Shaw saw the dying gunman lift his pistol with all the effort he had left. One final bullet from Shaw nailed the man in the forehead and flipped him backward, sending his shot straight up in the air.

Up the street, Dawson watched as the last of the fleeing gunmen slipped into the mission church through a side door. He helped Caldwell onto his feet, holding a bandana pressed to the bullet wound in his shoulder.

"We've got to get them out of the church without any harm coming to the priest," he said, glancing at the blood-soaked bandana on Caldwell's wound. "Jedson needs treating, fast."

"The woman is in the church," Shaw said as he walked to Dorphin's body and pulled his Colt from the dead gunman's belt. After checking it, he shoved it down into his holster, where he'd been carrying one of the Russians. "I saw her in the bell tower."

Uh-oh. . . .

Dawson and Caldwell looked at each other with trepidation. "Which woman?" Dawson asked Shaw warily. "The *bruja* with her sparrows, or Senora Rosa Reyes, who stole Jedson's horse—?"

"Don't talk crazy, Marshal," Shaw said. "I saw Senora Reyes. I wouldn't bring up the witch and her sparrows at a time like this."

Dawson and Caldwell looked at each other again, this time with relieved expressions. "We're both glad to hear that, Shaw," Dawson said.

After a pause, Shaw said quietly, "That is, I *think* I saw her. . . ."

Dawson only shook his head. Looking at Caldwell's back, he held another bandana on the exit wound. "At least it's a clean shot straight through," he said.

"Lucky me," Caldwell said drily.

Dawson helped him over to a post standing at the corner of a wooden overhang. He sat the deputy down and leaned him back against the post with the bandana pressed in place.

"Are you all right here while we take the church?"

"No, Marshal," Caldwell said with determination, "I'm not sitting this one out. Help me to my feet ... stick the bandana under the back of my duster ... I'll hold this one in place." He held the bloody bandana onto his wounded left shoulder, and managed to raise his Colt with his left hand. "See? Everything is working fine."

Dawson cursed under his breath. But he pulled the deputy to his feet and said, "All right, but don't die on me."

"I wouldn't think of it," Caldwell said.

For nearly an hour, Morgan Thorpe and Reilly Killer Cady had stood out of sight in the church's bell tower. They watched the empty street below, having seen the three men help the wounded man into an alleyway. From inside the church, the remaining Cut-Jaws gunmen had taken positions in the open windows overlooking the courtyard. They watched the ten-foot-high adobe wall, knowing it to be the most likely way for the four men to attack.

"I hope we haven't been left in a jackpot here," Cady said to the wounded Thorpe.

"If we have, it's too late to stop it now," said Thorpe, feeling a little better but still weakened from the loss of blood. "We had this thing all worked out. It should have gone through slick as grease."

"It went to hell when my brother and the Fist disappeared."

"I hate to say it, but somebody killed them," said Thorpe. "It might have been some of our own."

"I hope I live long enough to find out who," said Cady.

The two looked back and forth along the inside of the adobe wall. "I hate to think of all that gold lying out there in the hills, and me dying here, never getting my share of it."

"Think *the best*," said Cady. He gave a short grin. "That's what Santana always says."

"Santana . . ." He spat and lowered his voice, even though the priest was nowhere around. "I've had it with him too," said Thorpe. "Him and his damn *revolucion*. He needs to make up his mind, decide if he's an outlaw or some kind of *politico*—savoir of his people." He smirked and spat again.

"I can't complain up to now," said Cady. "He's always seen to it we got our share. What he did with his share was his business."

"The kind of money he'll make off of this job is going to push him to the top of the heap, though," said Thorpe. "He'll be able to afford himself an army. Once he gets that he'll be hard to stop."

"Good for him," said Cady. "He's no more crooked than any other sumbitch who wants to run other people's lives for them."

"He's a bad man, and a son of a bitch," Thorpe said.

"He's a priest," said Cady.

"So . . . ? He can be all three things at once." Thorpe grinned weakly.

"Yeah, I expect you're right," said Cady. "Did you see that poor sumbitch's face in the cellar?"

"Yep, that's Buck Collins," said Thorpe, "or what's left of him. Santana said he's *teaching* him."

"Teaching him *what*? How to take a bad beating?" Cady asked. The two chuckled.

Outside, having snuck up crawling on their bellies until they huddled close against the outward wall, Shaw and Doc Penton checked their guns. When they were finished, Shaw left his rifle in the dirt and held the two big Smith & Wesson .44s in his hands.

"Are you sure you can handle the doors, Doc?" he asked under his breath. "It's going to get awfully busy down there."

Doc gave him a look. "Are you doubting I *can* handle the doors?"

"Just offering," Shaw said, noting the prickly sound in the wiry older gunman's voice.

"Well, don't offer," Doc snapped back at him.

Shaw watched him raise his hat and run his fingers back through his gray hair.

Doc let out a breath and said, "Pay me no mind, I get as rank as a bad onion, times like this."

"Get going," Shaw said. "I've got you covered."

They both looked around at the empty wagon still sitting in the street, the team of horses standing at rest in the cool evening air.

From the bell tower, Thorpe and Cady saw Doc Penton's thin figure appear atop the ten-foot wall, then jump down quickly and race to the big wooden doors.

"Here we go!" Thorpe shouted, cocking and leveling his gun down onto the running gunman. "Get him!"

A barrage of bullets exploded from the open church windows and whistled past Doc Penton as he ran. Bullets from the two gunmen in the bell tower kicked up dirt in his wake, only inches from his boot heels.

But shots from both the church and the tower slackened when Shaw appeared on top of the adobe wall, firing round after round with deadly accuracy from the Russian .44s.

Of the three Cut-Jaw gunmen in the windows below, Ned Breck lay dead, draped over a window ledge. Blood ran freely from his body, dripping down the wall and onto the ground. Carlos Loonie and Charlie Ruiz had ducked inside as Shaw's bullets spun past them. But Charlie stood gripping his chest with one hand, his face as pale as chalk.

"I—I knew the first time . . . I laid eyes on him. That he was . . . going to kill me," he said.

"Hang on, Charlie!" said Carlos Loonie. "I'll get you patched up."

"Ha!" said Ruiz, blood running from between his fingers, down his belly. "There ain't no . . . *patching up* for this." He leaned back against the wall and slid down to the ground. He eyes went blank, staring straight ahead.

At the front doors, Doc jerked the long timber up from its frame and pitched it aside. He threw the doors open as Thorpe and Cady swung into sight and fired down at him from the bell tower.

In the courtyard, Shaw had jumped down from atop

the wall just in time to escape a shot from Reilly Cady, who had swung his gun toward him after seeing Doc disappear out through the open doors.

Shaw fired the big Russian in his right hand toward the tower. Cady fell backward with both hands grasping his face—the .44 bullet smashed through the bridge of his nose and caused the back of his head to explode on the large church bell. The bullet caused a resounding ring as it gave the bell a glancing blow, before it turned and thumped into Thorpe's stomach.

Through the open doors, the empty wagon came rumbling in and slid to a sidelong halt, Dawson standing at the driver's seat. Calwdell sat in the seat beside him, one bloody hand holding the bandana to his chest, his other bloody hand holding his Colt.

Carlos Loonie leaped out through a window with a loud yell and fired wildly toward Shaw. But one shot from the big Smith & Wesson in Dawson's hand sent him flying dead to the ground.

Behind the wagon, Doc stepped back inside the open doors with caution. Shaw walked sidelong toward the wagon, the smoking Russian .44s in his hands.

At the bell tower, Morgan Thorpe stepped into view, one hand held high, gripping a pistol, his other hand holding his bleeding stomach.

"Of all the . . . damn luck," he said, gasping heavily in his pain. "I take one . . . from off the church bell." He tried to give a dark laugh, but it ended in a painful groan.

"Gut-shot," Doc said, "the poor sumbitch."

Seeing the raised gun in Thorpe's hand, Shaw levered one of the Russians up toward him.

"Wait—don't shoot," Dawson said to Shaw. "Thorpe, drop the gun and walk down here."

"I'll drop the gun," said Thorpe, "but I'm not walking any damn where. I hurt too bad. I'm going to die right up here."

"Where's the padre?" said Dawson. "He can patch you up. We've got a wounded man here ourselves who needs his help."

"There's no help here . . . not from the good padre," said Thorpe. "He's gone."

"Where's the woman?" Shaw asked.

"She's gone too," said Thorpe. He laid the gun down on the ledge and shoved it away from himself. "Biggest damn haul we ever made . . . now the padre is on the run and here I am, dying." He sounded bitter.

Dawson, Caldwell, Shaw and Doc all four looked at each other. "Are you saying Father Timido had something to do with stealing Readling's stash of gold and currency?" Dawson asked.

Thorpe managed to laugh, this time judging the pain to be worth the effort. "Wait right there," he said, ending his laugh with a hoarse painful cough. "I'm coming . . . down after all. I've got to . . . see your faces."

Doc walked inside the church and met the bloody wounded gunman as he struggled the last few rungs down the ladder.

Out front, Dawson had stepped down from the wagon; Shaw had walked over and stood beside him. While they waited for Thorpe and Doc Penton to walk out of the church, Shaw heard the slow drop of hooves walk in through the open doors. He raised a free hand around and patted the bay on its muzzle when it walked up quietly beside him.

"I didn't forget about you," he said to the horse. The bay chuffed and blew out a breath.

When Thorpe stumbled out into the courtyard, Doc right behind him, Dawson walked over. The wounded gunman leaned back against the wall and slid to the ground.

"Can I . . . get some water?" Thorpe asked.

Doc walked back inside the church for some water. Dawson said to Thorpe, "Now, what were you going to say about Father Timido?"

"Father Timido is Mingus Santana," Thorpe said, his stomach bleeding more from his climb down the ladder.

Seeing that the wounds were going to take him pretty quick, Dawson said, "You're saying Santana posed as a priest?"

"No posing to it," said Thorpe. "Mingus Santana is a priest. He always was. He just . . . changed his name. Something these . . . holy men can do, I reckon."

"I don't believe him," Shaw said over Dawson's shoulder.

"It's true," Thorpe said. "He's been . . . right here . . . almost three years. He had a church . . . outside Mexico City three years before this." He gave a pained grin. "Why do you think nobody ever caught him . . . or even saw him for that matter? Nobody knew it but me . . . and his other two right-hand men."

Doc appeared with a wooden bucket of fresh water and a long gourd dipper. He gave the dying gunman a sip; then he poured a few drops onto his palm and raised it to Thorpe's sweating forehead. Thorpe sighed in relief.

"What about the woman," Shaw asked him, "Senora Rosa Reyes? And don't tell me she's some dove he bought to keep him company. I know better. She told me about her father and her brother, how Readling was holding them hostage."

Thorpe shook his head. "All lies," he said. "No father . . . or brother held captive. She's *una monja*, is how they say it. . . ." Thorpe choked out in a gasping breath, gripping his stomach tighter.

"She's a *nun*?" Shaw said, translating his words. "No, I don't believe it! He's lying," he said, turning to Dawson, his eyes wild in disbelief.

"Believe it," said Thorpe. "I've got no . . . reason to lie to you."

Seeing the man starting to slump, Shaw grabbed him by his sweaty shoulders and shook just enough to keep him awake, knowing that once he shut his eyes, he'd never reopen them.

"Where's the priest taking her?" Shaw demanded.

"Anywhere he . . . wants to take her," Thorpe said, his voice getting weaker. "They've been together . . . a long time. Like man . . . and wife."

Shaw stared at him. "Like man and wife?" he said. "But you say she's a nun."

"Yeah . . . I know," said Thorpe, his voice turning faint. "Ain't that something . . . ?" His words ended in a whisper.

"Wake up!" Shaw said, shaking him again by his shoulders. "Wake the hell up!"

"Shaw, turn him loose," Dawson shouted. "He's dead."

"He was lying," Shaw said. He looked back and forth among them. "We've got to go after them. They can't be that far along the trail."

"We can't go," Dawson said. "I've got to get Jedson patched up. The bleeding's stopped, but put him in a saddle and it'll start up again." He looked around. "Anyway, we've put down the Cut-Jaws. We'll get Santana, whoever he is, when he shows his face again."

Shaw turned to Caldwell and said, *"Undertaker?"*

The deputy gave him a nod and said, "It's okay. You go ahead."

"I've got to find her," Shaw said. "I've got to."

"I understand," said Caldwell. "I told you it's okay."

Shaw gave Dawson a questioning look.

"Go on. Get out of here, Shaw," Dawson said. "I'll patch him up and let him rest the night."

Without another word, Shaw stepped into his saddle, turned the bay and rode away toward the trail running behind the mission church and off into the hillside.

After a moment, as Dawson filled the gourd with water and held it to Caldwell's lips, Doc said, "I expect I'll just go get my horse and catch up to him."

Dawson and Caldwell stared at him curiously.

Doc gave a tired smile and shrugged. "I wronged him a while back, damn near got him killed. I've got to work it off somehow."

They watched him walk out the doors and down the street, where he stepped into his saddle and rode away.

"Well, our man Shaw is off and gone again," Caldwell said after a moment.

"Yep," said Dawson.

"I believe he really thinks that Senora Reyes is his wife, Rosa . . . somehow," Caldwell said.

"I know he does," said Dawson. "The shape he's in, it's best to just let him ride it out, I figure." He looked off in the direction Shaw had taken toward the hills. "I know she's not Rosa Shaw," he said, "but I almost envy him thinking it is. To tell the truth, I could have just about gone off after the senora myself, Deputy."

"Oh?" Caldwell stared at him.

Dawson let out a breath. "But two men can't have the same woman," he said. "I know that now." He gazed off toward the evening sunlight, watching it spread red and gold on the hills mantling the far horizon. "I only wish I'd known it years ago."

Don't miss a page of action
from America's most exciting Western author,
Ralph Cotton.

GUN LAW

Coming from Signet in April 2011.

Kindred, New Mexico Territory

Neither of the two men standing at the bar saw Sherman Dahl ride into town. They tipped shot glasses at each other and threw back a mouthful of fiery rye. Sliding their empty glasses away, they raised heavy mugs of beer and drank through an inch of cold, silky foam.

"*Ahhh* . . . damn, this is living," said one to the other.

Out front, Dahl stepped down from his tan dun and spun its reins to a wooden hitch rail in front of a tack-and-saddle shop next door to the Lucky Devil Saloon. He pulled a Winchester repeater from its saddle boot. The tack-shop owner wiped his hands on his leather apron when he saw Dahl step onto the boardwalk. But he looked on in disappointment as Dahl walked past his open door to the saloon.

At the bar, the other man grinned and replied through a foam-frosted mustache, "You're by-God right it is."

On the boardwalk Dahl levered a round into his rifle chamber and stepped back for a second while two cattle buyers walked out through the saloon's batwing doors. The buyers looked him up and down and moved on. One took a cigar from his lips and gave a curious nod.

"It doesn't look good for somebody," he said, noting the serious look on Dahl's face.

The two walked on.

At the bar, one of the drinkers, a former Montana-range detective named Curtis Hickes, grinned and wiped the back of his hand across his foamy lips.

"Tell the truth," he said to his companion, Ernie Newman. "If it wasn't for me, you wouldn't be standing right here today, would you?" He poked a stiff, wet finger up and down on the bar top as he spoke.

"I don't deny it," said Newman. "You were right about this place."

"Damn right I was right," said Hickes. He took another deep swig of beer.

"I'm obliged," said Newman.

"Yeah? Just how obliged?" Hickes asked in a blunt tone.

"As obliged as I should be," said Newman. He gave Hickes a guarded look. "But I ain't kissing nothing that belongs to you."

"You know what I mean," Hickes said. He rubbed his thumb and fingertips together in the universal sign of greed. "Every act is worth its balance."

"I don't know what that means." Newman shook his head, sipped his beer and said, "The fact is, you was asked to bring a good man or two with you. So I might just have done you a favor *standing here today*."

"That ain't how I see it," said Hickes.

"See it how it suits you." Newman shrugged. "I'll do the same."

"Son of a bitch!" Hickes growled.

"Say it again. I dare you!" Newman's hand went to his holstered gun butt.

Both men heard the rustle and scuffle of boots as men cleared away on either side of the bar from them. The saloon owner ducked down out of sight and crawled away in a hurry.

But before either man could make a move on the other, Dahl's Winchester exploded from where he'd stepped inside the swinging batwing doors.

A half block away, the cattle buyers flinched at the sound of gunfire. "I called that one," one said without a backward glance.

"Indeed, you did," said the other in a dismissing manner. "Now let's talk beefs. . . ."

Dahl's first shot nailed Newman in the heart, from the side as the gunman turned facing Hickes.

Hickes saw the impact of the bullet fling Newman halfway up onto the bar. He swung around toward Dahl, snatching his Remington from its holster. But the gun never cleared leather. It fell from his hand back down into a tooled slim-jim holster as Dahl's next shot hammered him backward against the bar and dropped him dead on the floor.

"Good Lord Almighty!" the saloon owner cried out, rising from the floor at the far end of the bar and looking at the blood splatter and bullet holes in the shattered mirror behind the bar. "Somebody's gonna pay for this!"

He held in his shaking hand a sawed-off shotgun,

which he'd jerked from under the bar in his frantic crawl. Seeing Dahl swing the rifle barrel toward him, he turned the shotgun loose as if it were hot and let it fall to the floor.

Dahl lowered the rifle barrel, having levered a fresh round into the chamber. "Where's Ned Carver and Cordell Garrant?" he asked anyone listening.

"Cordell Garrant is dead," said a voice from a corner table. "He died a week ago from the fever."

Dahl swung around facing the voice as a man wearing a long swallow-tailed suit coat and a battered derby hat rose slowly from a chair, his hands chest high.

"Ned Carver left town three nights ago," the man said quietly. "Must've known somebody was coming for him."

"Nice try, Ned," said Dahl. The rifle exploded again. The shot flung the man backward from the table. His long coat flew open, revealing a sawed-off shotgun he never got the chance to draw.

"Holy jumping Moses!" shouted the saloon owner, seeing more blood splatter on the wall as customers once again ducked away and scrambled out of range.

Seeing one customer look past him wide-eyed in fear, Dahl realized there was a gun being pointed somewhere behind him. He levered another round and swung in a fast full circle.

But he wasn't fast enough. He saw the big Russian pistol pointed out at arm's reach toward him; he saw it buck; he saw the streak of blue-orange fire. He felt the bullet hit him high in the chest at heart level. A second bullet hit him no more than an inch from the first; and he flew backward, broken and limp, like some rag doll.

Dahl's rifle flew from his hand; he hit the floor ten feet farther back from where he'd stood.

"I'm Cordell Garrant," the gunman said.

He stepped forward across the floor toward Dahl, who lay struggling to catch his breath, his right hand clutching his chest over the two bullet holes. He cocked the smoking Smith & Wesson Russian revolver in his hand and started to raise it for a third shot.

"Guess what. Ned was lying about me being dead," he said with a flat grin.

Dahl managed to roll an inch sideways. His right hand dropped from his chest and inside his corduroy riding jacket. "No, he wasn't . . . ," he said in a strained voice as his hand swung out a .36-caliber Navy Colt and fired.

"Damn it to hell!" the saloon owner shouted, seeing the bullet bore through Garrant's right eye and string a ribbon of blood and gore out the back of his head.

Garrant hit the floor, dead. Blood pooled in the sawdust beneath him.

Dahl let his hand and the Navy Colt slump to the floor beside him. He let out a tense breath and felt the room tip sideways and darken around him. The pain in his chest seemed to crush him down into the floor.

Huddled in a corner of the saloon, a young dove named Sara Cayes stood up warily and ventured forward. Around her the stunned drinkers came slowly back to life.

"Oh, my, he's alive!" she gasped, looking down at Dahl, seeing his chest rise and fall with labored breathing.

"He won't be for long," the enraged saloon owner

said. He snatched the shotgun up from the floor, shook sawdust from it and walked forward, raising it toward Dahl.

"You stay away from him, Jellico," Sara Cayes said, hurriedly stooping down over Dahl, protecting him. "Can't you see the shape he's in?"

"Get out of my way, whore," said the saloon owner, trying to wave her aside with the shotgun barrel. "All I see is the *shape* my place is in."

"He's unarmed, Jellico!" the dove cried out, huddling down even closer over Dahl.

"Suits me," said the saloon owner, cocking both hammers on the shotgun. "Now get back away from him, else you'll never raise your ankles in this place again."

"She said leave him alone, Jellico," said a voice from the batwing doors. "While you're at it, empty your hand. Shotguns make me cross, especially pointed at me."

The saloon owner, the drinkers and the dove all turned and faced the newly appointed town marshal, Emerson Kern. The lawman stood with a hip slightly cocked, his left hand holding open one of the batwing doors. His right hand lay poised around the bone handle of a big Colt .45 holstered on his hip.

Upon seeing the marshal, the saloon owner stopped and lowered the shotgun barrel straight down toward the floor. But he didn't lay it aside. Sara Cayes rose a little over Dahl but remained in position in case the saloon owner tried anything.

"Marshal Kern, look what this murdering dog did to my place!" said Jake Jellico. He swung a nod around the blood-splattered saloon.

But the marshal was still interested in the shotgun

and the fact that it was still in the saloon owner's hand. He raised his revolver from its holster and cocked it toward Jake Jellico.

"If you don't empty your hand, I bet I stick a tunnel through your forehead," he said.

"Easy, Marshal," said Jellico. He stooped and laid the shotgun back down on the floor. "You can't blame me for wanting to kill him, armed or unarmed."

With the shotgun out of play, the marshal lowered his Colt and walked over and looked down at Dahl lying on the floor. The young dove eased back and allowed him a better view of Dahl's face and the bullet holes in the front of his shirt.

"Not a big bleeder, is he?" said Kern.

"He's not bleeding at all," said a man among the drinkers who gathered around closer.

Sara Cayes gasped slightly, noting for the first time, bullet holes, but no blood.

"Step back, sweetheart," said Kern, touching the toe of his boot gently to the young woman's shoulder, moving her aside the way he'd do with a cat or dog.

Sara moved back grudgingly, yet she stayed stooped down near the unconscious gunman. Dahl lolled his head back and forth in the sawdust and murmured something under his breath. Even with him knocked out on a sawdust floor, Sara thought him to be the most handsome man she'd ever seen. *Too handsome for this place . . .*

"What—what does this mean, Marshal?" she asked in a halting voice, staring at the bloodless bullet holes.

"What does this mean . . . ?" Kern squatted down beside her. He poked a probing finger down into a bullet hole and shook his head. "I'll tell you what it means."

He stood up and looked around at the gathered crowd. "I'll tell all of you what it means." He gestured a hand around at the bloody aftermath of the gunfight. "It means the town of Kindred is going to have to get busy gathering up the guns if we're ever going to be a respectable, upstanding community."

"Here we go," a voice whispered in the crowd.

"What's that?" Kern asked, taking a step forward toward the man who made the remark. "You got something you want to say, *Dandy*?"

"No, Marshal," said Ed Dandly, owner and manager of the *Kindred Star Weekly News*. He backed away as the marshal moved forward. "But it's *Dandly*, not *Dandy*," he corrected meekly.

Kern ignored him. "What I'm saying, gentlemen," he continued, settling back in place beside the unconscious Dahl, "is that this sort of thing is going to just keep happening so long as we continue to allow guns being carried on the streets of this town."

"The marshal's right," said a voice.

Kern raised a boot and rested it on Dahl's shoulder. Sara tried to shove the boot away, but a cold look from the marshal halted her.

"I might not know what this was all about," Kern said for all to hear. "But I can tell you straight up that it would not have happened if these men's guns had all been hanging on pegs in my office instead of hanging on their hips."

"For the record, is this where you're going to tell us that as soon as our new mayor takes office this sort of thing is going to stop?" Ed Dandly asked. He whipped out a pencil and a small leather-bound writing pad.

"Yeah, I'll say that," said Kern. "I'll say it, because it's the truth." Again he took a threatening step toward the newsman. "The people voted Coakley into office to clean this town up, and by thunder, that's what he's going to do."

But this time the newsman stood his ground, knowing he was doing his job.

"No need to come closer, Marshal. I can hear you just fine from there," Dandly said, scribbling as he spoke.

The sheriff stopped, realizing that whatever he said or did now would be in the next edition of Dandly's weekly newspaper.

"So long as there are guns carried, there will be guns fired," Kern said stiffly. "There will be gunfights just like this and people will die. Some of them will be innocent bystanders, like all of you here could've been." He looked around the saloon from face to face. "Thank goodness, Mayor Coakley and myself will be changing all this. That's what I'm saying."

On the floor Sherman Dahl moaned beneath the marshal's boot. Sara Cayes said, "Marshal, we need to get him some help."

"You go do that, Sara," the marshal said. He looked around at the gathered townsmen and said, "Some of you drag these bodies out into the street so Jake can get this place cleaned up and get to serving you again."

"I'm sticking with Sara and this man," said Ed Dandly, scribbling on the pad. "If he lives, I'll find out what this was all about."

"You do that, *Dandy*," said Kern. He gave the newsman a cold stare. "Maybe you'll find out what I said is true, if you'll look at it with your eyes open."

"I can assure you, Marshal Kern, my eyes are always open," said Dandly. "If men can't carry guns, what's to keep them safe?"

"Safe from what?" said Kern.

"Why, safe from the wilds, Marshal—safe from savages, safe from one another."

"That's the law's job," Kern said, tapping a thumb against the badge on his chest. "It's my job to keep all of you safe. That's what I was appointed to do, and that's what I *will* do."

"Without guns, who or what will keep us safe from you, Marshal?" Dandly asked, speaking boldly with his pencil and writing pad between himself and the lawman.

Kern gave him a smoldering look. "Safe from *me*?" he said in a flat yet threatening voice. "What are you trying to say, *Dandy*?"

The newsman stood firm in spite of the marshal's harsh demeanor. "I'm not talking only about *you* necessarily, Marshal," he said. "I'm talking about the law and the government in general."

"You're saying you don't trust *the law*," said Kern.

"Not entirely," said Dandly.

"You don't trust *lawmen*," said Kern.

"That's correct," Dandly said. "Not beyond what's reasonable."

"You don't even trust the *government*," the marshal said as if in disbelief. "What kind of a low, unpatriotic weasel are you, Ed *Dandy*?"

GRITTY WESTERN ACTION FROM
USA TODAY BESTSELLING AUTHOR

RALPH COTTON

FAST GUNS OUT OF TEXAS

KILLING TEXAS BOB

NIGHTFALL AT LITTLE ACES

AMBUSH AT SHADOW VALLEY

RIDE TO HELL'S GATE

GUNMEN OF THE DESERT SANDS

SHOWDOWN AT HOLE-IN-THE-WALL

RIDERS FROM LONG PINES

CROSSING FIRE RIVER

ESCAPE FROM FIRE RIVER

GUN COUNTRY

FIGHTING MEN

HANGING IN WILD WIND

BLACK VALLEY RIDERS

JUSTICE

Available wherever books are sold or at
penguin.com

S909-0930